The Grease Monkey's Tale

Paul Burman

 **PaperBooks**

Paperbooks Publishing Ltd, 2 London Wall Buildings,
London EC2M 5UU
info@legend-paperbooks.co.uk
www.legendpress.co.uk

Contents © Paul Burman 2010

British Library Cataloguing in Publication Data available.

ISBN 978-1-9074611-6-3

*All characters, other than those clearly in the public domain, and
place names, other than those well-established such as towns and
cities, are fictitious and any resemblance is purely coincidental.*

Set in Times
Printed by JF Print Ltd., Sparkford.

Cover designed by Gudrun Jobst
www.yotedesign.com

Praise for Paul Burman:

'Burman's first novel reveals an inventive, passionate
and insightful writer'
The Independent

'Tightly, expertly written... an exceptional debut'
Blogcritics.org

'That rare novel that goes deep into the inner life of its
characters, yet moves right along with the brisk pace of
a page-turner. Beautifully written, richly atmospheric
and movingly told.'
Diary of a Heretic

Other works by Paul Burman:

The Snowing and Greening

of Thomas Passmore (Paperbooks)

At the Rawlings' Place in

Ten Journeys (Legend Press)

What is this Truth?
And where does it steal from?
Who is its mistress today?
And who was its master yesterday?
A fickle beast of ruthless pedigree,
Best lay it to rest with a story.
Give me a good, honest lie any day.

Prologue

His voice is deep and lined with gravel, but fluid. It's the sound of riverbed pebbles chattering and grinding against the hushing of fast water. Hypnotic.

"Prop open your peepers, pin back your lug-holes," he croons. He widens his eyes and waggles one ear lobe between callused finger and thumb.

Watch. Listen.

His eyes may be the blue-grey of an overcast sky, but framed by wild fronds of hair sprouting from beneath a broad-brimmed hat, and planted in a face of nut-brown leather, there's a piercing brightness to them. He casts a roving glance – the broadest arc – to net his audience and sweeps a pointing finger to keep each listener in place.

"Gather round, gather close," he beckons. He places his hands together, palm-to-palm. "In these two hands I have a story. Watch as I open this book." He mimes the opening of a book, the turning of a page, and then, to the rhythm of a familiar phrase and in the manner of so many beginnings, he starts to draw the net in.

"Once upon a time, not so long ago, in a land not far away…"

Part One

1

Once upon a time, in a land too close for comfort, there lived a man. A young man who, even then, was on the run. He was a grease monkey – a mechanic – on his way to a new start; inching out through the snarl of city traffic, tapping a beat on the steering wheel of his pride and joy: a glossy black, 1972 E-Type Jag. His hands went tappety-tappety, tap-tap-tappety, and at his side was a rat called Polonius (sniffing the air) and a goldfish called Ophelia (swimming in circles). He'd given his little sister these pets as presents for her seventeenth birthday, and she'd named them and loved them as only she could. But his sister was dead – killed – and now they were his.

As for his name... well, a name's just a label, a tag, and signifies sweet nothing. It can't change who a person is, or where they've come from, or what they look like, or what they've seen, or the stories they know. It can't change any of that stuff. So, we'll know him as Nic. Nic the mechanic. And he was a fresh-faced, innocent-looking Nic back then; slow to anger, mostly amicable; an open book. His skin was olive brown, his close-cropped hair was black-bristled, and he was in his early-twenties. He was a grease monkey and panel beater extraordinaire.

With one foot hovering a whisper over the clutch and the other stroking the accelerator – inching through the snarl of city traffic – Nic was travelling towards a big, new beginning, seeking better fortune beyond a distant, brighter horizon. Polonius was in his cage, Ophelia in her half-empty tank, and he'd pulled the tan leather passenger seat forward to wedge both firmly in place on the floor pan. There was a long journey ahead, but when the traffic began thinning he'd tell himself he too might leave all congestion behind.

Everything that was stuffed up and couldn't be quickly sorted might be left behind. Let the passing of time do what it does best. If one path leads nowhere, try another. Wherever it was he was heading, he'd get there in the end.

Peering ahead beyond the crush of traffic to the slow drama of roadworks – temporary traffic lights, a generator puking exhaust fumes, two orange-jacketed Council workers with jackhammers and a third gripping a shovel – he mouthed his dad's motto at the windscreen. It wasn't something the old man chanted every day or anything like that. He never had it tattooed on his forehead or suggested it should be engraved over the fireplace. But it was a tenet his dad had lived by, more or less, and Nic wasn't sorry to adopt it as his own because the old fella had mostly given good advice.

"Look forwards, move forwards, never back." It had sprouted into his mantra. *Look forwards, move forwards, never back.*

His dad was dead too, and so was his mum. Dead and buried. All he had left of his family were memories, trinkets, two pets and the proceeds of blood money – accident insurance, estate proceeds – their blood, his money. Life was no fucking fairytale, for sure, and it had been when things seemed their most beautiful best that it shat unfairly but squarely upon the four of them.

He looked across at the passenger seat, to the manila envelope perched on top of his jacket. It didn't hold much, but it did contain enough instructions to start a new life.

2

The manila envelope. He couldn't get over the way Mrs King had turned up the way she did, like some quaint fairy-godmother or the like, and he was surer than ever it was Siobhan's doing. She'd orchestrated it somehow. To try and make up for what he'd gone through, thanks to her.

It was more than just the chance to work again, of course. It was an offer with knobs on. It was the job of a lifetime. And the old dear, Mrs King, knew it. And yet it was even more than all this, because, when it came down to it, what she'd arrived at his apartment to offer (a mere couple of hours after kicking Siobhan out) was the chance to leave the stink of the past behind and the opportunity to move on with the rest of his life at last. *Look forwards, move forwards, never back.*

All the same, it was no easy call. This city was his home, the place he'd grown up in with his sister and his mum and dad; the setting for his best memories (as well as the worst). So, once Mrs King told him she'd return in twenty-four hours for an answer, he spent the morning, afternoon and evening pacing his apartment, teetering between acceptance and refusal, balancing as many reasons for and against as sprung to mind – juggling the pros and cons, the good and the bad, the happy and sad – in between trying to phone Siobhan to talk things through with her.

Peering out the window, across the park towards the roofline of the Central Gallery, the Performing Arts Centre and the restaurants that fringed the river, he was confronted instead by his own clownish reflection: a mop of tight corkscrews of hair that spiralled every which way; bloodshot, startled eyes, and a beard that looked too big for him now. Wild.

"Fuck off," he said, and turned to stare elsewhere. At his bookshelves and the crooked stacks of paperbacks and each crazy stratum of spines (different colours, different fonts, different sizes), which, if nothing else, were a measure of having too much time on his hands for too long. He ran a finger along the edge of one shelf and was confronted by a family photograph perched in the middle (burnished brass framing a pose in a once-ordered world): a portrait of his raven-haired mother, sister and father, huddled on a bench on the city ferry, with the river behind them. His mum, on the left, had an arm round his sister, and his dad, on the right, had an arm embracing them both.

"I deserve a slice of good luck," he told it. "Maybe I should take the job. Maybe I should rent out the apartment and take the damn job."

"Every journey begins with a single step," he made his father say.

"Too bloody right."

"Language," his mother warned him, but with a hint of smile.

"Risk nothing, gain nothing," the old man added.

His sister looked on. She was laughing and her hair was blowing in the wind, but she wouldn't speak. Why should she? She owed him less than nothing.

By the time he'd paced his way through to nightfall, he was clear about one thing: it was the fantastic – unbelievable really – chance to manage his own garage in the not-too-distant future that tempted him. It was one of the things he'd always wanted to do, ever since he got hooked on cars as a twelve-year-old. This alone could be a treasure worth travelling for.

Twenty-four hours after she first appeared, Mrs King stood in the centre of his living room again. In her tweed woollen suit and her shiny brogues, with her hat pinned to her tight bun of ice-white hair and a fresh rose in her left lapel, she may have appeared quaint, demure and diminutive, but was as sharp as any hat-pin. She didn't mince her words; her eyes were a piercing green.

"Well?" she said.

Nic glanced at the pictures on the walls, at his sofa, his books, his mementoes, at the arrangements of objects that represented his past and who he'd become, and wondered what else he could do. What real choice did he have? Through the window, he caught sight of the elms and Moreton Bay fig trees that fringed the park; he caught sight of the bluestone church spires and the crystal-sharp skyscrapers of the city – the backdrop to childhood and family life – and doubted he'd ever be ready to leave it behind. Not ever. And then, for stark, shit-bitter contrast, he recalled the gut-wrenching abandonment that summed up the last few months and how no one would give him the time of day anymore, let alone the chance to work… except Siobhan, perhaps, his former lover (whose tidy wit and enchanting laugh and oh-so-pretty arse he'd kicked out of his life too damned well). Siobhan and this Mrs King.

"Yes," he said, "I'll take it. Might as well. There's nothing to lose."

She stood clutching her bag and a manila A4 envelope in front of her. "Hmm," she nodded. "And everything to gain?"

"Too right."

She dabbed the A4 envelope in the air and almost smiled for the first time.

Its contents were a disappointment. He'd expected a glossy brochure, detailed maps, background information on the company he'd be working for, fliers, brochures, leaflets from the local Tourist Information Office promoting the region he was moving to and selling the delights of Gimbly. But there was none of that. Instead, there was a basic contract to sign and a photocopied, hand-drawn map that approximated the town's location, with a couple of scrawled instructions on how not to miss the junction for the Gimbly road. That was all.

"Don't lose that," this fairy-godmother told him. "It's not an easy place to find, what with the forests and the logging tracks. So many tracks which lead nowhere that's anywhere. There's a telephone number written at the bottom in case you get lost – not that you'd get much reception on your mobile."

"Oh, I see," he said, and ran a comb of fingers through his straggly hair, then smoothed the beard beneath his chin. He turned the map over, but it was blank on the back. A raven landed on the balcony table with a hasty flurry of wings, and immediately leaned forward to caw at the window. Nic watched it a moment, then placed the papers on the table and gnawed at the skin of one knuckle.

She pulled a pen from her handbag and tapped the air with it, and the raven hopped down onto the tiles and cawed again. "You'll have to sign the contract while I'm here. I did explain."

"Yeah."

He looked for the small print, but there wasn't any. It couldn't have been more straightforward. And still he hesitated.

"Can I get you a drink?" he said. "Tea? Coffee? How about a glass of water?"

She let the offer pass and raised her voice over the nuisance bird. "The wage is better than you'll get anywhere else. Guaranteed. You wouldn't get this sort of money even in the city."

He nodded. "Relocation expenses, a rural living allowance, fringe benefits – you mentioned all that stuff." It had to be a reputable business, surely; else they'd pay a basic wage to any local cowboy who could swing a spanner. And it remained a flattering offer, even though he saw the elegant hand and seductive, silver tongue of Siobhan behind it. He'd never been headhunted before.

If only he could talk it through with her – ask what she knew about the place – but he'd told her to get lost and she had. She'd vanished yet again, as only she could. For all he knew, she might be flying to the farthest ends of the earth at that very moment.

She wasn't answering her phone and had turned MessageBank off, which was her way of saying, "You too, Nic. Get stuffed. I can live without you too." Maybe he'd never see her again; not ever.

"Remember, it's a three month contract to start with," Mrs King added. "Not too long, not too short. To see whether you like us and whether we like you. To see whether your face fits, as it were."

"I understand."

A second raven landed, except it had a chunk of bread gripped in its beak. It dropped the bread and croaked once, twice, three times, and the first one took a sideways step towards the glass of the sliding door.

She talked over the birds. "It'll get you back on your feet again."

"I know," he said, and smiled at the raucousness coming from the balcony. Two days in a row. They were giving her a hard time. "I appreciate that. Thanks."

"So we'll see you in a few days?"

He took the pen and signed the contract, and then she was gone.

Left to his own devices, but with a sense of direction now – a destination – he tugged at his wild tufts of hair again, went to the bathroom mirror and examined the image.

"Time to find a pair of scissors," he said to his reflection. "Time for a new start."

Look forwards, move forwards, never back.

3

Nic tapped on the steering wheel and snatched a glance in the rearview mirror of the diminishing city: a landscape of glass, chrome, concrete, iron, crafted stone and timber; of structures that reflected the movement of water or slices of an ever-changing sky. He felt privileged to have inherited the old man's affinity for the diverse shapes of the place and for its resilient (if unforgiving) textures, because these were the designs and materials his dad had devoted his life to, and would always remain a part of his story even though he'd gone. Just as its shapes and textures, pavements and streets, parks and schools, alleyways and arcades, pubs and clubs, would remain part of Nic's story, wherever he was. It was who he was. It'd always be his home.

With a flash of lights and the flick of a wave, he let a delivery van pull out from the kerb and take a place in front of him. Then accelerated a tad too hard before a soccer mum in her gleaming Bimmer X5 cut in from a side street.

This was still his belonging-place, even if he had to leave a while. In a year or so he'd be back – maybe sooner – and then all would be sweet again. For one thing, he'd no longer be lugging a suspended sentence around his neck.

He'd had a narrow shave, but that was behind him now. Best not dwell on it. Even so, if he ever saw that Chris bastard again, he'd... well, he didn't know what he'd do. Only what he'd like to.

"Look forwards, move forwards, never back," he reminded himself once more, running a hand over his head. Wasn't used to the lack of hair, nor to so many bristles, but he thought the close-cropped look suited him – tougher, meaner, less of a walk-over – as if a new image could change who he was.

Lyrics to a song from the radio washed over him, and then the song faded and a string of commercials began. Selecting a CD, he slid it into the player. Bob Marley and the Wailers: *No Woman, No Cry*.

Spot on.

Like any orphaned beggar boy or any knight errant in any fairytale, all he was looking for was his own happiness. Ever-after happiness.

The traffic shuffled down stretches of suburban high street, crawling in small steps from one harness of traffic lights to the next. Cracked pavements edged by dying plane trees, against which padlocked bikes and shop signs leant, and dogs pissed. Beyond the cobweb of tram cables and powerlines, two aeroplanes sliced a hazy sky, flying east, north, wherever, and he thought of Siobhan. Of course. Wondered where she was. Didn't want to, but couldn't help it. Always.

Siobhan.

The traffic picked up pace until it was trotting past parade after parade of scruffy, narrow, shop facades; then gained more speed as the road widened into a semi-industrialised zone of small factories, over-advertised car yards, Mr Friendly Garden Centres and grey warehouses. From burbs to urban fringe, the traffic galloped from point to point.

When the city began petering out and Nic arrived at the spaghetti of overpasses and underpasses and the roundabouts of ring roads (a couple of hitchhikers holding up rough, cardboard signs), he took a moment to pause, relax and draw a longer breath. Ignoring the exhaust fumes from the convoy of carnival trucks in front, he imagined he could already get a faint sniff of a different, distant landscape – fresh air, fresh prospects – and he cracked a smile.

The E-Type Jag was jam-packed with luggage: clothes, CDs, a few books, a photo album, a rat, a goldfish, a toolbox, a recorder, a tin whistle... but as little emotional baggage as he could possibly escape with. Long after the music stopped playing, the words and rhythm of *No Woman, No Cry* remained in his head.

4

The first time Nic met Siobhan was at the bum end of a gruelling week in early autumn. It was Friday afternoon and he was sweaty and smelly and stale. For five days in a row, the sun blistered the bitumen, scorched the concrete, sizzled the city and left him parched. He'd been on his own for a week while the boss took a holiday, but had grown sick of his own company within forty-eight hours. He had another week to go. It made all the difference in a day, he came to realise, having someone around to turn to once in a while, even if they said bugger-all. The crucial thing was knowing somebody else was there. And too much had gone pear-shaped that week. The engine parts he'd ordered arrived late and turned out to be for a newer, altered model. To top it off, instead of soothing a difficult customer who wanted an expensive job finished on the cheap and wouldn't take no for an answer, he refused to bite his tongue any longer. The city wilted and his patience shrivelled with it.

"Do it yourself if you're the expert," he told the prick, "or take it someplace where they'll give you labour and parts for nothing. Either way, it'll cost you for the work I've done, plus materials. You've done sweet F.A. but mess me around since you booked it in." What he wanted to add was: "Fuck off, numskull; crawl back to your hole."

The customer – a self-important plonker who probably reckoned he was an expert because he'd changed the spark plugs on his car once – blinked, reddened, but then recovered. "Should've known better than come here in the first place. Just give me my bloody keys and I'll take my business elsewhere. Thought you'd know what you were doing. Where's your boss? I wanna talk to the owner. Nah, forget that – just give me my keys."

In the background, the buzz of traffic might have been the buzz of agitated bees.

Nic happened to be holding an adjustable wrench in his right hand and there was a large spanner tucked into the leg pocket of his oily overalls; there were two grease tracks across his forehead and another below one eye. He leaned towards the little prick, but relaxed when the guy danced a quick, backward two-step. He tried not to smile. The boss wouldn't have handled it this way – could be a bit soft at times – but maybe he'd still be proud of him. He liked a good story and he'd certainly laugh when he was told about it.

"When you've settled the bill, I'll return your keys."

The customer huffed and puffed, but then dug deep and dragged out a credit card, slapped it on the workbench. "I want a receipt and an itemised invoice. I won't be coming back here again."

"Suits me fine," he said. "We're not a fucking charity, you know."

The boss would back him on that.

Snatching his keys, the man strode towards his car spewing a litany of mumbled complaints. But not mumbled enough. "Bloody amateurs. Cheap-skate wog bastard. Fucking dago."

Nic grabbed the adjustable wrench and stepped out. "What? What did you call me?"

The buzz of traffic changed tone. It paused, as movement became suspended between one intersection of lights and another. Somewhere a swarm of cars was revving to race into a higher gear – waiting. And then it began again: a moment of heightened frenzy followed by the normal hubbub.

"Nothing. Nothing at all, mate. Was talking to myself. Said I'll be glad to see the back of this fucking place."

"The feeling's mutual."

In the last blistering half-hour of that working week, as he lay on an inspection trolley and eased himself under a mud-baked ute, he licked his lips at the thought of sculling an icy cold beer at the pub on his short walk home. One frosty beer would refresh him, two might cool him, three would start to slake his thirst. Could've rolled straight into one of two-dozen beer commercials at that moment: hot, thirsty man meets crate of ice-packed beer.

Several beads of sweat tracked between the grit and grease on his forehead and ran into the corner of one eye, stinging and half-blinding him. Lifting an arm to mop himself with the sleeve of his overalls, he knocked the muffler and copped a face-full of dirt and rust-flakes.

"Shit," he said. And because there was no one to answer him, he said it again, but louder. "SHIT." His hands were clammy and the spanner slipped in his grip.

All the same, what better way of earning a crust than scratching about with a motor? For sure, every job had shitty days, but there was little to beat the pleasure of tuning a machine to its peak, until it purred. Making a broken vehicle come alive again – sleek and fast and powerful. Taking a car apart and rebuilding it so it was better than before.

He was a grease monkey and a panel beater too; a doctor in mechanical parts – carburettors, CV joints, gaskets, distributors – and a cosmetic surgeon in panels and paint. Sleek, powerful cars were his passion, but every vehicle fascinated him. Hadn't found one yet which he didn't enjoy working on. Like a skilled piano tuner, he could identify the make and age of most idling engines, and how their music might be improved, just by listening, eyes shut. How he loved the velvet softness of warm oil trickling between his fingers: smooth, juicy lube.

One day he'd run his own garage, and he'd slap up a sign and shut up shop early on a stinking hot day like this, high-tailing it to the beach if he felt like it. At other times he'd work flat-out through the night if he wanted to. He'd be his own boss and specialise in exotic, fast cars... one day.

"I wish, I wish, I wish." Three wishes.

"Our best achievements begin with a dream and a wish," his dad would've beamed.

"Be careful what you wish for," his mum would've cautioned. A stock reply.

The car entered the work bay at lightning speed. He flinched, winced, pulled his legs in, swore again. "Fuck." If the driver had misjudged the distance, he couldn't have slid out the way fast enough: one car would've slammed into the other and he'd be crushed to a pulp. Minced meat. Life could be a fragile thread, casually snapped. He knew this too well.

The car braked, reversed and straightened, creating a piercing screech of tyres on the painted cement. The engine was turned off. A Porsche 911, from the thrum of it.

Rolling out from the ute, he opened his mouth to give the driver a piece, but took a breath instead. One argument in a day, in a month, was more than enough. Besides, the week was all but over and nothing should spoil the sweetness of that. But he was curious too. Who'd bring a Porsche here when there was a dealership down the road?

Standing, he dragged the rag from the back pocket of his overalls, wiped his hands, then tucked it back in place and wiped a sleeve across his brow. Rubbed at his eye; tried blinking out whatever speck had fallen in.

The Porsche was metallic Midnight Blue – a favourite colour – and shimmered with newness; sparked with sophistication, sensuality, energy. As the driver climbed out, she removed a pair of sunglasses and, in one brief glance, seemed to take stock of the work bays, tool racks, the counter, the back office, before returning her focus to the mechanic.

"Hello," she said.

"Got problems with your brakes, have you?" he said.

She let the door fall closed, then reached through the open window to drop her sunnies on the dashboard. "No, I don't think so."

"Good. That's a relief."

She had the grace to smile at that. "Sorry. It needs some work on this panel though."

He nodded, stood back to admire the lines of the car; crouched down to focus on the damage; drew the tips of two fingers along its bruise to gauge the contours of the dent.

"Ouch," he said. At the centre of the dent, a fingernail of paint had chipped away. "Someone put the boot in, did they?"

"It's possible." She had the light build of a ballerina and possessed the self-assured, agile step of a dancer too.

"You wouldn't rather take it to a Porsche dealer? There's one just down the road. You might still catch them open."

"I heard you were good – very good. You come highly recommended."

"Who from?"

When she didn't answer, he turned round. She was wandering round the garage as if it was the most fascinating place she'd ever been; as though she couldn't resist exploring it, but also as if something might jump out and bite her. He watched her peer tentatively beneath the hydraulic lift at the underside of the car perched there, then glance quickly in the direction of the spray room and back at the office again.

When she realised he was watching her, she span around to face him and stood still. "Sorry again. I was being nosey." She bit her lip and walked back towards him. "Can you make my car new again? As good as new? I've only had it a fortnight."

Beyond her calm self-assurance, every now and then a ripple of something less certain. Once he'd noticed this, he looked for it and wondered who she was, what she was doing here.

"The dealership's not two blocks away," he said, and with that decided he wasn't going to do the job. Once she thought about it, she'd realise it didn't make sense for the dealership not to do it. "It's not far. I won't get it done any quicker than them. And they might already have the paint in stock, whereas I'll have to order it."

She reached for the door handle, a scent that held the suggestion of vanilla brushing against him. "I know that, but if you can't manage it, don't worry." She opened the driver's door, obliging him to move aside, but made no effort to climb in. Instead, she looked him in the eye and screwed her nose up in an impish smile, and it left a pause between one moment and whatever followed.

"I can do as good a job as any, if you really want me to," he said in a hurry and took another step back. He guessed this'd be a cash job, to hide the work from an accusing husband or father – a sugar-daddy, perhaps. He looked for a wedding band or a flashy engagement ring, but saw neither.

"I know you can," she said. "I wouldn't have gone to the trouble of bringing it here otherwise, now would I?" She hesitated a beat before adding: "Besides, I've admired that E-Type you drive; I know you'll look after this beaut."

He blinked, dragged the sleeve of his overalls across his forehead again, and looked for something in her face that was familiar. Her big, round eyes almost swallowed him up; they were deep and warm, but she knew she'd piqued his interest and they were laughing – teasing – too. Maybe he'd seen her in a nightclub. Should he know her? Had he danced with her, perhaps? Or hooked up with one of her friends? Surely he'd remember if he'd seen her before.

Taking the rag from his pocket, he rubbed it across his hands once more, then folded it flat, laid it on a corner of the workbench. There'd be no more work done today.

"Do I know you? How do you know about my car?" Maybe she knew someone in his apartment block or lived in the same area.

"It's a small world." The pixie smile returned and then she climbed into the driver's seat. "Monday morning okay? You'll need it a few days, I suppose?"

"I'll not be ready for it until Wednesday," he said. "I'll get the paint details then. I've got work coming from all directions and I'm on my own at the moment. Sorry, that's the best I can do."

She started the motor, replaced her sunglasses and with them that slightly superior façade returned. They were a mask to hide behind. "What about overtime? Fit it in Monday and I'll pay you extra, double-time, whatever."

There was no urgency in what she asked. She was bartering because she could afford to, not because she needed to. A playful condescension: Lady Fanny and John Thomas, the princess and the grease monkey. But he wanted those eyes to smile at him again. They were big enough to swim in.

"I have a life. I don't need the extra cash. Thanks all the same. You can drop it off on Monday, but I'll not get round to it until Wednesday." Maybe the Porsche dealership wasn't able to do the job as soon as she'd wanted either. Perhaps she was a spoilt prima donna, needing her own way quickly, before someone close to home witnessed the damage. She'd probably raced across the blocks from one garage to another, trying to sort it out before they all closed for the weekend. "If I have a chance to start earlier, I will, and that won't cost you a dollar more."

At that, she took off the sunglasses again and looked up at him more intently than before. Once more she bit her lip and once more she hesitated, as if this was the moment she'd been steeling herself for all along but hadn't known how to get to.

"Dinner then. How about I buy you dinner if you manage to fit it in?"

For a moment he was lost, aware only that he was standing there like a dummy. He made himself shrug and tried to look nonchalant. Over the six-cylinder song that her engine sang, he said: "We'll see."

She exited with a squeal of tyres and he didn't expect to see her again.

5

Apart from his sister's pets, Nic lived alone in a flash apartment in a fashionable quarter of the city, not a long stroll from where he worked. An apartment of redwood, polished bluestone and green leather, it was the sort of place featured in glossy coffee table magazines like *House & Garden*, *Town & Country*,

Architecture Now! The sort of magazines you'd find in a dentist's waiting room. Its entrance was approached along a pavement of shining slate, a handrail in matt chrome, sunken lights; the lobby was expansive enough to accommodate a large pond, cascading water, boulders and pebbles, a couple of tree ferns – the pretence of a natural environment. His neighbours were inner-city dentists, managing directors, established barristers, who banked five or ten times his salary – fastidiously-preened empty-nesters. As such, it was a quiet set of apartments, where the loudest intrusion might be the music and laughter from a cocktail party, or the clicking of leather heels along speckled-brown marble corridors, and he was its oddest sight, arriving home from work each evening in oil-smeared overalls and a grease-streaked face.

The residents' basement garage was a showcase of the latest models from BMW, Mercedes, Lexus, Audi, except for Nic's black, 1972 E-Type Jaguar that was parked smack in the middle of them. The coupé, not the soft-top roadster; a car whose sleek lines suggested not only the power and speed of a sprinting panther, but the sexiness of feminine curves and depths. It was a glistening, polished blackness on the outside, with tan leather upholstery on the inside, a walnut dashboard, a graphic equaliser... In short, a magnificent beast; a V12 charger for a knight in shining armour.

Among the stable of other cars, it was a refreshing idiosyncrasy that drew his neighbours' attention to him when he first moved in, and possibly they imagined he was a famous actor, moody musician or an eccentric sportsman. Until they discovered he wasn't joking when he said he was a lowly grease monkey. Which, in turn, would've begged the question: how come you can afford to live in a flash apartment in a fashionable quarter of the city when you're so young and only a mechanic? Except no one asked because no one got to know him well enough to do so.

Undoubtedly, they assumed his wealth was ill-gotten and that he must be a criminal of sorts, or that he'd won the lottery and would blow the lot before the year was out. Either way, it was the un-neighbourly nature of the place and the long hours everyone worked that meant it was easy to avoid knowing one another's real story, and he was glad of this when he first moved in. He preferred to be left to himself in those early days because he was still raw from his loss and had ample grief for company.

And though his flash apartment and his magnificent car arrived at the cost of a father, a mother and a sister, he slowly learnt to be as happy with his lot in life as grief allowed, knowing that he need never want for anything nor go hungry for the rest of his days, unless he was very unlucky or exceedingly foolish.

Always, however, in the quietest and stillest moments of the early morning or late-evening, when the shadows were stretched to their longest, he knew he'd rather be a struggling mechanic, paying exorbitant rent in a squalid unit, with only the dream of an expensive car and a luxurious apartment, if it meant he still had his family to return to… to sit at the family table and break the bread and chew the fat with… to connect with and argue with and be driven mad by… to share the tale of each day with.

All the same, he wasn't going to mope about his flat and mourn for the rest of his days. "Life's for living," his mum used to say, and it was good advice. It meant that more and more Monday mornings saw him arrive at work heavy-eyed after a weekend of pubbing and clubbing – after too much empty play, too much alcohol-induced dehydration – but moving forward and living his life. And so it was on the day the ballerina girl delivered her car.

When she drove up, he'd just dragged open both roller doors to the work bays. The city traffic sounded nervous and querulous – a rush hour of horns and impatiently-revved engines and sirens – and it mirrored his mood. The rich, pungent smell of cigars and coffee drifted down from a café fifty metres away, mingling with the dry acridity of exhaust fumes. Strong black coffee – he could've drunk a jug of the stuff.

"I'll need a name and a contact number," he told her, wondering if he'd have enough space to park the Porsche until he was ready for it.

"Siobhan," she said, and was amused when he looked puzzled. Biro poised, he'd paused mid-stroke through the S. "I'll write it down for you."

She printed it: neat block letters, no loops. He watched her hand flit across the paper. Elegant fingers; neat, short nails that weren't overly manicured.

"How do you get what you said out of that? Looks like *Sy-ob-han* to me."

"Take it from me, it's *Shur-vorn*. It's an Irish name. More straightforward than it looks. It means Jeanne in French, as in Jeanne d'Arc. She's my namesake." And she laughed as if she'd admitted something ridiculous.

"Who?"

"You know: Joan of Arc."

"Oh yeah." He tried the name out for himself: "Siobhan." He nodded at the sound of it, tucked the sheet of notepaper into the pocket of his overalls. "How about that? I've learnt something new today and it's not even nine o'clock. Cheers." It nudged him beyond his Monday-morning weariness into a more charming mood.

She took the high hem of her dress and curtsied. "And may your world be a richer place for it." She laughed and her eyes widened, before jangling the keys in her hand, dropping them onto the counter and turning to walk out.

"I'd offer you a lift," he called after her, "but..." and he motioned at the garage.

"I know, you're on your own. It's alright, I'll catch a taxi."

"I can phone for one. Get it to collect you."

And with that, she raised an arm at the stream of traffic and a cab immediately pulled over to the curb. "Catch you later, Nic," she called over her shoulder, as if he was an old friend, throwing in his name for good measure.

When he picked the keys up, fitted a plastic wrap over her driving seat and climbed in ready to park it out of the way, he sat there a minute or two. How did she know his name? He stared through the windscreen and saw nothing. The usual symptoms.

6

It was that time of year when the shortening of the days becomes apparent and when each new, shorter day has a calmness about it that suggests a lull between the drama of one season and the next. The leaves on the avenues of elms and London planes had begun to yellow, but the stillness would hang, like a moment suspended, for a week or two yet; until the heat of the sun had waned and the first flurries of a cooling, leaf-rustling wind arrived. There was a brooding expectancy about each day, as if the season was its own waiting room. And yet, the afternoons climaxed in a fierce heat for several days in a row, as if the sun was overcharged and couldn't help but ejaculate the last of its summer glory, even though a new, startling chill accompanied the nights.

Of an evening, before preparing his meal or phoning for a takeaway, he'd spend five minutes watching Ophelia drift, like a slice of carrot, between the rocks in her tank or suck food from the surface, while Polonius ran outside his cage, hugging the apartment walls, or nestled in the folds of the mechanic's pullover and groomed himself. Simple pleasures. As twilight arrived, Nic might sit next to the balcony window with the TV on and watch the roses and ferns in their pots (some of his mum's favourites, that he'd managed to keep) fade into shadow. Once or twice or more, he found himself thinking about the girl with the Porsche, wondering where she lived, how much she knew about him, which of his friends or neighbours she was friendly with. She became a fresh shadow to his thoughts. Maybe he'd seen her at a nightclub or standing with a group in a pub, chatting and laughing and dancing the night away.

"Siobhan," he said to Ophelia or Polonius or the world in general. He practised saying her name and told himself he did this because it was an unusual name.

"She seems like a nice girl," his mother would've said. *Nice*? Such a bland word.

"'Hot' then," he heard her say. But this wasn't the sort of thing his mum would've said and so she unsaid it.

"Ask her out," his father would've prompted. "If you like her, then ask the girl out."

Nic smiled, but shook his head.

"What's to lose, except a little pride?" the old man would've pressed.

Beginning work on her car on the Tuesday afternoon, he stayed at the garage later than usual to bring it along; triple-checking every stage to make sure it was flawless. On Thursday, he sent her a message that it was ready and found himself waiting for her to arrive. Yet, despite the urgency, she didn't collect it until mid-afternoon the following day.

He didn't see her walk in. He'd just settled another customer's account and had reversed that car so it was ready to drive away. When he stepped back into the workshop she was there, examining the tool boards, strolling around.

"You're very tidy," she said. "A place for everything and everything in its place. Painted silhouettes of every tool. How neat." There was a slight burr to her accent, he now noticed; a soft rising at the end of her sentences, as if the habit of every statement was to question. He heard it and noted it, and then it vanished again, so that he wondered if he hadn't just imagined it after all.

"Have to be," he replied. "Although that's my boss' doing. It wouldn't do to leave a screwdriver rattling around in a customer's engine compartment, would it?"

"A spanner in the works? Absolutely not."

Nic fetched her keys and account and she paid in cash. Peeled the notes out of a snakeskin wallet. No sign of the usual credit cards.

"You don't mind cash?"

"It's all the same to me."

"Now," she said, thoroughly absorbed it seemed with placing her wallet in her handbag and re-shuffling its contents, "what about this dinner? Are you doing anything tomorrow evening?"

He laughed at that. "You don't owe me anything. Besides, it wasn't finished when you wanted it."

She looked up then and held his eyes with hers for a moment. "Perhaps you have a girlfriend who'd mind me taking you out?"

He shook his head, glanced at his rough hands, his stained overalls. "Not at all. Have you even looked at the car?"

She followed his glance and smiled. "It's very nice. Perfect. Thank you." Then she cocked her head on one side and seemed to be reappraising him. "Do you always play hard-to-get when someone's going out of their way to be friendly? Or maybe I'm not your type?"

"No, it's not that."

"What then?"

"Nothing."

"Well?"

Outside, the traffic was building up into the Friday night rush hour. Here was the hustle and bustle, the hurly-burly of a city's population putting a frantic week behind it, moving towards the ritualistic frenzy of another weekend socialising. One-night stands and hasty retreats. Everyone, it appeared, had somewhere to go and someone to be there with. So why, with beautiful ballerina-girl actually asking *him* out, did he feel like a thirteen-year-old schoolboy baulking at his first date?

He shrugged. "Okay. Thanks then. That'd be good. Where? When?" A hurried slurry of words before he could chicken out.

7

She chose a restaurant by the river, close to the casino, and booked an outside table warmed by patio gas heaters, where the world could be watched strolling by. A saxophonist, busking under the arches of a nearby bridge, entertained them with the loneliness of one wailing jazz melody after another, and they were comforted by the galaxy of a million bud lights that mapped the constellations of branches of every tree along the promenade. On and on the galaxy stretched, past restaurant after restaurant, couple after couple, with the river ribboning behind. Where they sat was sheltered by an extensive awning, like a sail, and this outside area was further defined on three sides by a low balustrade, on each section of which the name of the restaurant was advertised: *Khan*.

At the end of that first dinner (an *hors d'oeuvre* of nervous small-chat, followed by an exotic but substantial main course, which left them abstaining from the promise of the sweetest of desserts in favour of a sobering coffee), she chose not to go on to a pub or a club, but suggested they stroll along the river, through the city and along the edge of a park, back to her apartment.

"I've got an early start tomorrow," she told him, and he nodded.

He didn't feel like being in the crush of a pub or a club tonight either. Not tonight. However, this is what he'd expected she'd want to do, just as he'd expected the whole evening to be as frenetic as that first occasion she'd appeared – squeals of brakes, flashes of drama – but she'd surprised him in being a much calmer and even presence, and together they'd eased into a mellow mood instead.

She removed her stilettos after they'd walked a hundred metres or so and carried them most of the way back, but wouldn't change her mind about catching a tram or a taxi; she said she loved to walk on nights like this. They talked as they walked and she had a natural spring in her step, a lightness of foot and a fluency of energy, which had been contained when she wore stilettos but which thrilled him and enervated him.

Occasionally they lapsed into silence and then one of them would point something out – some drunk, some car, some building, some piece of street art – as if, tonight, they must resist any prolonged silence because the newness of the other's voice was delicious. So they discussed the meal and the city and its restaurants and its nightclubs, and he drew her into describing some of the other places and other cities she'd been. And whenever he thought he might risk blabbering on too much himself, or that she might drift towards an awkward silence, he'd introduce another question.

"So this apartment you're in..." he said, looping back to an earlier topic, willing her to let him step closer to her personal life now; yet finding himself more nervous, not less, as he realised how rich it was to be next to her.

"The company I'm working for arranged it," she said. "While I'm in town."

"You're doing consultancy work for them, yeah?"

"That's right."

"I thought you might be a ballerina that first time I saw you," he confessed. "Some sort of dancer."

She laughed. "No? What made you think that?" She held onto

Nic's arm and tried standing on her toes, *en pointe*, but couldn't.

"I'm not sure. The way you moved, perhaps."

"Hmm, I don't know about that," she said. "Those first two times I saw you, at *Dinos*, I thought you must be someone famous. It's the E-Type that does it. It's out of the ordinary."

"And you asked the bouncer if he knew who I was?" Nic said, remembering that part of the story she'd given him earlier. Still warmed by it.

She grinned and nodded. "It can be a small world at times."

"And then you copped that dint to your car?"

"Yep. And immediately thought of you." She paused, smiled in the way that wrinkled her nose. "Actually, it wasn't quite immediately. I did go to the Porsche dealership first if you must know, but they couldn't fit it in for ages."

He laughed at this. "I guessed as much." But he twinged with guilt as he remembered thinking of her as a prima donna. "Oh well, I'm glad about that."

"You didn't seem too pleased at the time."

"Well, it had been a crap day and... well, things change."

They were standing outside the foyer to a five-storey apartment now, only several blocks from where he lived. Spotlights illuminated a large pond and water sculpture to one side, threw sharp shadows back from the peppermint willows that overhung the area. A penetrating chill had slid into place in just a few minutes and its keenness began to fog their breath as they stood talking, and he held her hand and traced the outline of her fingers.

"So, how long will this job keep you in town? How long does it usually take to do whatever it is you do?" After an evening of sitting opposite her, walking next to her, being near to her, he wanted to stroke his fingers through her hair, knowing how fine it'd feel across his skin, but they hadn't quite arrived at that closeness yet. "Will you get another job here?"

She looked down, dabbed at the footpath with the toe of one stiletto, then looked up again. Her eyes drew him in. "I move around a fair bit, Nic; interstate and overseas. Though I've been based here a few weeks this time around, I'm not usually in one place so long. I travel a lot. Don't know where I'll be next."

He tried to hold her gaze, but couldn't, and looked up into the darkness of branches overhead. Was she telling him there might be no relationship between them at all, but if there was it couldn't be a long-term one? Sex, not love. Another one-night stand? After their evening together, he'd begun to crave something less fleeting. Although that could be a starting point. Every relationship began somewhere. He let go of her hand and nodded, tried to find a way around what she'd told him.

"And what is it you do exactly?" he asked. "What do they consult you about?"

"Oh, this and that."

He waited a moment, raised his eyebrows. "Really? Wow. Sounds interesting."

"I don't want to bore you."

He moved closer to her, wondered whether he should put his arms round her shoulders. She was a good deal shorter and was wearing a perfume he didn't recognise – missing that hint of vanilla she'd worn before – but it smelt expensive, exclusive. "Try me. You won't bore me. Perhaps you work for the secret service? Are you a spy? An undercover cop? You want to play twenty questions?"

She laughed, he laughed; it was getting colder.

"No big secret," she said. "Like I said before, my qualifications are in accounting and business management. Mainly, I audit cashflow and profitability strategies; identify problems, propose solutions." She waved a hand in the air as if to shrug the subject off, then grinned and added: "I'm an alchemist. I turn base metal into gold. It's what everyone wants, isn't it? More for less?" When she spoke, she worked her feet, rocking or standing on one foot or tracing circles across the damp stones; she was rarely still, always dancing.

"Hmm."

"Perhaps I should say I'm a corporate mechanic. I get a kick out of fine-tuning the way a business operates; from making the wheels of capitalism spin smoother, faster, more efficiently." She paused a moment. "Will that do?"

He wondered how tall she'd be without stilettos, tried to remember what she was wearing when she'd driven the Porsche, but couldn't. He'd had to push the driver's seat a way back for himself. "A mechanic?"

"Yes, definitely," she said. "Yes, I like that. You see, we're not so different, you and I."

He stroked the palm of her hand, wanted to kiss her wrist, her throat. "Fair enough." She'd told him everything that wasn't much at all, but it didn't matter. He just wanted to know something about her. Anything. Even these crumbs would do. It was a way of connecting two lives. "You've done well for yourself."

She smiled at that and said nothing, but let go of his hands and glanced at her watch; it was almost midnight. "Look, I'd ask you up for a coffee or something, but you'd end up staying the night and I've got an early start in the morning..."

He knew not to make a mistake at this crossroad. Avoid showing any sign of expectation or disappointment. If he was to stand any chance of seeing her again, he had to say the right words, make the right choice. "That's okay. If you're back tomorrow afternoon, perhaps we could drive down the coast?"

"Sorry. Tomorrow's out completely. And the day after. That's why I'm having an early start. Sorry."

He stared down at his rough hands, which were still warm from her touch, and wasn't surprised by this dismissal. Maybe he'd asked too many questions. Anyway, she'd be accustomed to the pick of smooth-talking, sharp-dressing, executive fly-by-nights, suits pressed to a knife's edge, competitive ruthlessness similarly honed, and he knew he was no competition. All the same, he gave it one last shot: "How about next weekend?"

"Oh, before then, perhaps. If you're free. I'll be back in town on Tuesday. What about the movies on Tuesday night?"

"Excellent," he said, and took her hands in his again. "Tuesday then."

8

A life without love is a barren table – measly meal after meal of stale, cold porridge – but a life attended by love is a smorgasbord. It's food to burn bright with, to glow from, and Nic and Siobhan ate well. Movies, dinners, nightclubs; wining, dining, dancing; talking, laughing, embracing... savouring the most profound silences of one another. They feasted.

Without speaking of it, it was as if they tried cheating the shortness of her stay in the city (and the inevitability of separation) by stealing every opportunity to be together and by fully living as much of every shared fleeting minute as possible. Nic should have dragged his feet when he arrived at work each day, but was illuminated instead – was brilliant with it. And he began to hope at first, and then to *believe* and then to *know*, that this relationship burnt so bright it could easily outlast any periods of separation. Together they'd find a way to be together. She was the woman life had been drawing him towards, to wrap him up with. Inextricably. Always. He knew it. *The* one. It was such a simple thing to discover, but sent him reeling nonetheless.

"Someone's fallen head over heels then," his boss observed.

"What?"

"Love. You look like you've fallen arse over tit in love. Got yourself a woman, have you?"

He smiled, didn't bother denying it. He unscrewed the drain plug on a Mazda 3 and let the oil trickle through his fingers; thought of Siobhan and his grin grew. Began the first job humming a tune and whistled it all morning, all afternoon.

"God help us," his boss declared. "I'll wear ear-muffs tomorrow."

A man in love is an entertaining spectacle.

When he'd first kissed her – on the Tuesday, before entering the cinema – and felt her standing on tip-toe, pressing against him, making the moment happen as much as he was, it was as if the fugginess of years began to dissolve. Afterwards, as they walked back to her flat, he couldn't remember what the film was about. All his grief from the past and his doubts about the future appeared manageable; he was ready to lay them to rest and to live in the present again.

And how shallow his years of kiss-me-quick, fuck-me-fast encounters now seemed. From their first meeting in the workshop to his absolute enchantment with her days later was too much of a maze to map. Having arrived at a magical place, why would he ever want to find his way back out? If he could lose himself with anyone, Siobhan was the one.

Before long, they'd whispered and sang and shouted words of love to one another, and she somehow stretched another four weeks of working in the city into six. She did it for him. She did it for them. It was the most ancient of stories.

9

The first time Siobhan stayed at his apartment – what began as a brief visit one afternoon finished with brunch the following day – she browsed his CD collection, pulled out a couple of paperbacks, then picked up the photo of his parents and sister.

"Nice photo," she said.

"Thanks."

"Is this your family?"

He nodded.

"You've got the same eyes as your mum. And your dad – your mouth and chin are the same. It's uncanny. This your sister? She's pretty. How old is she – seventeen, eighteen?"

He looked at Ophelia in her tank, Polonius sniffing about in his cage, and he nodded again.

"Do you see them much? Whereabouts do they live? Are they in town? I'd love to meet them."

"They're dead," he said.

"What?"

"They're dead. All three."

"Shit." She put the photo down.

He walked towards the balcony window, away from her. "That's life," he said, "I guess. It happens. No one's immune." And he sort of shrugged.

"How? What...?" she began, and took a step towards him, but then let herself sink onto the edge of the couch.

He stood facing the window and gazed outside, focused on how the world was faring – children playing in the park, a pregnant woman pushing a pram, an elderly couple resting on a bench – and then turned back to her.

"I'll tell you the story of my family," he said. And to lighten a moment made heavy, he added: "Are you sitting comfortably? Then I'll begin." And this is almost the story he told her:

Once upon a time there was a man and a woman and a girl and a boy, who were also a husband and a wife and a daughter and a son, as well as a father and a mother and a sister and a brother. When the man started out in adult life he was apprenticed to a Master Builder, and it was the daughter of this Master Builder – his only child – that the apprentice met and loved and later married.

For a wedding present, the Master Builder made his new son-in-law a partner in the business, which might have happened in

*the fullness of time anyway, wedding or not, for the man had fin-
ished his training by then and had proved himself a fine builder.
He'd become well known for his craftsmanship, hard work and
good sense, and was respected by those who knew him. The wedding day celebrated more than one union and the future was full
of the brightest promise.*

*Within a few years, the young woman gave birth to two chil-
dren – first a boy and then a girl – and the business of the two
builders gave birth to success after success. They no longer built
plain homes for ordinary working people, but were involved in
the construction of giant dreams instead: luxurious apartments,
cathedral-like shopping malls, futuristic university halls, government installations.*

*Neither the childhood and adolescence of his son and daugh-
ter, nor the death of the Master Builder, dulled the man's dreams;
they only burned brighter. His business grew and his workforce
grew and he contracted out numerous projects to other busi-
nesses; he moved among politicians, leaders, successful and
wealthy people. This became his life.*

*By this time, the son was old enough to begin finding his own
way in the world, and although he wanted to work with cars – to
be a doctor in mechanical parts and a cosmetic surgeon in panels and paint – rather than follow his father's footsteps, his
father was wise enough to understand what it was to dream and
grow ambition for oneself, and was only too pleased for his son.
Besides, he'd always been interested in these things too. So the
son left home and began fending for himself.*

*One day, all the man's dreams came to fruition. He success-
fully tendered for a major building project that would bring
international renown and which bigger companies declared
impossible to complete to the specifications and deadlines
required. He knew he could do it. It would be tight, but he could
do it. It would be a crowning achievement and guarantee future
prosperity for his company and everyone who worked in it, and*

he invested everything he had in ensuring its success.

When the project was nearly finished, and he'd almost completed the task that so many people had said was impossible, there were those who grew more and more disappointed by the day. They'd have liked nothing better than to see him fail, and this was largely because they felt his success would diminish their renown. And because, with hindsight, people would accuse them of poor judgement in declining the project. Some cheered him on, hoping he'd fail, while others openly jeered and criticised, envious of the prizes he'd win.

A few weeks before the completion deadline, the man took his wife and daughter, three managers and a couple of investors on a helicopter flight. The man's son – the mechanic – was asked to join them, but had to sit an apprenticeship exam that day. They were intending to inspect the progress of the project from the air, before flying along the coastline to admire some landmarks of great natural beauty. However, the purpose of the joy flight was also to help everyone feel good about the way things were going and acknowledge their hard work, patience and loyalty. There was to be a slap-up meal and trip to the theatre later.

As it turned out, the helicopter crashed into one of the landmarks of great natural beauty and everyone on board was killed. No enquiry could fathom exactly what happened, but, all the same, that was the end of the man and the woman and the girl, the husband and wife and daughter, the father and mother and sister. Robbed of its director and managers, and with the company reeling, the project faltered and stalled, and the long knives were quick to be drawn. His company crashed as surely as the helicopter, taking a good few and a few good with it, and his biggest competitors carved the empire up and shared it out among themselves. Everyone who knew grieved in public, but there would've been much dealing in private triumph throughout various bedrooms and boardrooms.

The end.

When he'd finished telling his story, Siobhan sat ashen-faced, staring at the carpet. She opened her mouth to say something, but then stopped. A couple of seconds later, she began again.

"It's a terrible thing to lose somebody you love. But to lose... " She shook her head. Her voice was little more than a ripple.

"One thing that's always bothered me," Nic said, more matter-of-fact now, "is that because they couldn't discover any other reason, they more or less pinned the accident on the pilot, poor bastard – pilot error. That's something for his family to live with. Sometimes people feel they're owed an answer and need something definite or someone to blame, I guess." He paused. "But life isn't that neat and tidy, is it? There's times when it leaves us dangling, never knowing the answer or the reason for something, and it doesn't matter how much we kick our feet about with one guess after another, refusing to accept that we might never be sure... we're still never gonna know."

He shrugged his shoulders, took a deep breath and sat next to her. "That's it," he said, "my family history." The telling of it had taken him outside himself, as telling a story often will – as if the story became somehow more significant than his part in it, as if he could lose himself in it and thereby find himself closer to his lost family again.

"You must miss them very much."

Her colour was only slowly returning and her voice was still a murmur, but Nic was fully back in the room now and next to her. It was a relief, a catharsis, to be able to tell it, rather than have it attached to him and trailing behind like a shadow. It may have still been there, this shadow, but he suspected it felt slighter lighter.

He took a deep breath and smiled. "Yep. I do."

She traced several circles with one finger on the seat of the couch between them, but without focus. Still somewhere else.

"It's alright though," he assured her, to bring her back. "It's getting easier. It was a while ago now."

She stopped the circles, clasped her hands and focused on him. She said: "I'm sorry, Nic. My life's complicated, messy. I'm probably the last thing you need."

He sat a moment in waiting. She was trying to tell him something, except the words fell short. "What? What are you talking about? You're exactly what I need. Who I need, who I want to be with."

"You say that now, but – "

"No," he said, and shook his head at her silliness, placing one hand over her clasped hands. "Don't. Everything's gonna work out fine. It already is."

"But –"

"What?"

She shook her head. "Nothing." She bit her lip, but now took his hand in hers. "The last person I loved got hurt... I think. That's why. I don't want you to get hurt."

There was a moment before they both realised what she'd said – it was the first time she'd used the 'L' word – and then she shook her head, seemed unsure whether she was smiling or blushing. "The last person I 'quite liked' is what I meant to say."

He grinned. It was hard to believe how quickly things could turn.

10

Siobhan was a pale-skinned beauty. She was petite and impish, graceful and athletic. Cat-like in her agility, sex could be animal-fierce and acrobatic; she scratched and bit, licked and kissed, and taught him to move in ways he hadn't even fantasised about. Her voice had a sing-song lilt to it, inherited from her parents, she declared, and reminiscent of her Irish ancestry. Her round pools of eyes were the deepest brown and her paleness was accentuated by the earthy darkness of her hair – 'the colour of a peat bog,' as she described it once – which she wore bobbed.

She was standing behind him, her arms round his waist. It was early evening and he was at the bedroom window, glancing through the slats of the blinds. Beyond the crowns of the avenue of trees, across the dark sea of shadows and space he knew to be the park, the lights of a carnival illuminated the night. Everything else seemed darker, flatter, more two-dimensional in contrast.

"I'd forgotten about the carnival," he said, and pulled the bath towel tight around his waist. "It comes for a fortnight each year." He'd learnt to measure autumn by it, in the way that others once learnt the passing of the seasons and their place on the planet by the movement of the constellations. The dancing lights of the Ferris Wheel, the Octopus, the Gravitron, the Zipper, the whole she-bang, were a galaxy of neon stars on the furthest edge of night.

"Let's go," Siobhan said, pulling the slats wider. "Let's run away together and join the carnival. I wish we could, Nic. The two of us. Away from all this." She waved an arm that encompassed not only his apartment, but the city and their entire past lives. Her laugh had an edge to it.

Nic turned. There was something flat in her tone, or an added ingredient he couldn't quite place. Maybe her job wasn't as ideal as she made out; maybe their relationship had changed too many things; maybe she knew she couldn't leave him behind. He was framing the words to approach this when she swung the mood back again.

"Tell you what; we'll leave all this behind and stow-away on boats in the Tunnel of Love. How about that?" Tried to dismiss the moment with a dose of self-mockery.

"Is everything alright?" he said.

She looked at him and stepped away from the blinds. "I've had a hell of a day, that's all. It'll be good to go out and be silly.

I haven't eaten candy floss in years. Not since... not for years and years."

He slid a hand to her neck and then across her shoulders and eased the tension there, the way she liked it, and she turned so she was leaning into him. "I saw you this morning," he told her. "I'd forgotten about that, but I saw you."

"You saw me? Where did you see me?" Her neck was stiff and her shoulders tight, but he pressed his thumb into the muscle and traced a slow, deep circle.

"I was in a customer's car and he was driving, otherwise I'd have hooted or pulled over. I'd forgotten all about that."

"Where?"

"In front of the casino," he said.

"Oh," she said, but there was a finality about the way she said it, as if that was the end of the subject.

He laughed. "Like a bit of a flutter, do you? Got a bit of a gambling problem, perhaps? It could've only been ten-thirty or eleven at most. Never took you for a Pokies player." He ran his thumb round each knobble of her spine and then stretched his hand around the back of her neck. He pulled his hand back, drawing his thumb and fingertips together to massage the muscle there, and then moved it up a fraction and did the same again.

"That's good," she said.

"Black Jack or roulette?" he teased.

She laughed. "Not at all. I hate gambling. Seems kind of pathetic all those people pouring their life savings into bloody machines. One tragedy after another. It's a quick way of filling someone else's pockets."

He moved his hand onto her head and pushed his splayed fingers across her scalp, through her fine, dark hair. This is what she really liked. "So you're consulting for the casino, are you?"

"I didn't say that."

"Aha, so you are."

"What is this, the Inquisition?" She rolled her head, stretched her neck. "As it happens, I'm not consulting for the casino. I'm actually not. I was meeting a client there, that's all."

"Those two little guys in suits?"

She paused and turned to face him. "Leave it, Nic," she said. "I'm not gonna tell you who I'm working for. I can't. I always guarantee absolute confidentiality. You understand that, don't you? You have to understand that."

He nodded, drew her towards him again. "Okay. Sorry. I just wanted to show a healthy interest in what you do."

She smiled at that. "It wouldn't be."

"What?"

"It wouldn't be ethical if I talked about it and it wouldn't be healthy if you asked any more questions. I'd probably have to... I'd have to turn you into a frog or terminate you with extreme prejudice or something."

"A frog?"

"Like I said, I've had a hell of a day."

"Then we'll have toffee apples and candy floss for supper. We'll do it. We'll go on the shooting range and I'll win you a giant pink teddy or a fluffy frog or something." He wanted nothing more than to make her happy. "Do you like dodgem cars?"

They'd wander from stall to stall, soaking up the spinning lights – white, red, blue, green – and the disco sounds, the banter and the spruiking and the generators chugging, the laughter and the squealing screams, the smell of doughnuts and diesel and hot grease; buying into the magic for just a few coins. They'd be part of the throng and, like all the other lovers, separate to it. As they walked, played and laughed, frittering away their coins on one game of chance after another, each one loaded against them, they'd be making a gentle, insinuating love, which would lead them all the way home again, where they'd dance and couple and burrow deep, to softly explode one more time.

"Best take a jacket," he said. "It'll be cold in the park. You can wear one of my jumpers if you like – fold the sleeves up." She'd worn one of his jumpers the evening before, and he thought it looked sexy, a turn-on, seeing her swamped in something so large. He thought it highlighted a sense of vulnerability, as if she needed him to protect her and be her knight in shining armour – and that, if he did, she'd be his prize.

But that night it wasn't cold. It had become a mild night and the pathways they traced through the park were full of lovers orbiting one another, radiating warmth, gravitating towards this fleeting galaxy of delight. Lovers and families.

"When I was a kid I wanted to run away and join the circus," he said. "We went one Christmas. I wanted to be a clown with a big red nose, orange hair and enormous yellow shoes, do tricks that'd make people laugh. They had a magician too. I must've been four or five at the time." His foot connected with a piece of bark and he kicked it to one side. "But I was fourteen, maybe fifteen, last time I properly went to a carnival. Went for the rides, rather than just to walk through."

"Me too. Who did you go with? A girlfriend? A nubile Year Nine girl you'd got the hots for?" She dug him in the ribs with her elbow and wrinkled her nose in mischief. "Did you make her wear your jumper too?"

A family of five were walking a few metres ahead. Parents, two sons and a daughter. The youngest boy was holding his mother's hand, the daughter had linked arms with her father and they were marching in step; the oldest boy seemed to be sulking and dragged his feet.

"No. There was no girl then. I went with mates from school. We used to go as a family, when I was younger. My father loved the atmosphere of the carnival, my mother just liked going out as a family – anywhere. She liked having us around her, I suppose." He stopped.

"Family was important to her," she observed, and gave his hand a squeeze.

He nodded. Family was *everything* to her. The memory

flattened him. They walked in silence a while. Sometimes grief knocks you flat to the floor and never properly lets you get off your knees again; every time you begin clambering up, something sparks a memory and you get knocked flat once more. You become a mass of bruises and cuts and aches. You just have to roll with it, and wait and hope. Eventually, time and fresh air will heal most wounds.

There was a dark centre to the park, where the path dipped into a hollow, leading to a round garden bed, from where a number of other paths radiated, like spokes to a wheel. The path they took ran parallel to a stream, a man-made watercourse, which dropped through a series of waterfalls into ponds. They passed a couple of benches and a large memorial to a half-forgotten explorer. But the spotlights weren't on that night, just the sounds of water and footsteps and the chatter of people up ahead and somewhere behind them. They walked without speaking a while and he warmed at the touch of her hand, the sounds their shoes made as they scuffed through leaves.

When the path brought them out of the hollow again, he said: "My father liked the machines at the carnival too, especially the old-fashioned carousels. He'd stand and watch the guys pulling the levers, adjusting gears. All that grease and oil. You could see him wanting to roll his sleeves up and get his hands real dirty. He was that sort of bloke; always wanting to be in the thick of it."

It was a relief and a release to talk, and to begin to fill the silence that had been weighing him down for so long. A healing. Her presence had begun to draw the hurt out of him, and she knew what to ask and how to listen. Sometimes it takes an age to realise how much the hurt of grief needs to be talked out – and to be able to talk it out.

For her part, though, she offered almost nothing about her upbringing. Occasionally, she scattered crumbs of information, like small gifts of her past, but then changed the subject or asked him a question about himself again. He wondered what hurt she might be hiding, but sensed a resistance in her that told him not to probe too deeply.

"All in good time," his mother would've told him. He knew there'd come a point when she was ready. And, truth be told, he delighted in the element of mystery she dressed herself in and played upon during those early days: the deliberate vagueness when she talked about her work; the sudden change in direction to some of her sentences; the suggestion of secrets that couldn't be shared or alluded to. She treated it like a game, mostly, so he treated it like a game too.

It was the opening night of the carnival and brimming with mobs of teenagers, entire families, young and old couples, and swimming with excitement. He bought her a helium-filled balloon in the shape of a heart and she threw her head back when she laughed, arching and exposing her throat, before tying the balloon to her wrist. She seemed relaxed again now, and the tension of the working day had dissolved.

"How romantic," she said.

He thought she might be mocking such sentimentality and so shrugged his shoulders. "Hearts are cheaper than round ones."

She punched him on the arm and boxed his head with the balloon. "I meant it. It's a good thing. Don't go and spoil it."

"Thought I might buy you twenty more and watch you float away."

"You're not romantic at all. You're a heartless, cynical bastard."

Placing an arm around her shoulder, he drew her closer. They moved among crowds of other balloon-anchoring, embracing couples; threaded around buskers and jugglers and mime artists, and passed a small queue of children jostling one another to have their faces painted by a couple of teenage clowns.

It was the best carnival ever.

In the open space at the end of one lane of stalls, a leather-faced performer, clutching a small, chrome-plated harmonica, created a flourish by playing a few harsh notes at the milling crowd – abrupt enough to startle a few and grab the attention of others. A small crowd were already gathered, waiting for whatever might come next, and a few more looked on as they walked past or paused to watch.

The guy looked as if he was used to living rough and Nic thought he was just a homeless bum looking for money until he began his delivery. He wore a patched ankle-length, oil-skin coat and a tattered, wide-brimmed felt hat drawn low; it appeared as if his few belongings were rolled into a bundle at his side, next to which a shaggy-haired mongrel lay panting, its tongue lolling out.

"Prop open your peepers," he crooned, reaching out. "Pin back your lug-holes. Gather round, gather round. In these two hands I have a story. Watch as I open this book." A true showman, he mimed the opening of a book, the turning of a page, then pointed a finger at the arc of his audience and let his roving eye draw them all in so they couldn't pull away.

"Once upon a midnight dreary," he began, "while I pondered, weak and weary, Over many a quaint and curious volume of forgotten lore – While I nodded, nearly napping, suddenly there came a tapping, As of some one gently rapping, rapping at my chamber door..."

Nic made to walk on towards another section of booths and rides, but Siobhan stepped closer, into the story-teller's arc – became part of the audience – and so he stepped next to her and they stood leaning against one another, soaking up the story behind the rhythm and the rhyme. He was larger than life, this story-teller, as if he'd stepped out of a tale or a ballad himself, with his theatrical delivery and his long, grey, matted beard and his skin that was dark-tanned leather. His eyes were as animated as his mouth and his hands, which danced with excitement as he brought life to the words and gripped his audience and drew them in.

"Ah, distinctly I remember it was in the bleak December, And each separate dying ember wrought its ghost upon the floor. Eagerly I wished the morrow – vainly I had sought to borrow From my books surcease of sorrow – sorrow for the lost Lenore..."

On the grass, half a step from where he stood, was a fire-blackened billycan, a quarter full with coins and a couple of notes. The dog sat up when a young girl, directed by her parents, stepped forward to drop a coin into the can. It lifted a paw in a doggy salute and the old guy winked his thank you at her, while continuing with his tale.

Siobhan laughed at this and cuddled closer to Nic, and other children standing with their parents wanted to give money to get doggy salutes too.

"And his eyes have all the seeming of a demon's that is dreaming. And the lamplight o'er him streaming throws his shadow on the floor..."

At the end of his recitation, he paused a moment, holding his audience that second longer in an electric silence, and then took a flamboyant bow that released them to their applause. Siobhan cheered and Nic dropped a gold coin into the can. She took out her wallet and peeled off a twenty. It seemed a lot, but she was glowing and so he shrugged and added another couple of coins too.

When the dog couldn't keep its paw in the air anymore it raised its muzzle and yelped a series of excited barks, and the story-teller took a final bow before kneeling at his bundle to pull out a bottle of water.

"Magic," Siobhan said. "I've always loved that poem."

Nic nodded, but considered the billycan of coins, the small bundle of belongings. "Not much of a life," he observed.

"Who knows? Depends what you want. Maybe his freedom is worth it."

"Who knows?" he agreed.

The carnival was everything he remembered it to be, but so much better because Siobhan and he were the nucleus of it. They steered one another from stall to stall, from ride to ride, talking and laughing louder as the mass of other people talked and laughed louder, and as one piece of music drowned out another, or was swamped by the shrill sirens and claxons announcing the beginning, end or drama of each new ride.

They wandered down the side of one set of booths, away from the crowd, and found themselves at the outer fringe, where five or six drunks were lolling and teetering, clutching bottles disguised by brown paper bags or swigging from cans of beer. Several fairground caravans and a few prime movers were parked close by; the cab of one was tilted forwards and a couple of men, stripped to their stained singlets, worked on the engine. In the seconds that Siobhan and Nic stood there, a fight erupted between two drunks. He tried steering her back into the alley of stalls and side-shows, but again she held back, wanting to watch. They were shoving one another around the guy ropes of a tent, too pissed to come to blows. When they fell over and, instead of swearing, started laughing on the ground and hugging one another, she shook her head and laughed too.

From a nearby speaker, Bryan Ferry sang: "Love is a drug and I've got to score."

"See, they're just messing," she said, and turned back to the carnival. "I could tell they weren't serious. They're all show, just like this place."

"All piss and hot air."

Five minutes later, as they sat in the Octopus, waiting for the ride to fill, she said: "At school – at Sisters Of Mercy – I got suspended for fighting. I gave the Head Girl a bloody nose. She was a couple of years older and a good bit taller, but knew she'd asked for it so wasn't going to say anything. But one of her friends blabbed to the nuns and, when I refused to apologise, they suspended me."

"You? You're joking?" He tried imagining Siobhan getting angry and lashing out, but couldn't.

"Too right I did. I've always hated mean, arrogant people." Above the safety bar that restrained them, she squared her fists at the memory and winked at him. "The nuns were worst of all. Vicious bitches mostly."

He put an arm round her and drew her closer. "What did the Head Girl do to start it?"

"Can't remember. I think she'd been picking on a friend of mine. Something like that."

"Standing up for someone, eh?" He nodded. "I like that."

"Maybe. Or maybe I was just in a scrappy mood, like those guys back there – a bit of mischief to get the adrenaline flowing. I don't remember now."

When the ride finished and they were standing next to one of the food stalls, cupping a styrofoam beaker of cappuccino each, he said: "How did your parents react?"

"To the suspension?"

"Yeah."

"They were alright. They understood."

He waited, then said: "What are they like?"

"Who?"

"Your parents, of course. Tell me something about them. How often do you see them? Are you close?"

"You want to know all that stuff?"

"Yeah. Of course I do. I want to know everything about you."

She blew on her coffee and sucked some of the froth from the top, seeming to dismiss what he'd said as if he couldn't possibly be interested. Then she smiled and conceded. "Oh well," she began, "they live in Ireland, like I said before. They left the place just before I was born – moved here – then returned for a holiday a couple of years ago, to visit relatives, and decided to move back permanently. After twenty-odd years, and to the town my mother grew up in, of all things. I told them they must be cracked, but they seem to like it, three doors down from my grandmother. And in a village where the priest still believes he's God's right-hand finger!" She held up her middle finger to emphasise the obscenity of the notion. "No accounting for taste, eh?"

He nodded. Perhaps there was bad blood between them. Perhaps she felt abandoned by their departure. That'd be understandable.

"You didn't want to go with them?"

"You're joking, right?"

"So you waved them goodbye, watched them fly off into the sunset?"

"We see each other. I've been to Ireland a few times." There was an abruptness about the way she said this: a closing announcement, not an intimacy. She'd narrowed her eyes and was looking past him.

"They must have missed the place and the people for all those years, and realised how much they missed it all when they went back."

"Hmm."

"Where is it they live? What's the name of the place?" He needed her to open other parts of herself to him. How could he understand her if he didn't know her?

Her gaze shifted back once more and she took a breath, smiled. "Have you ever been to Ireland?"

"No, but I'd like to. I've always wanted to go there. One side of my father's family – the milky part of the chocolate – comes from the south-west coast." He hurried on. "I'd like to visit the towns where the ancestors are buried and do the family history thing."

She nodded, considered. "My parents live in a small town, not far from Dublin." Then she wagged a finger in the air and began laughing again. "My mother used to tell a joke which her mother passed down to her. In many ways it was her motto, I guess. She told it whenever anyone was doubtful about what they were doing in life, where they were going. She – my mother – is the one with the get-up-and-go. My old man prefers the quiet life; as long as he has his beer, his TV and his horses."

"What was the joke?"

She cleared her throat, acquired a strong Irish accent and an affected turn of phrase. "There was this American professor, or some such; on holiday in Ireland, he was; doing the grand tour, don't you know, tracing his family history. Anyway, he'd got well and truly lost driving himself down and around and up and along the narrow country lanes of Ireland, as any tourist would, and so he stopped at a gate to a field and called over to a potato farmer for directions. 'Hey, Paddy, is this the road to Dublin?' asked the professor in his swanky American accent. Well now, the farmer stopped what he was doing, so he did, and he waded across the field to the gate in his gumboots, and he thought about the question for a minute or two, then he scratched his head like this, you know, and said, 'B'Jesus, man, this road will take you anywhere you want it to.'"

Nic waited, then smiled. "Is that it?"

"I guess you have to hear her tell it. She'd always tell it serious and then crack up, and that would get me going, along with anyone else that was listening. She thought it was right hilarious, but I guess it was really a piece of folk-wisdom. When I was a kid, she used to say the potato farmer was her own father – my pop – and that the American went on to become the President of the United States." She paused. "Each road leads anywhere and everywhere, I guess."

He'd finished his coffee and was playing with the beaker, squeezing it together until it began to split. "My dad was always telling stories too. I suppose it's one of those things most parents do. Except he thrived on having an audience to string out a yarn to, a bit like that guy back there. He loved it."

They swayed and tapped their feet to the beat of an unidentifiable eighties' tune, and he looked at her and wanted to kiss her and make her part of his life. He'd have liked her to have known his family, but the prospect of sharing some sort of future together would have to do instead. He folded his beaker in half and it snapped, leaving a small bead of coffee to run down his fingers. He licked it off and she raised her eyebrows, then she drank the last of hers.

"Each night, when he was home," Nic said, "Dad would tell us a story, my sister and me, before we went to sleep. My mum always read from a book, but he usually made his stories up as he went along – or built on the ones he'd begun before. Adventure stories, fairytales, folk-tales, extensions of TV episodes, stories with punch lines or twists... anything. We'd ask for a story about something or other and he'd make it up on the spot."

Like many people, Nic often measured the rhythm of his words with his hands – he talked with his hands. Sometimes he clasped them together as if in prayer, or as though they were the covers of a book, and sometimes he chopped sentences up into slices of ideas. Sometimes his boss would laugh at the way he'd use his hands to explain a job to a customer or to tell him something. Occasionally, if struggling for an expression, he'd use his fingers to draw out a string of words as if stretching chewing-gum from his mouth. It was a habit to rest his chin on them or hold a self-silencing finger against his lips when he was listening intently. He worked with his hands and he spoke with them.

"There was one story I remember him telling my sister after she'd been upset about something. It's a bit like your mum's joke: that even the longest journey begins with a single step. The story he told her was about a girl setting out on a journey to seek adventure and fortune, but who complained constantly that she wasn't getting anywhere fast, and who was really having one adventure after another without realising it. 'Each step is a journey to savour and enjoy,' he'd have told her at the end, or 'The journey is more important than the destination itself' – something like that. He liked stories to have a moral."

Siobhan stopped moving to the music for a moment. "You know what you should do, Nic, to honour your dad – your family? You should write the stories down before you forget them. These things shouldn't be forgotten. Not ever." She looked at her coffee. "Like that busker back there reciting *The Raven* more than a hundred years after Poe wrote it. Wasn't it fantastic? Our stories define us. I can't imagine who I'd be if I hadn't got hooked on *The Raven* when I was sixteen." Then, as if to dispel the embarrassment of having unravelled this truth, she pulled a face and eased into swaying with the music once more.

"I'm not much good at writing stuff down," he said. "I couldn't stand English when I was at school. I enjoyed reading, but that was about it."

"So what? What's that got to do with the price of fish? It'd be different if you're doing it for yourself. Just write them down as if he was telling them to you."

He nodded.

"I'm not just crapping on about this to be nice," she said. "I don't do that. I'm crapping on because I mean it."

He smiled at that and she took his crumpled beaker and slid it into her own before dropping them both into a nearby bin. Then she held his right hand and examined the oil-stained calluses on his fingers and across his palm.

"I don't think you're that different, your dad and you," she observed.

"You sound like you knew him," he said.

"From the way you've described him."

As they began walking again, she stroked the back of his knuckles, and they passed a unicyclist juggling three machetes who was staging an argument with a fire-eater. There were more kiosks selling toffee apples – red cellophane tied around each glossy apple-on-a-stick – and candy floss and popcorn and baked potatoes and hot dogs, and he steered her towards the dodgem cars, weaving between the throng exiting the Tunnel of Love.

It was edging towards midnight when they strolled back through the park away from the carnival. Siobhan held a pink bear with a heart-shaped balloon tied round its neck and Nic carried a coconut and a cheap tin whistle. As they reached the hollow and the water features in the centre of the park, the music of the carnival ended. Pulsing into the night one moment, silent the next.

They huddled closer to one another, then he put the tin whistle to his lips and sounded out a few soft notes with the fingers of one hand. Rough, tinny notes, played soft.

"Can you play that thing?"

For answer, he unlinked his arm from hers and gave her the coconut to carry, then played a few bars of *Waltzing Matilda*.

"You *can* play."

"A little."

"Anything other than *Waltzing Matilda*? Someone should bury that thing once and for all."

"How about this one then? This might suit you." And he played *Cockles and Mussels* all the way through the hollow and up to where the path lights were shining again.

When he stopped, someone in the scattered parade of people behind them carried on whistling and someone who knew the words began singing in a semi-drunken falsetto: "In Dublin's fair city, Where the girls are so pretty, I first set my eyes on sweet Molly Malone..."

"Very good," she said, drawing him close again, and burrowing her hand into his jacket pocket. "Next time I'm plagued by rats, I'll know who to call."

Information boards declared there were bats in the park, roosting boxes perched in a number of trees, but they saw none as they walked. Just a few faint stars and the glow of the city and, huddled at the base of a tree, trying to lose themselves in the shadows of night, a couple of junkies shooting up. One looked about eighteen and the other fourteen or fifteen at most.

Siobhan and the mechanic looked at one another, said nothing for a few steps. He glanced about, as if there might be other junkies squatting under trees like strange, fallen fruit, or else someone about to leap out and mug them.

"What a couple of tragics," Nic said. "What a bloody waste."

She said nothing for a few moments, until he thought she wasn't going to, then she said: "It's the fuck-wits in Government who make me sick. Them and their bloody zero-tolerance." They walked on a few steps, and she added: "They're the ones who push kids like that into filthy squats and back alleys – sweeping the issue under the carpet and into dark corners. It's because of them these kids shoot up every bit of shit they can lay their hands on."

There was a new tone to her voice, one he hadn't noticed before; he tried to catch her expression, but she was looking away, into the darkness of the park. "Some bastard dumped a syringe in front of the garage a few weeks back," he said. "I hate that. I hate having to pick those things up."

"Wouldn't happen if they provided safe injecting rooms like they promised, Nic. Clinics and health support might work better than detention centres and prison, don't you think? Generally politicians are such short-sighted, gutless bastards."

The families walking behind them had fallen silent. She took a breath and lowered her voice. "Their policies have made it worse, you know, just like Prohibition did in the States."

"Prohibition?" He looked back towards where the druggies were sitting, but it was too dark to see that far.

"Prohibition didn't end alcohol, did it? It just invigorated the black market. Racketeers thrived, while ordinary people drank themselves blind on moonshine. It's no different here. Those kids back there, they'll be dead inside a year because they'll end up buying any old shit they can. But hey, what does that matter?

They probably don't vote anyway."

He hadn't seen this anger in her before. It jolted him. "You know more about it than I do," he said.

"I... " she began, but stopped herself and shook her head; tried shaking off the moment with a grim smile. "Let's forget it, eh, Nic."

He squeezed her hand. "What? Tell me."

"Doesn't matter," she said. Then: "I read the papers. That's all. Anyone can read this stuff in the papers."

"That's not what you were going to say. What were you going to say?"

"My sister..." she began, and faltered again.

"You have a sister? I thought there was only you." But he guessed what was coming. The evening had led to this moment.

"I *had* a sister. Quite a lot older than me. She overdosed a few years back. That's the reason... well, it's the reason for so many things."

He stopped and wanted to hold her there, but she carried on walking. "Siobhan," he said.

"It's alright," she replied, brisker again now. "It was a few years back. I'm only telling you so that you know, so you under-stand why I get so peed off with bloody politicians and their bloody Law and Order campaigns. There's so much they're refusing to do that could really help."

"What was her name? What was your sister's name?"

"Her name?"

"Yes."

"Moira. Her name was Moira."

He felt relief, as if they'd arrived somewhere important together, as if the wonderful craziness of the evening had all along been helter-skeltering towards the unburdening of this moment, and he placed an arm round her shoulders.

"So you see," Siobhan continued, "we've both lost a sister."

He nodded. He'd guessed there was something like this; he'd

just known it. It was probably why they understood one another so well. He glanced up into the branches of a tree to find a moment of stillness among this rush of understanding, and then he said: "My sister, she didn't want to go on that helicopter flight, but I said it'd be a good experience. It was just a frigging joy ride, but I said she should go. She'd have stayed at home with a book otherwise." And in admitting this, his memories of family life, which had been growing thin, less substantial, for not having had someone to narrate them to, seemed closer and sharper again now; thanks to Siobhan.

She slipped her arm round his waist. "You did what you thought was right. That's all anyone can do."

"I suppose."

As they approached the edge of the park, the headlights of traffic on the avenue were no longer strobing between the trees, but flooding the fringe of grassland and footpath, and the sound of tyres became slick on the bitumen. The rumble and electric crackle of a late tram grew more pronounced, while, further off, a fire tender's siren scratched a dotted line across the western edge of the city centre. Gradually the lightness returned to their steps.

"Are you tired?" Siobhan asked.

"No, are you?"

"God no, the night's still young," she laughed. An impish, suggestive laugh.

A few spots of rain fell and the two lovers quickened their pace.

11

It wasn't long after this that Nic got in trouble with the police and was sacked by his boss.

One storm-wracked Friday, having been half-drowned in a torrential downpour as he ran the last block home from work, and just seconds after opening his apartment door, Siobhan phoned. There was a desperate urgency in her voice, which gave him precious little chance to think straight or ask the questions he otherwise might have asked.

"What's the matter?" he said. "What's happened?" Maybe there'd been an accident and she was phoning from hospital, or she'd been mugged, or she was having to leave the city more suddenly than she'd anticipated – be phoning from some distant place on the other side of the country or overseas? Her tone suggested all of these. His wet jacket was dripping onto the floor.

"At last. Been trying to reach you. Listen. I'm sorry. Can you do a favour? A big favour? For a friend. This bloke. Needs your help. Shit. Sorry. I'm out of breath. It'll wreck our evening, but he needs help."

"Slow down. Are you okay? Tell me what's up."

"I'm okay. He's up shit creek. Really. I'm out of breath. Running around, sorting stuff out. Then this stuff with Chris. He needs a favour. Straight forward. I wanted to catch you at work. Must have just missed you."

"What is it? Who's Chris?"

"He had an accident. In his work van." She paused and took a deep breath. The words came easier. "Bust up the headlights, pushed in a panel. Look, he'll lose his job if the business – his boss – finds out. He can't deliver his consignment until it's fixed; not at night, not without lights – the police'll pull him over. Look, he's on a final warning – bit of a dill, I reckon – and if he doesn't finish his delivery tonight or if he returns the van damaged he'll lose his job. He's snookered himself. He's got a wife and two kids."

It was a flood of words. He'd never heard her like this before. "You want me to open up the garage and fix his van tonight? You're kidding?"

"No. I wish I was. It won't wait until tomorrow. He managed to buy the parts he needed and was going to try doing it himself, until he realised he didn't know where to start. He'd have ballsed it up for sure. That's when... Well, I said I'd ask you. You don't really mind, do you?" She was calmer now. "It'll wreck our evening, but it'd get him out of shit creek. He sounded desperate. I'll make it up to you tomorrow, big time, I promise."

The storm clouds had sucked most of the light from the day and his apartment was swamped in gloom. Looking around the room at the darkening corners, he waited before speaking, in the hope a different solution might step out and present itself – anything rather than say no to her. He dropped his bundle of mail on a chair, dragged his wet shoes off, tried to peel off his jacket while holding the phone, flicked the light switch on.

"Nic," she said, "are you still there?"

"Yep, but I don't know, Siobhan. I'd have to phone the boss. Tell him what's going on. I'll have to ask if it's okay." He'd been set on having a hot shower, before meeting her at a fashionable restaurant that she'd somehow managed to get a reservation for. But the evening was washing down the drain and he couldn't hold it back.

"Of course you do. He won't mind, will he? He's an okay guy isn't he? Look, I'll have to tell Chris something. Let's assume your boss is okay about it – after all, he left you to run the place for a fortnight and something like this could have happened then – and I'll tell Chris to meet you there at six. I'll be there too."

"That's only thirty-five minutes."

"You're the best. Look, I'll have to go now, my battery's running flat. It's been a shit of a day. Everything happens at once. There's other stuff I have to tell you, that we have to talk about. Probably for the best we're not going out tonight; I'd more than likely fall asleep sitting up. Don't worry about the reservation, I'll cancel it." And she was gone. Hung up.

Outside, another cloudburst rolled through and the rain beat against the windows of his apartment as he tried to phone his boss. The rose bushes and ferns shook feverishly in their terra-cotta pots and leaves scudded like whirling dervishes across the balcony.

His boss's landline and mobile both rang out, no answer machine on either. He vaguely remembered half a conversation; something about taking the family to see his mother, but even as he scanned through the couple of hundred listings of that partic-ular surname in the telephone directory, he couldn't remember where she lived or whether the location was even mentioned. It might've been in the suburbs or a few hundred kilometres away for all he knew. He might not have got home yet; he might be caught in traffic; he might have gone shopping.

Glancing at his watch, it was already six o'clock. There was-n't time to take a shower or even grab a bite to eat. Only time to remove his damp, dirty overalls, grab a clean pair and his car keys, ride the elevator to the basement and drive back to the workshop.

"Fuck, fuck, fuck," he said.

It was twilight, except in the narrow alleys where it was already dark, and a mud-spattered white transit van was parked close by. The rain had abated and the wind had eased, but the traffic hissed along in the wet and the black bitumen glistened with the reflections of city lights. There was no sign of Siobhan.

"Are you Chris?" he called to the figure climbing down from the van. When the guy nodded, Nic said: "Where's Siobhan?"

"She said to tell you that something came up: business. Wasn't a happy camper at all. Should've heard the language on her. Said to tell you she'd phone later." He was wearing driving gloves of all things, but removed them as he walked over to where the mechanic stood.

"Let's get on with this," Nic said. "You'll need to drive into this first bay, once I've opened up. I can't see it properly out here."

"I appreciate your effort, mate," said Chris, shaking his hand. "I'll see you right for helping me out like this; make it worth your while, for sure. What's your favourite beer? I'll get you a slab of something."

"No matter. What are friends of friends for?" Nic muttered, and went to switch off the security system, open a roller door, scrub up for a touch of patch-and-paint surgery.

The damage to the van was obvious but easily repairable. Chris' determination to yack on about nothing in mate-to-mate small talk was the biggest problem. Nic didn't want to know anything about him, nor to talk about Siobhan with him. If there was anything worth knowing, then she'd tell him later.

"Is that your Jag?" he said. "The old E-Type is it? Pretty special car, that one, mate."

"Yep." Nic peered in the back of the van. It was full of boxed TVs, DVD and CD players. Thousands of dollars worth. "Who do you work for, Chris?"

"City Electrical Discounts. Rip-off merchants, they are. Bastards'll sack me if they find out about this."

"Yeah, Siobhan told me."

"How long have you owned this beauty, mate? Shit, it's a nice looking car." He was standing by the E-Type now, peering at the dashboard, then had the door open. "I used to dream about having a car like this. Must have cost an arm and a leg. You don't mind if I look inside?"

Nic frowned. "I usually charge," he said.

"You're a legend."

"You're a wanker," Nic mumbled under his breath and got on with the job. Somehow the moron had cost him an evening with Siobhan, although she said she'd make it up to him and he guessed what that might mean. But other stuff had got in the way too. Maybe she'd wrapped up her work and it was time to move on. She couldn't drag it out any longer; there was another job to go to. Another city, another state; maybe overseas. That's probably what she needed to talk about.

When he was an apprentice fresh out of school, he'd learnt that long distance relationships were doomed to fail – had spent an electric summer with a girl called Maria, until her family moved away – but Siobhan meant more to him than anyone he'd been with before, in a way he'd never dreamt of. He didn't know what they'd try to make work between them, or how they'd cope with not trying. Shit, what a night it was turning out to be.

A couple of minutes later, Chris was standing next to him again, leaning over his shoulder – a space invader with garlic breath and lank, greasy hair.

"Looks like you know what you're doing. How about I go and get us a couple of take-away pizzas? My shout. Get out of your road for a while."

"That'd be good," he said. "Anything'll do." Felt like adding: "Get out of my face too."

There was something freaky about being in the workshop that night – it smelt wrong, tasted wrong, prickled at his skin – although tiredness, anxiety, disappointment, would've played a part. He fumbled with the tools, felt someone was watching him.

He looked over his shoulder, then stood, went to the open door and peered into the night. He came back to the van, turned on an extra couple of lights. Thought he heard shuffling beneath a workbench.

"Siobhan," he called. There was no answer, but the scrabbling stopped. A rat or a mouse, perhaps.

He tried phoning his boss again, but without luck. Always turned his mobile off after work. Nic looked through the office to see if he could find a telephone number for the guy's mother or a mobile number for his wife; half-hoped there'd be a list pinned to the wall or scrawled down one edge of the greasy calendar, a flashing neon arrow directing his attention to it. Nothing. No clue.

He got on with the job. Expected the Chris-fella to return after twenty minutes, but, despite his growling stomach, was glad he didn't. The bloke was a creep. He can't have been a close friend of Siobhan's.

And then his world and the order of his life changed forever.

He was pulling the last of the panel straight when the sound of the traffic flow outside drew his attention. The sudden silence was too specific, too focused, too complete. Pausing in what he was doing, he listened. From somewhere not too far down the block, the sound of three cars (a Lancer and two Commodores) separated from the silence, accelerated down the road and screamed to a halt just a few metres from where he was kneeling. The workshop filled with the blinding brightness of three sets of headlights on full beam and, in the contrast of sheer darkness created behind, the suggestion of three blue beacons flashing and the strobing blinks of red. Carnival lights.

The three cars blocked the entrance to the garage. The rushed opening of car doors and racing of feet in all directions... Too much, too quickly. It was a scene from a film – from any number of films. It was absurd. In the next second, he understood he was being robbed – or was snagged in the middle of a robbery – and didn't know why until he remembered the van loaded with electrical goods. Then the beacons became police lights – of course – and the confusion left him reeling. There was shouting – voices shouting at him – and the meaning behind the shouting took a moment to reveal itself. Like surfacing from beneath the dream-silence of water, to find yourself drowning.

"Stand up slowly! Slowly! Slower! Put your hands above your head! Up! Come on, we said move. Now! Come on, do it! Over here! Move over here! Now, face down! Get down! Lie down! On the ground!"

He stood up. He moved. He lay down. Mechanically, without thinking.

The day had become a dream, a film scene, spliced out of place into his world. He lay face-down on the cold, painted cement, with his arms pinned behind his back, half-glad of the chance to recover his balance, but comprehended instead another piece of information that had been there all along: the police had their guns drawn and pointing at him.

When he had sense enough to know that he could open his mouth and the right sounds would come out, he spoke: "What the fuck's going on?" Even then, his throat was dry, constricted, and his voice was less than a warble.

"Pipe down. We'll be getting to you in good time."

Something about the language and tone placed him back at school, standing outside the principal's office. Sent there by some bullying teacher.

A number of voices came from different parts of the garage, and he tried quelling his panic by counting how many cops were in the place. He made seven.

"Hello, hello, hello, what have we got here?" The open mockery of a pantomime policeman, loud enough and obvious enough for Nic to know the comment was directed at him. "Not only do we have one stolen van in the process of being tarted up, but it's still stacked with the proceeds of an armed robbery. A little slow off the mark, were we? Where are your mates?"

"What? You want to tell me what's going on? I don't know what you're talking about," he croaked, his face still pressed against the cement. How many times had he swept and scrubbed this patch of floor?

"Over here!" another voice called, with an urgency that made him try to turn his head and look.

A couple of minutes later, a calm, low voice spoke so close to his ear he could feel breath on the back of his neck: "Is the black Jaguar your car, sir?"

He swallowed, cleared his throat. "Yes. Yes it is."

Close to one policeman's foot, a mob of ants were dissecting a half-dead moth.

"Nice car," the voice continued. "Top shelf sound system.

Very expensive. Pretty good on a grease monkey's wage."

"Flash bastard," another voice said from across the garage, but contempt travels.

"I must be in the wrong job," the first voice continued. "You win the lottery or something?"

Nic closed his eyes. "Or something."

"You can stand up now, sir. I think we have everything we need to be going on with. Give him a hand, will you."

Two pairs of hands grabbed under his arms and pulled him to his feet.

"Are you a registered firearm owner, sir?" The plain-clothes cop held up a clear plastic bag for Nic to recognise its contents. Filling the bag and weighing it down was the bulkiness of a black revolver. The gun was like something from the cowboy movies of his childhood, but with a longer barrel than he'd imagined. It was the first time he'd seen a gun like that – up close and way too personal.

"No," he said, "and I've never seen that before either."

"In that case, perhaps you could explain how it came to be placed under the driver's seat of your car?"

He shook his head. There were no words left.

"Now that's what I call an optional extra," some smart Alec said.

12

Truth is often a matter of perspective and it was the numerous gaps revealed in Nic's explanation that damned him more than anything else. But then, if he'd been in the cops' shoes, he wouldn't have believed his story either, not as things turned out. The pillars supporting his world hadn't so much crumbled as vanished, with no trace of ever having been in place, and the sky came tumbling down.

Hello, Chicken Licken.

There's no prize for guessing that, while the police pulled the garage apart, the parasitic prick who called himself Chris failed to return clutching two boxes of pizzas and declaring Nic's innocence: "I'll cop it sweet, detective – the stolen van, the stolen goods, the armed robbery, the gun, the lot – but leave the grease monkey out of it; he didn't do nothing. Honest."

At first, Nic imagined the lank, greasy-haired bastard coming back from the pizzeria, stopping at the sight of the police cars and promptly side-stepping into the nearest dark alley of dog shit, garbage bins and discarded needles – where he belonged. But much later, when unanswerable questions outweighed hypothetical answers, he suspected that the ploy to fetch pizzas was a portion of a larger conspiracy and that Chris, if that was his name, had waltzed down the street to phone the police and let them know where they could find the van, the goods, the gun and the mechanic. The whole neat package bundled together, ready to go; an easy take-away. A classic set-up with no rhyme nor reason he could grasp. What he wouldn't have given to be left in a room with the bastard for just ten minutes; one minute if he had a monkey wrench to swing.

But, hell, this wasn't the worst of it.

This was sweet nothing compared to the completeness with which Siobhan waved her magic wand and vanished.

Pfft! Gone.

Not only did she disappear into a bubble of air but she left so few traces of having ever existed at all that he began to wonder whether he hadn't just wet-dreamt her into being. Maybe, all along, she was some sort of erotic sprite, a sylph, a shade, a spectre.

Being crucial to his explanation about that evening's events, when she couldn't be found to confirm what he'd said, and even her identity couldn't be verified, the police suggested she was a figment of his bizarre lie. Her non-existence made him culpable, his guilt became palpable.

It left him dizzy with doubt. And the doubt began throbbing in both sides of his head, in his temples. How could anyone confirm the past – even the recent past – if all proof of it had vanished without trace?

The detectives visited her apartment so she could 'assist in their enquiries', but the tenant's lease had ended that day. Someone confirmed that she sort of fitted the description offered by Nic, but there was no forwarding address or other details for her. The flat had been rented under a fictitious name and paid for up-front, in cash. The detectives called her mobile phone number, but a cattle farmer from way up-country, somewhere in the back of beyond, bordering the Never-Never, answered. The farmer hadn't heard of her or anyone who sounded like her; his phone hadn't been stolen and was in daily use. Another dead end. The detectives searched their computers for licence details, for any official documentation – or so they told him – but found not a single reference.

"Siobhan McConnell," he repeated for the umpteenth time. "That's her name. Maybe you spelt it wrong, maybe you're looking under the wrong spelling." He gripped the edge of the interview table and would've snatched their notebooks to see what they'd written if he could. How could he make them believe him? His head pounded. His legs would no longer support him.

Nothing made sense. He was hopelessly lost.

"We've tried a million variations, mate. Either she don't exist or that ain't her name." One cop walked to and fro behind him, one sat in front; the latter had turned his plastic chair round and had straddled it back-to-front, his arms resting across the ridge of its flimsy back and his head resting on his arms as he stared at Nic.

"What are you saying? Of course she exists."

"What about her business? Self-employed, you said?" And a

meaningful glance passed from one to the other; the edge of a smirk.

"Like I said before, I don't know the name of her business. She was a freelance consultant or self-employed or something. Perhaps she went by her own name."

"Oh, of course – how bloody obvious – a name that's not registered anywhere. Jesus H. Christ, you've got to be the world's worst bleeding liar!"

"She didn't like talking about her work."

The detective behind him laughed; more a snort than a laugh. "I bet she didn't."

Whenever they left him alone a few minutes, he'd close his eyes and try finding one clear thought, but then he'd give up and stare at the emptiness of the opposite wall or count the cigarette burns on the table instead. The police station was airless, dry; smelt faintly of sweat, urine and stale cigarette smoke. The styrofoam beakers of lukewarm brown liquid tasted like nothing he recognised. He couldn't fathom how he'd arrived at such a place.

"You said you did a job on her Porsche. What was that about? When did you do that?"

How could he have forgotten? This was his proof. The car registration would be listed in the garage accounts. That'd prove Siobhan was real. They'd trace it, find her and she'd tell them all she knew. She'd explain everything the best she could.

Or that's what should've happened. But it made things worse.

"You're wasting our fucking time," they came back at him. "I don't mind telling you, I thought there might've been one bloody crumb of truth among all the crap you've given us, but it's obvious you're protecting your mates."

He'd sat upright when they'd re-entered the room, ready to be told everything was okay and he could finally go home. "Why? What's happened? What about her car? A blue Porsche it was. Metallic Midnight Blue." Already panic was gripping his stomach and twisting.

"They should give you a bloody Oscar, they should. Not that you ain't a crap actor – they should give you a bloody Oscar for trying."

Nic turned to the second detective. "What's he talking about? What's going on?"

"You've been telling us pork pies."

"What?"

"Lies. One little porky after another. Story after story."

"No."

"There was no Porsche on the books whatsoever," he continued. "No such account. And why would there be, you dummy, when there's a dealership just a block away?"

"No."

"Well, if you're keen to do time for the bastards who did that job, then you can. You can do the lot."

Nic shook his head and the throbbing became a lump hammer on each side. The buzz of the fluorescent lighting grew louder and he closed his eyes, put his hands over his ears.

There had to be something he was missing, something about Siobhan he might remember. Whatever it was, though, he couldn't find his way back to it. If it was even there to begin with. The trail of their shared past had vanished, been wiped out. He'd been dancing with a phantom. He really had.

Except he wouldn't give up. On himself, on her, on the simple truth of what they'd shared. He mustn't. Without that there was too little left to believe in and he might as well admit his guilt for a crime he didn't commit – it'd be a world where truth counted for nothing.

Muffled by the pounding in his head, he thought he caught an echo of his mother's voice at her most sentimental: "Keep true to who you love and love will be true to you." But then he wasn't so sure it was her at all. Not there, in that place.

"There's a reason for everything and a solution to every problem, Nic," his dad would've told him, although his dad would've never got in such a situation to start with. "Don't let a door and a small room shut you down; it's a big world out there."

Though he'd have liked to have heard Siobhan's voice. To know where she'd vanished and why.

"If you don't cooperate and give us a few names, we can't help you," the leather-jacketed detective told him.

"Never been in a prison before, have you?" the other said. "Don't reckon you'd last a week, let alone week after week, year after year."

"You're looking at twenty to twenty-five, you know."

"They'll have you for breakfast, lunch and tea, and nobody'll hear you screaming."

"The newbies usually get done in the showers, you know. If you survive that, you can keep the HIV or Hep C as a souvenir."

"It's dog eat dog in there, and you're a pussycat."

"Hold on. Can he be a pussycat and everyone's bitch at the same time?"

"I guess he can."

Nic rubbed his face with his hands. "I don't know any names. That Chris guy is the only one I spoke to. I've told you this. I've told you. Why won't you believe me?" If he could've made up a few names to give them, to get them off his back for a few minutes, then he might've done. But he had to hold on to who he was and had always been, and had to fight becoming someone else he didn't want to be. In this nightmare, it was beginning to seem possible that he might slip into becoming someone else.

"You know what I reckon?" one of the cops said. "I reckon there's a strong chance the courts will decide you bought your fancy apartment and that flash car with the proceeds of criminal activity. That means they can be impounded and auctioned off. Do you realise that? I might put in an offer on the Jag myself. What do you reckon?"

"Do you seriously appreciate the deep shit you're in?"

One torment after another, pinching at him. He was stunned.

So fast was the fall into Hell. He stared in disbelief, blinked several times, and was slow to realise they were conjuring nonsense.

It was all nonsense.

"Bullshit," he said at last, and the throbbing in his head slowed, eased. "That money was left to me in a will and paid out by insurance companies. After my parents and my sister died. I can prove it." He pushed his chair back with a scrape across the vinyl floor, looked at the door, found the strength in his legs to stand.

"I want a lawyer now. This has gone on long enough."

"A lawyer? What do you want a lawyer for? We haven't charged you yet."

"Then fucking charge me. For crying out loud, just bloody charge me."

So they did. Handling stolen goods and unlawful possession of a firearm, for starters. Even so, once a lawyer arrived, he was soon out on bail.

13

His boss called at the apartment on the Monday, shortly after midday. Nic had phoned in sick, was still half asleep.

"Got you out of bed, did I?" his boss remarked. Took in the dimensions and furnishings of the apartment in one long glance. "Didn't realise you had such a flash place." His eyes lingered on the wide, flat-screen TV mounted in the middle of a broad expanse of whitewashed wall.

"Come in," Nic said. "The police messed it up a bit. You on lunch break? Sorry I couldn't get in today. Shit of a weekend." He shuffled towards the kitchen, then stopped. Drew a hand across his face; realised he hadn't shaved in three days. "I'll get you a drink. Black tea, one sugar? Do you want a bite to eat?"

He yawned, moved towards the sofa and leant against its arm.

"No, I won't stay. Don't have time." His boss remained standing by the door to the apartment, looking down at his hands. He might have been wringing them. "I'm going to have to let you go. Wanted to tell you in person. Can't pretend I'm not disappointed."

Nic sat, then stood again, took a step towards his boss and stopped. Wasn't sure where or how to place himself. "But it was nothing to do with me. None of it. I've been set up. From start to finish. You can't seriously believe...?"

His boss looked down again, then looked up and met his eyes. "Well, that's as maybe," he said. "At the very least, you opened the garage without asking me; did some moonlighting. I can't have that. It's my livelihood – I've spent years building that business. The police dragged me away on Friday night in front of my children, my wife, my mother. Came back on Saturday. How do you think that looked?"

Nic sat down again – slumped down. "I tried to phone you; couldn't get through. You weren't home."

His boss stayed where he was, his back to the door. "Word's got round already. I've had cancellations this morning. I shut up shop to come and tell you in person. You can come and get your gear tomorrow, but you need to give me the spare keys now."

"You're serious?"

"I'll give you a decent reference, even though... Show there's no hard feelings, eh?" He made a point of glancing around Nic's living room again. "You won't starve," he said. And that was that.

It might have been easier if he could've cried – if he could've sat blubbering in a corner at this new loss – but he hadn't wept in an age and was stuffed if he'd start now. Not for this. Maybe he should have planted his fist through the plasterboard and railed against the world: "Fuck you, you bastards!" But he was too drained and numb to rage and shout. He stared at his own redundant hands a while, then curled onto the sofa and slept some more.

14

That a person should be considered innocent until proven guilty is a cornerstone of the judicial process, they say. Society at large isn't half so generous though: if shit gets thrown, then some will stick, and the stink'll linger for an age or two. You can't wash it off in the shower. Notoriety, whether it's deserved or not, attracts some people and repels others, but it took less than a fortnight for Nic to discover who his friends *weren't*... which left Ophelia (who was a cold fish) and Polonius the rat.

Standing in front of the photo of his family on the ferry, his mum would've wagged a finger if she could as she said: "Forget them. If they won't stand by you when you need them, they're not friends at all. They're narrow and shallow. Shame on them."

"And steer clear of the creeps who suddenly want to know you," his dad added. "They'll be trouble, for sure."

Nic nodded. He knew this stuff. What he really needed were good lawyers and character references.

"You can draw on my name," his dad reminded him. "Of course you can. Definitely. Call in a few favours. Pull a few strings. You have to, Nic."

"Look to some of your dad's old mates," his mum chipped in. "God knows, he did them enough good turns."

His sister's hair blew in the wind. Her smile was frozen in place.

The Right Honourable William Pennant MHR, who'd wined and dined with his dad, and who Nic had first met at one of their house parties, agreed to provide a character reference for the court. Although Nic didn't like the guy – he was as slick as an oil spill and in love with the sound of his own voice – he'd become a big name in politics and, to be fair, didn't hesitate when phoned for the favour. He didn't need to be asked twice; it was as if they'd only met yesterday. Nic had to admire him at least for that.

"Of course I don't mind you asking," he said. "Your dad was a good man. Besides, we all need a hand every now and then. It's what makes the world go round. I'm a politician, remember." He laughed at his own joke and droned on for a minute or two. Nic tried to listen and appreciate what he was saying, but there was nothing much to hear. It was the clipped elocution that Nic's always found most irritating. He spoke with a plum in his gob, as if he belonged to a ruling class of fifty years earlier. And the accent had become more pronounced with each political success, as if he was growing into a caricature of someone he thought he might be; just to save the cartoonists from interpreting him for themselves. He finished with: "Give all the details to my secretary and she'll sort it out. Glad to be of help. Any time."

Once the call ended, Nic held the phone and stared out his window at an empty park. It was a grey, cold day. Not a drunk or a junky in sight.

There were long weeks, months, between his release on bail and the court appearance, and each day of these saw a contraction of his former, peopled world. Each contraction assisted in giving birth to the wizened, shrunken chick that his new world seemed set to become, and he had several notions about the ugliness it could grow into. A faithless, loveless, suspiciously foul thing.

Autumn. Winter.

He lost weight, he endured short, dark days and long, cold, cheerless nights. Newspaper headlines mirrored his mood:

FOOD FACTORY FINISHED – 400 JOBS LOST
GREY AXES METHADONE CLINIC FUNDS
FLASH FLOOD KILLS CHILDREN
SYRINGE BANDIT TARGETS TOURISTS

There were times when he'd kneel to feed Ophelia – a pinch of dried fish food – and, five or ten minutes later, would shake off his trance, having emptied half the container into her tank. At other times, he'd forget he'd opened Polonius' cage so he could run around and have a taste of freedom. Once, he returned home and almost buried his pet rat with the heel of his boot – Polonius hiding behind the curtain, nestling in the warmth of its drapes, and Nic about to draw them both closed for the night. Another time, he returned to find he'd left the balcony door open, and (his attention caught by a raven croaking on the balcony rail) discovered Polonius peering over the edge, about to discover the universe beyond.

Forgetfulness. Distraction. Depression.

Winter in the city was usually characterised by two or three light frosts at most, but the frosts were harsh and bit deep that year; although he found no delight in looking at a glazed landscape, it matched the brittle cold he felt in himself. If he didn't know better, he'd have guessed that his heart, lungs and guts had turned to ice. Before long, his next breath would crystallise and choke him. It was part of the spell. In the park, he watched children try to slide on whitened grass, but found no pleasure in witnessing their excitement, only bitterness.

"Whose patsy have I been?" he asked himself. "Whose fool? Where's Siobhan?"

Not knowing was the worst thing. No explanation made sense. If she was involved, how was she involved and why? If not, why hadn't he heard from her? What if something bad had happened to her?

There was no way of finding out. He was worried sick about her; he felt cheated and betrayed by her; his life was withered and hollow without her.

Winter. Spring. Months of waiting.

After the sting of several pointed rejections, there seemed no sense in looking for work. The word, it seemed, had been passed around and good references counted for stuff-all. His only achievements were his transformation into a hairy man – wild corkscrews of black hair and the scraggliest of beards – combined with a shelf of reading.

Reading fiction was a comfortable escape from the ugliness of his closed world. A matter of sitting in front of the fire when it was wet and cold outside. It took him all the way back to childhood, when his mum would read to his sister and him, and he was reminded too of the stories his father told, which he began writing down, as Siobhan once suggested he should – but because he wanted to, not because she'd said so.

At first he couldn't remember the words, just the gist of one story. Then, as he jotted the idea down, the words came back like the unreeling of a tune, and he found himself remembering one story after another and could even recall the intonation of his dad's voice as he told them. With it, came the warm scent of the man: a distinctive aftershave he'd never been able to track down for himself, blended with starch from his mother's ironing and a body smell that reminded him of strong tea. It was like having part of him back again.

"Once upon a time there was a noisy man..."

The Longest Journey.

"Once there was a pirate called Jake Blake..."

He remembered the way his dad smiled out of one side of his mouth and his faraway look as he conjured a character and a country and the journey to take them there. And though Nic had never known where the rhyme originated, he remembered the chant that became the nightly anthem of childhood and the prelude to every tale: "Tell us a story, Jackanory. Tell us a story, do." These were things he'd forgotten until he started writing the stories down.

Tell us a story, Jackanory.

Remembering such details was a diversion, but for every new book he read and every old story he recaptured, his hair grew longer and more unkempt, and he was less sure about where his life could go. Sometimes he picked up a book and stared at one page without connecting to a single word; at other times he'd read a book, cover to cover, in one sitting, forgetting to eat or wash or sleep or deal with the pile of dishes blocking the sink. He read anything and everything; directionless.

In court, looking more the wild man than ever, he was painted by his own lawyer as naive, gullible, an innocent taken advantage of. He loathed hearing these things even though he understood the strategy behind such words. The public humiliation was punishment in itself.

An immaculately-groomed, sharp-suited David McKenzie, of Hepsburg & Conway, said, "A testimonial from a prominent member of Government should help, as well as your father's reputation, and the fact that you've never been in trouble with the police before."

And here was another connection with his father's world, for the old man had used this law firm for years and, having grown with him and profited from him, they were happy to ensure Nic had the best representation available – as long as he had money to pay.

"I think we stand a fair chance with the Handling charge," David McKenzie added, and glanced at the mechanic's straggles of hair before automatically re-straightening his already straight tie – a conservative pattern of blue and grey diamonds, sharpened into a Windsor knot. "However, the prosecution will push on Unlawful Possession. The courts have been coming down hard on firearm offences since the Gun Laws debate."

This proved to be the case. The charges relating to the stolen goods and the van were dropped, but having an unregistered gun without a licence and carrying it in his car brought a conviction and a suspended sentence. He'd been wrongly accused and unjustly found guilty. Justice was more than an ass: it was an arse and it shat upon him.

15

Three days later, Siobhan re-entered his world.

With the court case and the verdict behind him, he experienced relief, then uncertainty, then relief again. Relief that the ordeal was over, uncertainty about how it might affect his future; relief that the worst was known, uncertainty about how he might recover his equilibrium. Oscillating from one to the other, the underlying constant beat was his anger at the unfairness of the world. It was a steady rhythm behind his thoughts, which robbed him of sleep as it tapped away at his consciousness and as he swung from one state of mind to another. He didn't want to be an emotional pendulum, ticking off the remainder of his days, but knew that unless he found another job to occupy his waking hours and leave him dog-tired enough to collapse into sleep each night, this would be the pattern of his days for some time to come.

Three pink roses bloomed prematurely on his balcony, but the petals were ripped off by wild, spring winds and became confetti on the pathway below. Daisies, daffodils, jonquils, shook yellow and cream heads as he shuffled through the public gardens, trying to escape his own company and the confines of his apartment; but he wanted neither reproach nor sympathy.

There were, however, more minutes of daylight than in previous weeks and the sun's warmth was more pronounced. Summer ceased being a memory and became a prospect instead, as is the manner of each season.

Nic had gone late to bed that night, three days after his sentencing, worn down from watching two movies and gulping a couple of sleep-inducing whiskeys in the hope that a heavy sleep would pull the curtain down on the past. When he woke his determination to start afresh would help him recognise new possibilities. With a new day might come a new start. He'd recover the person he had it in himself to be.

Perhaps the real nature of optimism was simply a matter of perspective: that long, sunlit days inevitably succeed the long, cold nights of winter, rather than the reverse; that if the glass is half-empty, it must also be half-full. He remembered his mother telling him once that a good night's sleep could solve all manner of problems. He picked up a photo of her and dusted its frame with his finger. "The world will be a brighter place in the morning," she'd say with a wink and a hug; "you'll see."

So be it. He'd give it a try. Give anything a go.

Siobhan entered his sleep, his world, the morning of the next day, in the form of a succubus. Slinky and sexy. Afterwards, he'd consider that the dream she woke him from should've been, by rights, erotic; the steps her hands were dancing beneath the doona should have seen to that. Instead, he woke with a jolt, having dreamt he was being smothered; he'd moved interstate to get work and it was his first day as a miner, but the shaft cage crashed to pit bottom and, though he somehow survived that long, terrifying drop, he was now being suffocated by the broken bodies of those poor souls who'd been in the cage with him.

Gasping awake to the real world, Siobhan was kneeling at the side of his bed. Her hands were weaving a magic around his shoulders, across his chest, towards the waistband of his boxer shorts, and he started at the moist warmth of her breath close to his ear, at finding someone in his room intruding on his sleep.

"What the..." he exclaimed and would've sat up, except she laid her arm across his shoulders and kissed his face – his brow, his eyes, his lips.

"Ssh. Good morning," she whispered. "At last. Oh, it's been too long. I've missed you," she crooned. "How I've missed you. But so hairy. What long hair you have, what tight curls you have. Oh so very, very hairy."

It was blowing a gale outside and her hair was damp; a few strands were flattened against her cheek. Befuddled by sleep, he struggled to be sure what time of day it was, what time of year it was, whether the events of the last few months had been a bad dream, whether Siobhan had in fact ever been real.

It gave her enough time to pull his doona back, slide up from where she knelt and straddle his legs. She sat above him, looking down, and squeezed his hips with her knees. Glancing across the room and seeing it to be the same as he'd left it the previous evening, he recognised what was a dream and what was real.

"What..." he began again. He borrowed a moment and took a breath to keep in check his anger, his delight – any tone that might betray him – until he was sure of himself, and her. "What are you doing here?" There were months of questions shouting to be asked, but what if she disappeared too quickly?

"Hi, Nic. The key you gave me. Remember? I keep it round my neck, next to my heart."

He looked when she pulled at the brown shoelace she was wearing and drew his key from the top of her dress, but he shook his head. "Not what I meant."

She raised her eyebrows, giggled, was pleased with herself and the surprise she'd conjured. "How I've missed you."

"And you were missed," he said. "The police missed you. My lawyer missed you."

She paused and sighed, seemed to deflate a tad. A clock measured the moments. He could have counted to five before she spoke again.

"Yes. Well. I couldn't help that and I'm sorry – more than sorry. The last few months have been shit all round. If I could turn the clock back I would, believe me. I thought I'd lost you forever. Look, I didn't find out what had happened to you until it was too late to do anything that might help. That *really* might help."

"You knew? About the charges, that I'd lost my job, the suspended sentence?"

"I was out of the country. A long way from anywhere, from

anything. It took a while to put the pieces together. And then, to top it all, I got robbed. I lost my passport, ticket, phone, almost everything except your key. I only just flew in the night before last. Look, if I could've done something, I would have, but it was way too late by the time I found out. Way too late. And then... well, I've been worried sick about you."

She paused again, as if hoping that might do, then slid her fingers around his waist and dug her nails gently, provocatively, into his skin. "Oh Nic, it's so good to see you again."

Fat chance, he thought. His dream was more real than this. "That's too easy," he said.

"What is?"

He took a breath. "It doesn't explain why you never got in touch, the way you disappeared. Even the police couldn't trace you. And what's with your name? And the apartment... There's too much you're not telling me. How bloody stupid do I look?"

He tried telling himself he didn't enjoy having her back, didn't enjoy her sneaking into his bed, sitting on him, wanting him; that the anger outweighed all this. He placed his hands around her arms as if to move her, but looked into her eyes instead. He thought he'd known her before, but the more he looked the less he now knew. "What is your name? Your real name. Who are you?"

She crossed her arms, sat upright as she looked down at him in mock-disdain, pouted; wanted to play at being the upset little girl. "I knew how it'd seem. I guessed you might be like this. Really, it was ages before I found out what had happened and then there was nothing I could do. When I heard how you'd been treated, I got scared; figured they'd try linking me in too and throwing the same crap my way. And that'd finish me off; I wouldn't be able to work again. Didn't think you'd want that, even if it would've cleared anything up – and it wouldn't, I can tell you that for certain. We'd have been no good to ourselves, no good to one another or anyone else."

She looked away a moment, and he could tell she was considering what else she might say. "But you got off, didn't you?" she continued. "They gave you a suspended sentence. That's nothing. Everything's worked out okay, hasn't it? You're clear now. It's over. We can get on with our lives. Nothing's changed who we are with one another, what we had – what we have."

"You've been gone for months. You could've helped. You could've explained about that Chris-prick. Let the cops run after him instead of me. You could've done something."

He began sitting up again, realised he'd have to shake her off, even if it meant pushing her to the floor, but she'd closed her eyes and was shaking her head. When she opened them again, they appeared watery, and she placed a finger on his lips.

"I love you," she murmured, except it was almost a groan.

Her dress was a deep maroon; the colour of arterial blood. It was a light material and he could make out the shape of her breasts, her nipples, through it.

"What?" he said.

"I wanted to fly back to you and help. Really I did, Nic, but it was no good by then. And then I was too ashamed to even get in touch until I could make amends and sort something out. Until I could offer you something. You don't know how much it's hurt to stay away, but I can help now though. I already have. Let me try and explain. And if you want to throw me out at the end I'll go, and I'll never darken your doorstep again." She smiled at the pantomime phrase, wiped a hand across her brow in mock tragedy. Except her eyes were still watery. "You can even have your key back." And she placed both hands over her left breast.

And this is the story she began to spill, almost word for word; certainly the gist of it:

"Once upon a time there was a girl called Siobhan McConnell – "

"No, Siobhan. Stop. I don't want a story. Stop playing games. It's too late for that."

"But it's complicated," she said. "If you want to know properly, you must be patient. There's a lot to tell. You have to listen."

"Then tell me straight."

She shrugged. "Well, like I was saying, Siobhan McConnell *is* my name. Siobhan is my middle name and I use it because I don't like my first name – it's hideous – and McConnell is my parents' surname, but not the surname on my birth certificate. My biological father left when I was a baby and I don't remember the bastard. Mum remarried when I was three and we took on Dad's surname – McConnell – but my name was never officially changed or anything like that. I went through school as a McConnell and the only people who ever get to see my 'official' surname are the faceless bureaucrats I don't give a stuff about, like tax collectors and customs officers. Everybody I care about knows me as Siobhan McConnell. The police can't have tried very hard to look for me, but they don't always, you know; some are lazy, dishonest bastards."

She held up five fingers and tapped down her thumb, as if she'd proven her first point, and then she wiggled her index finger and continued her story. She'd begun to brighten again now.

"As for the apartment, I don't always sort out my own accommodation. The company I was acting for leased it on my behalf. I don't know what name they put it under or how they arranged it. Probably some secretary or temp sorted it out. But again, the police could've still found out who was paying the bills if they'd really wanted. Isn't that what detectives are supposed to do: detect? I don't reckon they even tried. They'd nabbed you and only you, and probably wanted to make their charge stick – not to lose their arrest. You'd be surprised at some of the stories I've heard. They're not all honest."

"What about the phone? Even if it was turned off or stolen, the number for the SIM card would've still been registered in your name. What about that?"

"Who knows? Maybe the transmitter was playing up, maybe they got a digit wrong when they tried ringing. But even if they bothered contacting the phone company, they wouldn't have recognised my name because I would've flashed my passport as proof of identity when I first bought it."

He studied her face and wondered what name could suit her more than the one he knew. "What is your name?"

She considered this, laughed and shook her head. "Tell you what, I'll give you three guesses, and if you guess correctly I'll be your slave for life. But if you don't, then you're all mine. Forever. To do what I want with. And we'll put the last few months behind us."

He closed his eyes and tried fighting off her affections. "Stop with the games, Siobhan. Just tell me."

"No," she said. "Not today. Not when you're like this. One day, perhaps, but not today."

He was ready to shout, pull himself from under her, but she pushed her fingers through his hair, experimented at pulling one of the tight curls straight; combed her fingers through his beard. "I can't get over all this hair. It makes you look different. Half-man, half-beast."

"Harder?"

"No."

"Don't you like it?"

"I'm not sure I do."

"I didn't grow it for you." He shook his head, wouldn't be won back so easily. "Tell me about that Friday."

She raised her eyebrows, sighed, and lifted up five fingers again. She tapped three down and wiggled her fourth. "Whatever you say, Captain." And saluted.

"It was the craziest of days from the start, that Friday," she began. "By lunchtime, I knew I couldn't stay in town any longer. I just couldn't. I had to make arrangements to be overseas – Africa – within forty-eight hours. And I didn't have a clue when

I'd be back here again. We knew it might happen like that, didn't we? I did say, didn't I? I was going to tell you over dinner that evening, but then all that stuff with that bloody van happened and then my flight changed, and there was nothing I could do to let you know.

"I was going to be at the garage – do you remember? – and I was going to arrange something special for our last two days together, but my flight plans got shunted forward again and I had to leave straight away. I had to dash straight to the airport. The gods were against us that weekend. Bad karma, perhaps. I tried phoning from the terminal, several times, but you didn't answer; there was no reply." She laughed, as if appreciating a newly-discovered irony. "I thought you were sulking, that you thought I'd stood you up for no good reason and was refusing to talk to me. I thought you were being childish, the frustrated lover, so I decided to let you stew until you phoned me – give you a couple of days at least."

"I was being held in a cell," he said, "thanks to your bastard friend." She sounded like the voice of reason, but there were other things she wasn't talking about that didn't make sense. "Why the hell would armed robbers bother repairing a stolen van? Wouldn't they just steal another? And as for that fucking gun, why plant that in my car? I lost my job; I've got a criminal record now. If I put a foot wrong they'll lock me up."

She looked down at him, pinned under her, and bit her lip; but then lit up again and giggled. "I wouldn't mind being locked up with you," she said, screwing her nose up in that impish smile.

"You think it's funny?"

"No. Not at all." She dropped her voice an octave: "I fully appreciate the gravity of your situation." But she was laughing as she raised herself on her knees and deftly undid a button on his boxers. "You're on your back and I'm on top."

He grabbed her wrists, pulled her hands away from him, held them there. "Stop. Just stop, Siobhan. The whole thing must've been a set-up. But why? Why would any bastard do that? I'd never met the guy before. But you had. The bastard was a friend of yours."

She sank at that and the smile dissolved again. She shook her head. "No," she said.

"What?"

"I hadn't met him before. He wasn't a friend of mine. Stop saying he was."

"What?"

"You're hurting. Let go." She twisted her hands from his grasp. "I never said he was a friend of mine. I'm sure I didn't. Why would I? I did think he was a buddy of someone who's very close to me, though, and it was this friend who asked me to help sort things out. It was all a massive balls-up. God knows what was going on – or why."

He shook his head.

She rubbed at her wrists. He'd left red marks there. "I'm not usually a sucker for a sob story. I'm not usually that gullible. But I wasn't thinking straight that night, probably because I'd had a shit day with everything else happening and it caught me on the hop."

His voice became acid: "That's brilliant. Thanks a million, Siobhan. So, what's the name of this guy you're very close to?"

She shook her head. "No one you'd know."

"But at least we can get him to tell the police who this Chris-prick is, so I can get my life back. To prove I was innocent all along and clear my name. Not that I owe them anything."

She put her hands to her face. Shook her head. "No, Nic. No, we can't do that."

"Why? Because your friend was involved and you're trying to protect him? You'd rather I was in the shit than he was?"

"No, not at all. It's nothing like that. It wouldn't affect him either way. Honestly. He wasn't involved and the police wouldn't touch him. But – "

"Then why? Tell me why. Tell me why or you might as well...
you might as well go."

She stared at him and her face and her voice were expres-
sionless when she said: "Because this guy – Chris – he'd kill
you. No two ways about it. He'd kill you."

"What?"

"He's an absolute whacko, Nic. I've found out a bit about him.
It wouldn't be just him, either. The thugs he'd hang around with
would all be head-cases too. You're naive if you think he's the
sort of person you'd cross and get away with it. They'd put a bullet in your head – and mine – as soon as look at you. I'm not kidding, Nic. You just have to thank your lucky stars you didn't
come off worse. A suspended sentence is nothing. Really. You
don't mess with people like that." She added: "My friend's sorry.
He didn't know at the time either."

He stared at her.

"Sorry," she said.

He shut his eyes. Tried to think.

"It's only a suspended sentence, Nic. It means you got off –
otherwise you'd be in prison now. Best leave it alone and move
on, eh? These aren't the sort of the people who'd let you dob
them in to the police and live to tell the tale. The only thing to do
is cut your losses and get on with the rest of your life."

It was too much to take in. All the same, perhaps the worst had
passed and life might come good again.

She sniffed, then leant down against his chest, kissed his lips,
drew back and kissed him on the nipples. She lay like this for a
minute and he lay there too.

"You're very hairy," she said.

"Yeah, well." But he wasn't with her yet.

She slid one hand down to his waist and flicked her fingers
under the waistband of his boxers and she slid the other hand
through his beard, and he didn't stop her. "So very hairy," she
said. Then she whispered against his ear: "What big hands you

have. And what big teeth you have." She was giggling again now, trying to return them both to a better mood.

Sitting upright, she began hitching her dress up to remove it, and he knew she'd be naked beneath – except for his key on a necklace of shoestring. But he took her by the shoulders this time and clamped her there so she couldn't move.

"No. Slow down," he said. "I need to think. I don't know about anything anymore. Besides, the world's moved around a few times since you were here last."

"What's to think about? Have you met someone else?"

"No."

"Then relax. Trust me." Her hands slid back to his boxers. "Besides, you look like you've missed me. Like you want me." Still that cock-sure smile.

He closed his eyes. "Perhaps you should go. I'm not sure this is a good idea."

"Don't be so uptight, Nic. Relax."

"Really. You should go."

She ignored him. Her eyes were half-closed, her tone became a crooning once more. "I've saved the best till last," she sang. "I have a proposition for you: a new job. I found one for you. You'll love it. Job of a lifetime." Her voice was almost a whisper, a series of sighs. "After," she said. "I'll tell you after."

He wanted her; wanted her back so badly. Too badly. But it hurt him that she could re-enter his life and offer him something he wanted, and that he might sop it up like a pet dog begging for treats. Pride had to count for something; self-worth had to count for something.

"I think you best go, Siobhan. Please. I need to think." Dragging himself from under her and pulling himself up against the head-board, she lost balance, fell backwards and sideways.

Landing on her back on the floor, her feet in the air – a dark flash of pubic fur – she scrabbled to unscramble herself and stand, and she was rubbing at her wrist.

When she straightened her dress, her eyes were narrow slits. "Fuck you, Nic," she said, holding her arm.

He shook his head. "Not today," he muttered.

He closed his eyes, took a breath and he heard her push the bedroom door back as she left. But a moment later she was standing in the doorway clutching her coat and her bag. "I am sorry, you know. Very, very sorry. I don't think you realise that." There was a catch to her voice and he could tell she was crying.

"Okay," he said. But then she was gone.

16

A couple of hours later, Nic was halfway through stripping the sheets from his bed while listening to *If The Sea Was Whiskey*. Siobhan had bought him this album of early Blues recordings soon after they'd met – her first gift. She'd heard a couple of tracks being played in a café or somewhere, and had been won over by the gravel-lined voices and tinny instruments, the stories of lust and broken hearts and cold comforts. Here were the likes of Muddy Waters, Blind Willie McTell, Leadbelly, Lightning Hopkins – even their names painted pictures of men whose lives had been lived with little but words to a song or two and the beat of their music – and there was comfort in hearing them play out a tale of betrayal or bleak hope on such a morning.

Part-way through *Little Red Rooster*, two short buzzes on the intercom followed by a longer one: the way she'd usually announce her arrival. He allowed himself a brief grin, tossed a pillow onto the mattress and released the breath he felt he'd been holding all morning. She'd stormed out with the key still round her neck, as far as he knew – at least she hadn't thrown it at him – but there were rituals to arguments like this, he supposed, and it wouldn't have been right if she'd let herself in. Not this time.

All he'd needed was a couple of hours and Big Joe Williams' *Baby, Please Don't Go* to begin getting his head around what she'd told him. That's all. She'd have cooled down and realised as much; he was ready to talk now. It had been a fuck-awful few months, for sure, but it'd be good if they could somehow pick up the pieces and get on with their lives, one way or another. The past had passed. It was time to move on.

He sprung across the apartment to answer the intercom, his finger hovering on the door-release button, and was ready with a smart-arse comment. However, he was greeted by the brusque voice of an elderly woman instead. Against the background rumble of traffic and a crackle that had crept into the speaker, he had to ask her twice, but she either told him she was from Something Correctional Services or from Something Personnel Services. She wasn't collecting for the Lost Dogs' Home or selling God through instalments, that much was clear.

She was a short, bespectacled lady – the stereotypical image of a fairy-godmother, down to her brogues and tweed woollen suit, her tight bun of ice-white hair – and, once she'd been invited in, she stood in the middle of his living room, waiting to be offered a seat. Quaint.

He ran both hands through his hair. Didn't like to ask again where she was from – he'd work it out. "Have a seat," he said. "Please." Wondered what the day would throw at him next.

In her buttonhole was an early white rose; a small double bloom. In one hand she clutched her handbag and in the other a large, manila envelope; the only thing missing was a smile. To Nic, she looked old enough to have retired from whatever it was she did; as if she should've been playing bowls or organising a crochet or croquet club instead. Her name was Mrs King.

"I come bearing gifts," she began. "Or, more precisely, I come bearing an offer of employment."

"Oh yes?" He leant forward in his chair.

The employer she represented, it seemed, was aware both of

his 'straitened circumstances' and 'considerable skills', and was, in short, offering him a once-in-a-lifetime opportunity to help manage the workshop of a rural garage, which also dealt in selling new and used cars. His references were excellent, his conviction of little consequence – well, everyone deserved a second chance – and he'd received the strongest recommendation. If he proved himself and fitted in, there'd not only be opportunities to become involved in the sales side of the business, but it was possible he'd be groomed for a management role too.

He'd be provided with modest accommodation and arrangements could be made on his behalf to let his apartment if he wished. Remuneration would be higher than he was accustomed to and living costs much lower. However, he'd have to complete a three-month trial contract and respond to the offer within twenty-four hours because the need to fill the vacancy was urgent and there were other candidates she might approach.

"This is Siobhan's doing," he said. "Siobhan recommended me, didn't she?"

"Who?"

"Siobhan McConnell."

Mrs King raised her eyebrows. She didn't appear to recognise the name.

"Never mind," he said. "It doesn't matter."

She tapped at the envelope, which she still held. "It's the job of a lifetime and a once-only offer," she repeated.

A raven landed on his balcony railing, leaned forward and spewed out the roughest cadence of caws. It might have been laughing or it might have been scolding.

Mrs King paused at its row and narrowed her eyes to peer at it, then turned back to Nic and wrapped up her offer. "Take it or leave it, but you'll never get another offer like this one; I promise you that much."

She wouldn't stay for a cup of tea, nor was she at liberty to reveal the name of the employer; all relevant details would be provided in good time if he accepted the position. She'd return in twenty-four hours to receive his response. And that was that. The "Good day" she left him with was as brisk and brusque as the "Good morning" she'd arrived with. Whatever was in the envelope wasn't going to be revealed until her return, it seemed.

"Siobhan, Siobhan, Siobhan," he said, leaning against the door as Mrs King's footsteps faded towards the elevator. "Siobhan, Siobhan, Siobhan."

So this was the job she'd wanted to tell him about, until he'd given her the bum's rush. It was being offered to him on a plate. How had she wangled such a deal? No wonder she'd been excited – or hyper, more like it. He shook his head, sighed and pushed himself away from the door. Not only would it help him back on his feet, but he might even be managing a garage before long. That's what the woman had said.

Siobhan.

He needed to see her again. He had to. He'd made his point, that she couldn't take him for granted, but now he needed to see her. He'd forgive her for abandoning him; she'd forgive him for pushing her away. He'd evened the score a little, that's all. They'd forgive one another and make love. He could almost smell her, taste her skin on his tongue again, could feel her body pressing against his, drawing him deeper. They'd been perfect together before and they'd be perfect together again.

And yet he'd thrown her off... Would she even listen now? What would he say? What *should* he say?

He paced from room to room trying out phrases, trying to draw the best words out, chewing against his knuckles, at the same time as agonising whether to accept or reject Mrs King's offer – teetering from one to other. Straightened a couple of pictures, tidied away his shoes, peered out the windows. Stared at familiar objects, as if finding something new in them; as if he might come across the elusive, right words sitting on a chair or on the end of his bed or perched on the windowsill, waiting to jump into his mouth.

He picked up the phone, put it down, then picked it up again and pressed her number. It rang and rang, but there was no answer and, this time, no MessageBank.

"Shit," he said, and shoved the phone back into its cradle.

Ten minutes later he pressed the redial button, and then half-an-hour later, and then half-an-hour after that. He spent the day trying to phone her and pacing, wanting to talk it through with her, needing to talk to her, and wondering whether he really had to leave his home, his city, to move forward with his life.

"I deserve a slice of good luck," he told a photograph of his mum, his sister, his dad. "Maybe I should take the job. Maybe I should rent out the apartment and take the damn job."

"Every journey begins with a single step," he made the old man say.

At twelve o'clock that night, with his lines for Siobhan rehearsed and word perfect, but wasted on too many unanswered calls, he calmly placed the phone back in its cradle for the last time. By then he knew he'd lost her. She'd found him the job he needed, and he thought he might take it, but he'd lost her.

17

Next day, having signed the contract and seen Mrs King to the door, he stood in front of his bathroom mirror and examined the image that frowned back. Pulling his hair tight with one hand and obscuring a portion of his beard with the other, he looked to find the person he really was. It was time to leave the past behind. Again.

"Time to find a pair of scissors," he said to his reflection. "Time for a new start."

Look forwards, move forwards, never back.

Taking up the scissors, he began hacking hair off in clumps. The beard trimmed down easy enough, but he had to saw the scissors' blades through the tangle of curls to get anywhere close to his scalp. In this manner, he cropped himself. Then he plugged in his shaver and ran it back and forth across his face, neck and scalp until his skin was smooth. Baby smooth. Almost.

A new start.

"Welcome to the new me," he said.

18

This, then, is how Nic came to be on the road, viewing his departure from a city of tall buildings through the rearview mirror of his glossy black 1972 E-Type, Series 3. Once he'd overtaken the slow cattle truck he'd got stuck behind, he'd accelerate towards the freedom of a new start, towards an unboundaried sky and limitless horizons. New people, new places, new life. The past would diminish into the tiniest of specks and then disappear, because everything vanished after its time: good and bad, happy and sad. Any last doubts he had about this journey would vanish as surely as the road unravelled.

Driving beyond the dry, deserted plains of old market gardens, where billboards and elaborate facades advertised city-expansion housing estates and off-the-peg, instant suburbs, he thought he could smell a faint whiff of newness blowing through the air vents and brightening the windscreen. Yes, he was sure of it. Unwinding his window, he took a deep breath as he peered at the hazy green distance and its horizon of rising hills, patchwork farms, forest shadows; he wondered how long it'd be before he returned and what new, whole person he'd have become.

Sometimes you've just got to leave a place in order to begin again. Sometimes you have to leave in order to return.

Sometimes you return only to find that nothing can be the same again.

Anything had to be an improvement on the last six months.

19

He stayed the night at a scabby motel in a small town he'd never heard of. But then he'd never heard of any of the places he shot through towards the end of that day. They were hamlets mainly and meeting places for the local farmers: a church, a pub, a couple of houses and bugger-all else. This one had a river running through it and a near-horizon of mountains breathing swabs of moist, cool air across it, and also a High Street, shops and a motel. Perhaps he might've reached Gimbly in one haul, if he hadn't spent the morning cleaning his apartment, waiting for the agent to collect the keys and sign-off on the inventory, or if he'd have pushed on through the night, but there are journeys when it's important to relish a sense of arrival, and this'd be no treat if it was the middle of the night when he rolled into Gimbly, too hungry and dog-tired to care.

The motel room felt damp and stank of something sweetly artificial like carpet deodoriser or toilet cleaner. But the heater worked, and he cranked it up to shut out the chill of night, turned on the TV and fell asleep.

In the morning, he woke to a persistent knocking at the door. There was a tangle of sheets about his head and the fragment of a dream clinging to him.

"Hold on," he shouted, still half-asleep, struggling to get out of bed. Perhaps the alarm had failed to wake him and it was time for his breakfast tray to be delivered. "Just coming." Then he caught sight of the clock and it was only six-thirty.

The knocking turned into a tapping on the glass of the balcony's sliding door. A single tap, followed by another, then another.

An element of the dream resurfaced and for a moment he knew it was Siobhan, throwing pieces of gravel from below to rouse him. Somehow, she'd tracked him down to this place and this room to join him on the rest of his journey. He swung out of bed, dragged his pants on and went to the curtains. One foot was still numb with the awkwardness of sleep. He had an inkling that she'd displayed anxiety in his dream, and that this was somehow connected to her fear of losing him – he was pleased.

There was another tap as he snatched at the curtain and pulled it back.

What he saw was a magpie, pecking at the window with its beak, confronting its morning reflection. He dragged the curtains further apart and it took fright, hopped back a step, and then feigned a lack of interest in its vanishing other-half.

Sleep eluded him after that. He boiled the kettle, brewed a cup of tea, watched a mist evaporate on the mountains. The day promised to be fine. A fine day to herald a new beginning.

20

It became a day of birds. Two galahs flew to the spare seat on his balcony and perched there preening and chattering as he ate breakfast. Close to, in the branch stumps of a heavily pruned elm, a murder of crows squabbled for position while, along the main road, cockatoos flocked through the tops of Norfolk pines, pinching out each tender tip. And when he carried his baggage down to the car, he found a raven striding across its bonnet, leaving a trail of muddy prints, pronouncing itself hoarse in a single mocking croak, framing Nic's arrested movement in the cocked head of one white eye – challenging the world to ever know any different.

He got in but the E-Type wouldn't start. Nothing. He climbed back out and lifted the bonnet, and then tried again, but the battery was dead. Not flat, but dead. From four or five metres away, the raven stared at him slouching in the driver's seat with the door wide open, then strutted a few paces along and peered at him with its other eye.

"Caw!" Nic croaked. The raven said nothing.

There was only one thing to do. He'd have to wander down to the local garage and hope they had a compatible battery.

"Shit," he said.

"Caw!" the raven croaked and jumped into the sky.

Half-an-hour later, he was folding the flap from a cardboard box over and over, to pack out the difference in size between his old battery and the new one so that he could properly clamp it in place. It wasn't ideal, but it'd have to do.

He worked to the sound of the river, which ran along one side of the car park – an incessant pounding and gushing of water over rocks. Every time he breathed in, he could taste, across the back of his throat, the bitter coldness it brought tumbling from the mountains. And it was weird but comforting to think these waters probably grew into the same river that eventually meandered, broad and quiet, through the parklands of his city, before swilling into the bay. This rugged, bleak place may have felt distant and foreign, but the city wasn't really that far away. Just a few hours by car. He was reminded of Siobhan's story of the potato farmer and American President – how even a narrow, muddy, farm lane can lead anywhere and everywhere. He could always drive back to the city for the weekend, any time he wanted.

Nic drove and the road unwound. From lowlands to mountains; from wheat lands to dairy country to forest. The first fringes of desert not many hours distant. He gripped the morning and his machine gripped the road, slicing each climb and twist of rising-hill country.

Battalions of plantation pine stood sentry to the side of the road, in front of him, behind him, reducing the early sun to a dazzling stroboscope of light for at least half-an-hour. A few native trees – eucalypts probably – straddled the side of the road in places; every now and then a larger stand broke the regimented monotony of pine. Rosellas darted from nowhere to nowhere; just flashes of crimson, brilliant blue, streaks of green. Wagtails hopscotched the road ahead of him, magpies gossiped at the side or played dare. An eagle spread its wings at the sound of his distant horn and made its slow, lumbering take-off in front of him; he ducked automatically, saw the limp tail of its prey dangling from a clenched talon, avoided pinion feathers by centimetres. So many close misses, near hits, but the world was hunky-dory and the day had put a smile on his face.

Until, that is, he turned a blind corner at speed and came too fiercely across a few relatives of old white eye the raven, plucking at road kill – a semi-pancake of feral cat. Instinctively, he swerved to avoid such a group and the day changed its grip in an instant.

Hitting the gravel at the side of the road, one front wheel locked into a rut and took him in its own direction. He knew to steer into the skid and to ease slowly off an unsealed verge, but there was a fallen branch looming ahead, getting too near too quick, and he stamped on the brake and swerved again. All this on a loose surface. The car swung into a one hundred-and-eighty spin and sent it skating across the road onto the opposite verge. He fought with the steering wheel, was aware of dirt, gravel and mud kicking up and spattering the windows, felt the centre of balance teeter into the brink of a roll as it slid across a porridge of soil and grass and gravel towards the enormous girth of a magnificent, sky-kissing eucalypt.

Gripping the wheel and gritting his teeth, he was about to end in a broken mess.

And then it stopped.

It just shuddered to a stop. A metre from the tree.

He sat there. Then let go of the wheel. Staring at the windscreen. Pushed his door open. Turned off the ignition. And breathed. Took a long breath. Unfastened his seatbelt and almost fell out the car.

He was greeted by the sounds and movements of a forest in the morning. The bush. The melodic pipe-call of a butcherbird. Somewhere in the distance the laugh of a currawong. A hundred metres or so ahead of him, three ravens croaked priority over their road kill and continued tearing at viscera.

"Back-back-back!" they cawed.

"Shit." He took another deep breath.

The air smelt good. Better than he'd known it could. A blend of damp moss, rotting vegetation, decaying timber, pine resin, eucalyptus... burnt rubber. The bitumen had two snaking, black lines tattooed along it, across it; the gravel shoulder and grass verge carried two fresh wounds, and his car was the colour of dirt. But he was alive. And unbroken.

He drew a finger through the dirt on the door to reveal its glossy blackness, then walked round the car a couple of times. Inspected the tyres once and immediately inspected them again. Ran a hand along the panels, knelt down and peered underneath from three different angles. Shook his head.

Miraculously, for all the compressed drama of his four or five second slew, not only was he unscathed, but, apart from a blown tyre and a couple of scratches, the car wasn't damaged either – as far as he could tell. He'd take a proper look later. Polonius was on his back legs, sniffing the air-holes of his travelling cage, and only a little of Ophelia's water had spilt.

The eucalypt he'd nearly collided with was colossal, its girth greater than the width of the car. He took a piss behind it –

exchanging one union for another – replaced the tyre, eased the car slowly back across the verge and onto the road, inspected it once more for broken hoses or buckled joints, then set off again.

"Stupid," he told himself, frowning in the rearview mirror. "What a fucking idiot." And then he laughed. "Stupid, stupid, stupid."

Hills became mountains and pine plantations gave way to virgin bush. Each bend in each damp stretch of road became a dog-leg or a fiddler's elbow or a hair-pin, and the journey stopped being a matter of moving forward and became the zig-zag agony of one mountain pass after another. The road had been blown and cut through gargantuan outcrops of rock – strata of granite and quartz – and ferns, algae, rivulets, tree roots, all clung to and coursed from these precipitous embankments. To the side of the road, deep gutters were choked with fallen boulders, scree, fronds, bark.

The trees were giants and gnarled witches, conjuring gloom, blocking the warmth and light of day. Weaving an impenetrable barrier. Twice he turned on the headlights.

For over an hour, he drove through this type of country. Oppressive, smothering, claustrophobic. He was itching to stop, stretch his legs, have a bite to eat and a strong coffee. But there was no place to stop. No building, no café, no pull-in. Nothing. Just one blind bend after another.

It was soon after the mountains subsided into hills again, and the battalions of radiata pine stood sentry once more, that he missed his turn for Gimbly. If it hadn't been for the photocopied map and scribbled instructions Mrs King provided, he might've carried on another twenty minutes or so. As it was, he drove a couple of kilometres before realising he'd missed his turn. Retracing his route, he almost went past it a second time – the road he needed seemed little more than a loggers' track, and any signpost identifying the Gimbly junction, along with the distance to the township (thirty-two kilometres), was gone. One day, he'd wonder whether it had been obscured by forest growth or deliberately ripped down.

On his poor excuse of a map, Gimbly sat at the dead-end of a long and narrow valley, surrounded by an amphitheatre of hills, and was accessible only by that one road. Even so, after the first kilometre or two, he couldn't believe he hadn't misread the map and taken the wrong road after all. He stopped and checked it again, and wondered what sort of redneck, hillbilly town he'd find at the other end.

The road surface was sort of sealed, but had so many potholes and cracks – from caterpillar tracks of forestry equipment, or frost and heavy trucks, perhaps – that it might as well have been unsealed. It remained on a level to begin with, but struggled all the same to wind a tortuous route along the contour of the hill. After about five kilometres of this, it pitched down a steep incline.

Although the surface of that stretch was in better repair, there was little choice but to groan down in low gear, feet hovering on the brake pedal and clutch. At the bottom, though, it looked as if there was nowhere to go but through a river in full flood – across a ford – but the road right-angled at the last moment into a new stretch, which led to a bridge and then hugged the bank of the river for about a kilometre or two before crossing another older bridge and climbing to a higher elevation. Between road and river was a narrow flood plain, reedy in places and grassy in others.

Almost fifteen minutes later, the road emerged from a low tunnel of trees – a bramble of knotted branches and creepers that characterised the unruly wild of native forest – and he caught his first glimpse of the township. Such as it was. To the left, the river was still running parallel; a flock of ibis stabbed at the ground and a couple of heron stalked the water's edge.

It was what he'd been travelling for. His neck was stiff, his shoulders tight, his hands rigid on the steering wheel, and

Polonius was doing everything he could to scrabble out of his cage. So he cruised to a halt, slipped on the handbrake and turned off the engine. He stretched his neck, relaxed his shoulders, unclenched his jaw, and lifted Polonius up; then got out of the car and walked to the verge for a better view.

"Our new home," he said. It was a statement, but could equally have been a question. The amphitheatre or horseshoe of hills that surrounded the few buildings comprising Gimbly had, for the most part, been cleared for grazing. It was a still day and from where he stood he could hear the occasional bleating of sheep drift towards him.

Somewhere, not too distant, a generator was chugging, and he thought he could smell diesel in the air. The warmth and brightness of the sun was heartening after the damp shadows of the roads he'd been following all morning. But the smallness of the township startled him: just a huddle of buildings nestled to one side of the river at the base of the horseshoe. He saw a High Street of sorts, a few houses and a couple of sizeable structures, but that was about it. It was a fraction of what he'd expected.

"The bright lights of Gimbly, eh?"

What he'd envisaged arriving at had something to do with the dimensions of hope and promise. Not quite a new world, but a sense of something big enough, broad enough, dynamic enough to offer him a new beginning and, one day, to catapult him back into a metropolitan life based on success – swept clear of any trace of past disasters. Instead, it felt like he'd stumbled upon a lost town.

Polonius ran up his arm, around the back of his neck and down the other arm, his whiskers working overtime. The mechanic cupped him in both hands and stroked a thumb along the grey fur on his back. A simple caress.

"It's a new start, that's all. If it doesn't suit, we can always leave." He wondered how tight his contract was. "Might as well take a look, I reckon."

Turning to walk back to his car, he stopped. About fifty or sixty metres behind where he'd parked, tucked off the road and hidden from sight by a screen of bush, crouched a police car. He couldn't make out the features of the policeman sitting inside – just the dark shadow of an interior beyond the reflection of glass. But he sensed he was being watched. Nic raised a hand in greeting, nodded his head, smiled enthusiastically, and then climbed back into his own car. He returned Polonius to his cage and leant across to check the goldfish.

"Hello, Ophelia. Welcome to Gimbly."

Interlude

"Tell us a story, Jackanory.
Tell us a story, do."
"Pin back your ears, my little dears,
And I'll tell you a story true."

Once upon a time, in a land far, far away, lived a girl who was visited one day by a wise old bird – a raven. The wise old bird landed on the windowsill above her bed and told her she must travel to the other side of the world because there was a handsome prince who needed saving from a fearsome dragon... or because there was treasure to be found, or simply because it was time to have an adventure.

"But how do I get there?" the girl said. "The other side of the world is as far away as far away can get, and I don't have a bike and I don't have a horse and I don't even have any rollerblades."

"What do you have?" asked the wise old bird.

"Everything you see here and nothing else besides," she replied. "The clothes I am wearing and this piece of bread and this lump of cheese."

To which the bird added: "And eyes to see and a mouth to speak and a tongue to taste and a nose to smell and ears to hear. To say nothing of a head to think with and a heart to love with, a pair of capable hands and TWO STRONG FEET."

The wise old bird shouted these last words so loud that the girl fell back down on her bed in surprise.

She thought for a minute about the wise old bird's words and then she said: "But it will take forever and a few days more to walk from here to the other side of the world. I'll never get there."

"Ha!" laughed the wise old bird, as it hopped along the windowsill. "Don't you know that the longest journey in the world begins with a single step? If you learn nothing else, learn this. Everything else follows on from that."

And with that, the old bird pecked a meal from the girl's piece of bread – in payment, perhaps, for its wise words – then flapped its wings once and was gone.

And, what's more, before that day had breathed many more breaths, before the sun had grown much higher in the sky, the girl was gone too. Placing one foot in front of another, she was already heading towards the horizon in search of her Happy Ever After.

"Tell us a story, Jackanory.
Tell us a story, do."
"Pin back your ears, my little dears,
And I'll tell you a story true."

Once upon a time, not so long ago, in a land not far away, lived a noisy man who wouldn't be quiet and wouldn't listen. He was an old man, even though the hair on his head was blacker and shinier than a raven's feathers and even though he wasn't very wise, for it is sometimes as difficult to tell a person's age by the colour of their hair as it is to gauge their wisdom from their age.

He talked about the sea and the sand, but had never listened long enough to hear the surf's soft crash on the beach at night; he talked about the wind and the trees, but had never listened long enough to hear the leaves whisper in the breeze or to hear the boughs groan in the moon-shadows of passing clouds. There was so much this man talked about without ever having listened to create an understanding.

Anyway, because this noisy man would not be quiet and wouldn't listen, he never heard the growing chorus of people who, as one, were saying: "Be quiet and listen. Just stop talking. You might hear something. You might hear something worth talking about. You might learn. You might understand."

This happened for years and years until, one day, the man – who was even older now than when the story began – discovered his life was not as rich as other people's lives and began to walk round and round in circles shouting, "I've been cheated! I've been cheated! I've missed out on so much that was going on."

And the people nodded their heads and agreed with him. "You have," they said as one. "You've cheated yourself."

But still he didn't listen. All he saw was a large number of people walking past, nodding their heads in agreement. And so he went to even more people shouting: "I HAVE BEEN CHEATED! Everyone agrees with me!"

And he remained cheated for almost the rest of his life. Until, after many, many years of constant noise-making, he woke up one day and found he'd lost his voice. Vanished. It had got up in the middle of the night and left him.

So surprised was he at the delicious quietness of the world that day that his false teeth jumped out of his mouth too and went hopping toward the door, like a toad looking for a princess, and his wig, which was the same shiny black as a raven's feathers, spread its wings and flapped to a perch in the highest tree, where it built a nest. And the man smiled a toothless smile, scratched his empty head and was happy for a week and a day. His smile grew bigger and bigger with each new joy he found in the world until, one day, he was nothing but a smile, and when he opened his mouth he disappeared into a happiness he'd never even dreamt about.

Part Two

1

Once upon a time there was a town called Gimbly. It was the smallest of towns, much further beyond anywhere, hidden out the back of nowhere. Few people took the trouble to visit Gimbly; few people knew it was there. Unexpected visitors often found that a police car, driven by a churlish policeman – a tower of a man, with wolf's teeth and greedy, pig-hungry eyes – was lying in wait for them. Crouching, waiting. Strangers to the area might've suspected that, somewhere along this infrequently travelled road, it became known they were coming and were far from welcome.

Traveller beware!

Sometimes the patrol car would rush from town and meet them halfway, sometimes it'd be tucked out of sight, in a cavernous lair hacked from dense scrub and low tangled branches, waiting to spring out and pull them over from behind. Most visitors were snared by the leaping red and blue beacons, the snapping headlights, an impatient wail of siren, and a lengthy interrogation at the side of the road.

Gimbly's policeman was a giant, bull-headed brute, who sneered down with a curl to his mouth that sanctioned no discussion, and he could be trusted to hinder every journey. With only the one road (barely worth calling a road) into this dead-end town, any outsider arriving too close, whether by design or adventure or mishap, could expect to be stopped, questioned, turned around. On a good day, he might grunt that the road up ahead was impassable or the bridge unsafe, and leave it at that, but usually he'd issue an infringement notice too: reckless driving, dirty number plates, poor vehicle maintenance, crossing a faded white line.

Usually, it was merely the policeman's word against the driver's, which is all that it took. Enough to put most people off returning. And no point in complaining. The police car was a tollgate to the town, towards which only the unsuspecting came trotting unannounced. This grizzly bear of a bastard was a gatekeeper of sorts and had earned a reputation that few were prepared to dispute or dispel.

In Gimbly, he was affectionately known as the Gnome. Over two metres tall and with the solidity of a bull, he made most people feel small, and had learnt to find pleasure in what he couldn't avoid; would never stoop to apologise. However, it didn't take more than a couple of weeks or so for the mechanic to think of him as Gimbly's Troll. A toll-keeper troll; fol-dol-de-roll.

But for all that, on the day Nic the mechanic trotted towards Gimbly, he was expected. Expected and needed. No police car pulled out to pull him over, no wolfish smirk – "What big teeth I have!" – loomed down to suggest he step out of the car and try walking in a straight line. The Gnome gave him free passage.

2

What the grease monkey saw as he left the moist, shadowed darkness of the forest and carried on into Gimbly was a tiny, dusty town consisting of a cluster of buildings, huddled to a secretive whisper, pushed hard against the blunt end of a long, snaking valley. So small; too small. It was a town with a centre and nothing but a centre, as though everything else that should have been there – a parade of shops, a playground, public toilets, a telephone box, a few streets of houses – had wilted, shrivelled and vanished. What remained was the withered kernel of a town – no shell.

This recognition was accompanied by a yearning to slam on the brakes, do a three-point turn and return swiftly to his city of lights. Home, fast, and don't spare the horse-power. He'd been gone less than twenty-four hours, the adventure of Gimbly lay stretched in front of his nose, but nostalgia crept up and ambushed him.

If only he could've stayed among the tinted glass, matt chrome and neo-Gothic stonework of skyscrapers and apartment blocks, amid the flash impetuousness of fast traffic, the milling crowds of fashion-modelled office workers and tourists, within breath of exotic parks and manicured gardens... wide pavements cluttered with busy tables, the scrape of chairs, bright umbrellas and black-clad waiters juggling plates, trays, menus... the international cuisine of a thousand restaurants and cafés; chaotic illuminations and exotic aromas and erotic perfumes and the throb of different beats to songs without end, without end, without end, and the promise of ceaseless vibrancy, day and night – always somewhere open, someone awake, some place to go.

Maybe he shouldn't have left after all. Not for anything.

Certainly not for Gimbly. Not for a remote whisper of a town. What could anyone expect from somewhere like this but inbred rednecks? Sullen and ugly.

"Take it or leave it, there's still a choice," he told himself, and he almost believed he could hang a one-eighty, burn a little rubber, and rocket home – bugger the contract – if that's what he wanted to do. Even though it'd been instilled in him from childhood to remain true to his word, be as good as his promise, not let people down. And then he reminded himself of all those things Mrs King had offered him and how there must be more to the town than what he was seeing. There had to be.

He was tired, that's all. Road-weary and cranky.

"Never judge a book by its cover," his mother would've told him.

"Sometimes there's more to a place than meets the eye," his dad would've added.

Fingers drummed on the side of the steering wheel.

Rat-a-tap-tap.

Rat in a trap.

"Opportunity knocks," he said to Ophelia and Polonius, but his voice was flat. "One lap. That's all." He'd drive one lap. It wouldn't take a minute. "What's to lose?"

The first buildings, face-to-face on opposite sides of the road, were the garage and police station. Servo and cop shop. The garage to his left, the station to his right. His garage, if he wanted it, and a salary not to be sniffed at: almost double (somehow) what he was earning before.

A hotch-potch patchwork of plain cement block, fibro and corrugated iron – none of it rendered or even splashed with a coat of whitewash – although it stretched back a fair whack and had a new tin shed tacked on at the rear; to one side was a fenced car yard with a respectable range of cars.

Out front, two antique petrol bowsers slouched side-by-side on the edge of the pavement. Museum pieces really. Streaks of rust bled from ancient chrome fixtures, tufts of weed sprouted from the cracked bitumen around their bases, like old men's slippers. Senile old men, pissing blood. What's more, with the doors to its two service bays shut and a single door to one side yawning in the breeze, it seemed he'd caught it in the depths of an afternoon nap. A dive of inactivity?

A decent-sized garage for a one-horse town at the end of nowhere, but decrepit and ugly as shite.

Maybe there was another Gimbly and he'd found his way to the wrong one: "Sorry, town, my mistake; thought you were someplace else."

The cop shop appeared to be more police residence than station. A small house in brown, brick veneer. What his dad would've called brick venereal. An architecturally transmitted disease. However, in front was a rose garden to out-bloom all rose gardens – an amazing cornucopia of colour: clusters of lace-frilled creams, blushing pinks, swooning yellows and luscious, engorged crimsons. An elaborate maze of borders brimming with weeping standards, shrubs, miniatures, ramblers, double blooms, single blooms, colour upon colour, and disciplined not to stray beyond thin ribbons of lawn, precisely edged with white stone. It was a labyrinth of narrow pathways, archways, sideshows and centre-pieces, and would be a dizzying circus of colour and perfume at its peak.

He remembered the care his mum had lavished on her roses (she'd enjoyed the thick lusciousness of their petals and their rich scents in moderation, but cursed the viciousness of their thorns), except this garden went far beyond a passing interest in spending Sunday afternoons scratching around in the dirt, pruning, spreading bone meal. This was a vision, an enchantment, an obsession.

He lingered and looked. An ibis stood feeding on the wheel of lawn at its symmetrical centre, from which point the knot of ribboning paths radiated. A magpie, its head cocked to one side, hesitated between two rose bushes at the front, and two smaller birds – blackbirds, perhaps – were beaking for insects under the shadow of foliage next to the low fence. All four stood stock still, oblivious to the sound of his engine, the intensity of his scrutiny, which was absurd until he realised they were statues, made out of plaster or wood or some such, and carefully painted. So life-like it was uncanny.

Enough to break the spell.

He released the clutch and ambled forward. Past an empty block of land adjacent to the police house – coarse grass slashed short – and, alongside the garage, a narrower strip of wasteland, cluttered with tractor parts and a rusting chassis among long grass and nettles. And squatting next to this, an abandoned general store.

The assortment of faded signs tacked across the side of the building and beneath both front display windows suggested it had been all kinds of shop once – grocery, hardware, post office, pharmacy, newsagent, lolly shop – but in the hollow darkness beyond the smear of dust-coated glass, it was obvious the place had been empty for years. The interior would offer sweet nothing except dry rot, collapsed shop fittings, rat nests and cobwebs.

Across the road from this was The Crown Hotel, where he'd been told to report by Mrs King. The centre of Gimbly.

With two storeys and a steep-pitched roof, the hotel was head and shoulders taller than every other building in the township and, what's more, both floors boasted verandas with once-ornate posts and cast-iron filigree. Constructed from large slabs of dressed bluestone, its broad facade reflected the pride of a boom period, about a century or so earlier, although the faded scabs of burgundy and green paint on the woodwork told a different story. Spaced evenly across the ground floor veranda, seven jumbo-sized terracotta pots, spilling with spindly carnations and geraniums, added seven exclamations of brightness.

Nic's stomach tightened. What the hell had he got himself into?

Idling on, he passed a barricaded alley that separated The Crown from a derelict, weatherboard church and, next to the old store, two cottages begging nails and paint. Blinds drawn in one and a newish tin roof on the other. Couldn't tell whether they were inhabited or not.

The road continued straight ahead for a couple of hundred metres, towards paddocks and trees and the eruption of hills, before disintegrating into a track; so he turned right at the church and came upon an old school: red brick, slate roof, high windows, bitumen schoolyard. Out front was a sign: 'M.M.T. Security & Couriers Ltd'. Every visible window covered with reflective tinting, it was as if the building wore sunglasses, transforming it into a silent and mirthless place. A six-bay carport occupied one corner of the playground, under which a white panel van with an M.M.T. logo was parked, alongside a white minibus and a silver Lexus SUV.

Nic paused at the sight of the Lexus. Nice. But M.M.T. Security? He'd never heard of them.

Absurdly, given the deadness of the town, a row of eight drab motel rooms almost filled the length of the block across from the school. Though each unit had an empty parking space out front, the battered sign next to the driveway read: 'The Crown Hotel Motel – No Vacancies'.

He shrugged; drove on. The road swung right again. There was no other direction to take, no choice to make.

At the back of the hotel, just a spit from the tackiness of two shabby skillions, a corral of rubbish bins and aluminium kegs, stretched a row of garages. For hotel guests, perhaps. Opposite, across the road, occupying a large swatch of land that stretched all the way back to the rise of the hill, lay a fenced compound and yet another sign: 'P-R.G. LABORATORIES – TRESPASSERS WILL BE PROSECUTED'.

Nic stopped.

Massed together in the centre of the compound were a mixture of prefabricated and relocatable units linked to two substantial warehouse-type buildings, and the entire site was surrounded by a three-metre high, wire mesh fence, capped with razor wire.

He noticed a couple of chimneys and the busy clutter of extractor fans, vents, ducting and banks of air-conditioning units, and he spotted four, tall, skinny masts supporting surveillance cameras. And then he saw the security guard standing in a booth to one side of a pair of electric gates, with a phone to his ear, staring at him.

So this was the life-blood of the town: P-R.G. Laboratories, whatever that was. He sighed and touched the accelerator. Passed in front of the security booth and couldn't help but grin self-consciously as the guard's stare followed him, the phone still to his ear. The road bore to the right and took him to the side of the cop shop.

And that's all there was to it. Gimbly.

"Strange place," he said to his reflection in the rearview mirror. Couldn't see why anyone would set up business in such an out-of-the-way hole.

"Weird," his reflection agreed. "Weird as shit."

Time to decide. Stay, or break his word and leave? Return home to the city and remain unemployed – trusting the real estate agent not to have found a tenant for his apartment that quick – or give Gimbly a chance for three months.

He glanced at the petrol gauge, which was only a quarter full, and felt the hunger in his stomach, which was far less than a quarter full, and the decision was made. I'll give it a week, he told himself. Travelled too far to go back now.

"Nothing ventured, nothing gained," his dad agreed. The endorsement he needed.

It's what his folks would've expected.

And so, pulling round in front of The Crown, he drew on the handbrake, depressed the clutch, slipped into first gear and turned off the ignition. Except the engine didn't die. Not immediately. It idled several seconds too long before cutting out. The temperature gauge was okay; the oil gauge was fine. Could be the timing, a short, or the pump. He wondered if he'd get a chance to lift the bonnet that afternoon.

Then he pushed the thought away. All in good time. There were other things to think about and, with his stomach growling, he grabbed his bag, climbed out of the car and into Gimbly. Life's for living. *Look forwards, move forwards, never back.*

3

The Crown's double doors were closed. A wiry, black cat lay stretched across the doormat, watched him step around it to turn the handle, and didn't blink. A limp rufous whistler lay within the nest of the cat's outstretched paws; its white throat punctured red, one of its ripped wings lay on the veranda a few steps away.

He shut the door behind him with a clatter and rattle of loose brass fittings, but the sound brought no one to the bar. The place was empty. Apart from one black cat and a security guard, it was a ghost town. Even so, the hotel smelt of people: beer, cigarettes, polish, the inviting aromas of freshly baked bread and cakes. He counted three green vases filled with frilly pink carnations spaced across the bar but could see no bell to press for attention.

A moment later, he heard a vehicle enter the township and, dumping his holdall on the floor, he stepped back and peered above the etched frosting on the hotel windows to watch a police car pulling off the road.

"You found us then."

He span round at the sound of her voice. "Jeez."

"Did I startle you?"

Mrs King stood behind the bar. With her ice-white hair hanging loose, and wearing jeans and a T-shirt instead of her tweed suit, she looked less elderly, less quaint, but still had something of the fairy-godmother about her. Albeit a stern one.

"A little," he laughed.

"You've shaved off your hair and your beard," she said. "Wouldn't have recognised you if I hadn't been expecting you. We weren't sure whether you'd arrive last night or today."

"It's a smaller town than I imagined," he said. Though felt like adding: "Than you led me to believe."

"You must be hungry, thirsty. Let me fix you a drink and a bite to eat."

There wasn't much of a smile and her tone wasn't exactly friendly or welcoming – too curt for that – but her words were kind enough.

"What have you got?" He looked for a menu.

"Anything you fancy. Anything and everything."

"Anything?"

"We like to look after our own in Gimbly. We may not be a big town, but we're close-knit. If we haven't got something you particularly like, then we'll get it within a few days. We want you to be comfortable – we hope you'll want to stay." She touched a flower in one of the vases and it briefly nodded its head in assent.

"You own this place?"

"It's a family business. Sort of."

"And the garage?"

"Part shares. My husband – Archie – he's the manager." She paused, considered. "Hopes to retire before long. Not as young as he once was. You'll meet him later. Once you've eaten, settled in, refreshed yourself. You tell me what you fancy and I'll rustle it up while you're taking your bags to your room."

"What do you recommend?"

She didn't need time to consider, as if she knew he'd ask. "You'll probably want something light after being on the road, something on toast that'll keep you going until dinner. We've got some premium smoked ham at the moment. The best. What about a couple of slices of ham on toasted English muffins, topped with Eggs Benedict? A few fried mushrooms too, if you like? Beautiful oyster mushrooms."

He was surprised. "Sounds good." The moment she suggested it, he could think of nothing he'd rather have. And how hungry he'd become.

"You'd like a beer or something hot?"

"Tea would be good."

"What sort?"

"Irish Breakfast?" He was half-joking.

"Of course."

Too easy, he thought. Should've asked for something exotic like Jasmine or Orange Pekoe. He glanced around, took in the size of the bar, the high ceilings, the former grandness of the place, the spicy sweetness of warm cake and bread.

"That's a lovely smell," he said, feeding his need for homely small-talk. An ever-nagging hunger these days. "Is it baking day?"

"It's always baking day here. There might just be a slice of banana cake or gingerbread to have with your tea, if you fancy. Fresh out the oven. Do you have a sweet tooth?"

"Yep. Definitely."

"Good. A working man needs to eat well. I like my boys to have a healthy appetite."

Something brushed against his legs; between his legs and his holdall. The cat had crept in, probably round the back, and he picked up his bag and stepped to one side. He was all for rats and goldfish, but had an antipathy to cats. They made him sneeze, made him want to clap his hands and shout "Shoo!"

"That's Mog," she said. "Funny how cats always know the people who don't like them." She reached beneath the bar and pulled out a room key for him. "You can call me Mary."

4

Nic climbed the broad, mahogany staircase two steps at a time, but was overtaken by the cat, which came to a stop at the top and immediately began preening itself in the pretence it wasn't noticing him. His room was three-quarters along a light-starved corridor. Dark and dingy. His heart sank yet again and his stomach constricted into another knot. The hall carpet was worn down to the weft and warp of its jute skeleton, and he could imagine how grim, how pokey, this room would be.

Sagging a little, he placed the key in the lock, opened the door, and... Afternoon light flooded through a sash window that opened onto the balcony. The usual gloom of burgundy hotel carpets had been replaced by a light oatmeal, and the walls, ceilings and woodwork were painted a combination of white and cream – the trappings of a dairy theme – and, as if to emphasise the freshness of this, there was a lingering smell of paint that the airing of a faint breeze hadn't fully dispersed. The rest of the hotel might be gaudy and shabby, but his room was pleasant enough.

Dropping his bag on the bed, he looked around. Not only was there a TV but a new DVD player too, and a bar fridge, a microwave, a sizeable desk with a reading lamp and a bowl of fruit – three large green apples, three shining red ones – and the adjoining bathroom, while cramped, was fine too. A bathroom of large, white tiles, from floor to ceiling, and modern fittings.

This would do well.

The only thing out of place was the positioning of the bed in the room. So close to the wall it stopped the bathroom door from fully opening. If he swapped the bed with the desk – and there were indentations on the carpet to show how it had been – it'd solve the problem. But that'd wait until later. Until after he'd brought in Polonius and Ophelia, and unpacked his bags.

Despite Gimbly's shortcomings, three months might be manageable after all. It was more of a possibility than a few minutes ago. He'd view it as a working holiday. In his spare time he'd explore the region, drive to distant towns, get to know a few new faces. A change was as good as a rest. What was there to lose? Maybe there'd be someone to help him forget Siobhan – to try to forget Siobhan. Everything might turn out for the best.

5

His new boss was a head shorter than Nic, but a great deal heavier, stockier, more portly. One of those blokes without much of a neck, who shared a passing resemblance with a Pit Bull Terrier.

"Archie King," he said, pushing himself upright from the bench he was leaning against and extending a hand – a broad paddle of a hand but without much grip. He took a moment to hold Nic there and look him over. "So you got here then?"

"Yeah. It was further than I thought."

"That's what everyone says."

He had a newspaper spread out, a biro on top and notes scribbled across the *Racing Guide*. At his side was a mangy Blue Heeler, which swayed on its paws or slid its seated butt in step with its master's every movement.

Nic wondered whether the creature had a bad case of worms or was suffering some form of senile dementia. It had let out a rumbling growl and an abrupt bark when he first stepped into the garage but sank to the floor when Archie King had barked back: "Shut the fuck up."

Archie limped round the workshop telling Nic his hours and pointing out where everything was. "There's a bit of work to catch up on, but nothing desperate," he said parenthetically, between a wave at the racks of tools and a wave in the direction of his office where the accounts, work logs and a computer were kept.

"Servicing farm vehicles mainly and a bit of repair work – oh, and a couple of generators to look at – but nothing desperate. You can manage that without getting your knickers in a twist, I take it?"

"No worries."

"You can call me Arch or Archie. This place thrives on bloody nicknames – you'll find that out for yourself – and I'll answer to most of them; but I don't take well to rudeness or disrespect, and I don't suffer fools kindly." He reached out with one hand to steady himself against the tyre changer and he balled his other hand into a loose fist for the mechanic to observe. "I'll knock any smart fucker's head off sooner than tolerate rudeness."

The dog, which began growling again at the sight of the fist, tottered to its feet and barked once more in support. They were a team, these two; like Laurel and Hardy, Tom and Jerry.

Nic nodded, was more interested in seeing the car yard. "Fair enough," he said.

"The last guy we had was no good. Had to get rid of him. I hope you'll be a lot less disappointing. You understand you're here on trial, to see how things work out?"

"Yeah. And to see if Gimbly suits me."

"Hmm."

"I know my stuff. If I don't, then I'll ask."

"Oh, the silly bugger knew his stuff alright, but he had the wrong attitude and too much of it, if you know what I mean. Needed to grow up, learn what's what, keep his nose clean. I know you've got a bit more – what shall we call it? – 'life experience'. You've had your own run in with reality. Life ain't all sweetness and roses, is it? You've probably learnt that you've gotta look after Number One and let the rest of the world look after itself, and not to sticky-beak into other people's business."

"I guess," Nic replied, even though he wasn't sure exactly what was being referred to. Did the old fella mean his arrest or the loss of his family? The media glutted on that for a couple of days: 'CONSTRUCTION CHIEF KILLED IN CHOPPER CRASH.' They'd made it public property alright. Along with its subtext: 'How The Mighty Fall'. A short grab of entertainment for Mr and Mrs Bloggs and Joe Blow.

Archie King pulled a grubby handkerchief out of his pocket and loudly blew his nose, then huffed and puffed and spat out the door, before wiping his mouth and pocketing the hanky once more. "Don't you worry about your unillustrious predecessor though. You do right by us and we'll do right by you. Can't say fairer than that now, can I?"

They stepped into the yard, where fifteen second-hand cars were parked in three tidy rows, facing the road. Nothing older than a couple of years at most and popular models too.

"Not bad," Nic observed, although he figured the turnover would be painfully slow in an out-of-the-way dump like this. Couldn't imagine the district farmers bothering with the Gimbly road if they were after an extra car. Why not spend a day in the city and get a bigger choice?

Archie snorted. "Them? They're nothing. They're the ones I don't mind a bit of dust settling on. The real showroom's out the back." A note of pride crept into his voice. "If you think they're good, wait till you see these beauties."

Archie gingerly grabbed the chain that was hanging next to a roller door at the back of the workshop, gave it a gentle tug and a counter-balance sent the door clattering upwards to reveal a large tin shed on a rough concrete slab.

"Open sesame!" he said with a dramatic flourish.

There were no windows, no skylight. More cave than show-room. He flicked a switch and two fluorescent strips buzzed into life.

"Jesus!"

"Not bad, huh?"

Parked in a row across half the area were five absolute gems. Five gleaming jewels. A Lotus Elise in metallic Persian Blue, a grey Jaguar XF, a silver Audi A4 Cabriolet, a Lexus SC430 in maroon and, wearing its original olive green, a classic Porsche 356 in mint condition.

This was a treasure chest.

"Jesus."

"Jesus died on a hot cross bun," Archie said, and laughed.

"Wow." The world span rapidly on its axis, presented Gimbly in a sharper perspective.

"You, my boy, look like all your bloody Christmases have come at once. Ha! A bit of a surprise is it? I wish Mary could see your face right now. This is what we're about here. Those other cars ain't nothing."

Silenced, Nic walked between each car, yearning to touch them, stroke them, slip into each driving seat, lift the bonnets, turn the engines over – listen to them purr. He couldn't believe they were really here. It was too bizarre.

Next to the tin shed's entrance, at the back of the workshop, was a stinking toilet, a wash-basin and a storeroom – tacked onto the garage with fibro sheet walls, the cheapest and flimsiest of materials. If the darkening layers of sooty stains were anything to go by, then wet rot had well and truly saturated the structural timbers holding this area together. He looked about him for some sort of alarm system.

"What?" Archie said. "What's the matter?"

Nic shook his head. "You've got, what, hundreds of thousands of dollars worth of cars here? That's just these five. Where's your security system? A tin opener could get into this shed; a strong kick could get through the fibro."

"You're a suspecting bugger, ain't you? Probably what comes of living in the city too long." He was still smiling at the impression made on Nic. "No one bothers us in Gimbly. They wouldn't get far if they did."

"What's to stop them?"

Archie considered his words. "Believe me, it's a small and

bleedin' close-knit community we've got here, and a long road in. We usually know who's heading this way before they do."

"Really? Then who buys the cars?"

"Not a prime position for the prestigious car market? Is that what you're saying?"

Nic nodded and snatched one last glance before his new boss switched off the light and lowered the roller door.

"The magic of the World Wide Web," Archie said, giving the three words special emphasis, as if they evoked a mystery of wizardry that he appreciated but didn't care to fully understand. "We do business in a few ways, but mainly through an agent who runs a website and advertises on the internet. More of a broker really. Sometimes we track down a car for a punter and guarantee a rock-bottom price, but mostly we build up a bit of stock that our man sells through his so-called 'virtual showroom'.

"I've got one of those digital cameras in the office. Our cars can be delivered wherever they're wanted; home delivery and test-drives, if that's what it takes to flog 'em. Keeps costs down and sales up. Few other buggers can afford to sell as cheap as we do, not with their overheads." He sniffed and leant against a pillar of the car lift. "There's good money to be made from imports too. The friggin' paperwork puts most people off, but once you've done it a couple of times it's easy as pie. What's more, and I'll tell you this for nothing, it don't matter whether there's a recession or not, the rich bastards don't get any poorer and they buy these things as if they're just runabouts. That's all they are, you know: fast toys for rich boys and girls."

Now the place began to make sense. And for the first time Nic was warming to Gimbly. If, as Mary King had told him, he seriously had a chance to manage this place one day, then he'd consider cutting out the middle man and aim to trade some of the finest machines in existence. The best of the best. He'd build a name for himself the way his dad had. Forget about being a grease monkey and a panel beater – that'd be a hobby instead. He pointed back at the tin shed. "So why not go a peg or two further upmarket? What about the odd Lamborghini or Ferrari?"

Archie snorted. "Don't get ahead of yourself, buster. You gotta walk before you can run, and all this is a fine bloody balancing act. The higher the price, the smaller the market." He hesitated, rubbed the bristles on his chin. "What makes our business work is that it's just a tad separate from the mainstream; it's that first bracket of exclusivity which the world and his wife are panting to get their leg over. I'd rather a faster turnover and a bigger market than go looking for punters who've got half a million dollars to throw at a car. Not that I haven't thought about it, but best not put all the eggs in one basket, eh. Besides, it works – our turnover's faster than the bleeding cars themselves, so why mend something if it works?"

Archie paused, looked down at the dog, jabbed a thumb towards Nic's E-Type parked across the road. "You obviously appreciate a bit of class in a motor. Who knows, you might be able to afford something a bit more modern after a while." He laughed at that, then bent down to pat Bluey at his side, although the movement made him wince. "There might even be a bonus or two, if you're a good lad and you're happy to fit in."

6

On that first Gimbly evening, Nic arranged his clothes in the wardrobe and his toiletries on the bathroom shelf, the way a person does when they believe they'll be in one place for a while. Polonius, from his cage on the desk, surveyed the edge of this new world before nestling down to sleep; Ophelia, in her tank above the bar fridge, swam to and fro, to and fro. He glanced at his watch and gave himself another fifteen minutes. In fifteen minutes he'd head downstairs to the bar for a drink before dinner and to break the ice with the yokel-locals. Couldn't put it off any longer.

That was when he stubbed his toe for the second time.

Grabbing the end of the bed, he began pulling it away from the bathroom door to switch it across with the desk and chair. But as soon as he dragged it out from the wall, it revealed a massive stain – a monstrous thing – that had wrecked the almost-new carpet. A spilt tin of oil or dark paint perhaps, although it looked more as if someone had bled to death on the spot.

He'd choose his moment to talk to Mary about it. She'd probably ask if his room was okay, and he'd say: "Fine, thanks, but I kept stubbing my toe so I changed the bed and desk around – hope that's okay? – and do you have a spare rug to cover that stain? Looks like a dog died there." Perhaps it was a legacy of his predecessor's stay. No wonder the guy was unpopular.

Outside, it had grown dark and he was more than ready for dinner, but he stood at the window and stared into the emptiness of night and wondered which direction home was. The roads he'd travelled had wound every which way and, without noticing where the sun had set, he'd lost all sense of north and south, east and west. Away from the city, and the linkage it provided to his past and his family, he was alone in the world now in a way he'd never been before, and it left him feeling hollow – stark empty and hollow. It made him realise how much a person invested in a place to identify who they were and how they belonged. So he stepped back from the window and repositioned one of his photos on the desk.

His dad embraced his mum and his sister, and all three smiled at him.

Next to them, the bowl of apples seemed to say, "Eat me," so he picked a large green one and took a bite. Although the skin was waxy, the flesh was the sweetest he'd ever tasted, and juice ran down his chin.

"Delicious," he drooled. "Fantastic." And bit deeper.

7

The noise from the bar spilled up the staircase and he expected a larger crowd milling about and sitting close to the small tables – drinking, chatting, playing rummy, poker, backgammon – than the fourteen or fifteen who were there. One moment there was the slap of cards and click of dice, the clink of glasses and bottles, eruptions of raucous laughter, and then he appeared in the doorway and it all stopped.

Ridiculously, he was reminded of those old cowboy films, when the gunslinger, new sheriff or unwelcome stranger walks through the swing doors of the saloon for the first time, creating a tense silence that only pistol shots or the first chords from a honky-tonk piano can snap.

With the exception of two middle-aged women, they were all blokes and every single one of them looked at him, staring that moment too long, before someone said: "Your call," and someone replied: "Double three," returning to their games. Although several notches quieter, he thought. More guarded. Restrained.

There were no pistol shots and the jukebox remained silent, but there was no bartender to be seen either. Oh well, this was the country and he was the new boy in town. The appearance of a stranger was probably as exciting as it got around here.

Three guys, all dressed in the corporate uniform of security guards, stood chatting at the bar. On their black windcheaters was a discreet M.M.T. logo, and Nic thought the tallest one had been watching him when manning the gate at the laboratory earlier that day. It was this one who leaned over the bar, placed his near-empty glass under the tap and poured himself a free beer.

Nic pulled a few coins from his pocket and, for the second time that day, looked for a bell to ring. He jingled the coins in his hand, made a show of stacking them in a pile on the counter, hoped the sound would bring the bartender out.

One of the guards stared over at him and Nic nodded, smiled, but got nothing back.

Oh well, he could do without small chat for the moment, but it'd be easier if the TV behind the bar was on. Country folk could be friendly, the salt of the earth and all that garbage, but they could be as ignorant as shite too. They were laughing about a shooting outing they'd been on and about the mess one of them had made of an animal – a deer or wild pig, perhaps – which had got tangled in wire when it tried to clear a fence. Then they were ranting and winding up one another about a footy match.

Universal pub talk. The mindless forehead-thumping of 'mateship'. A yearning for Neanderthal commonality. And Nic was on the outside.

He rattled the coins again in his hand and stood there while another customer left his game of cards, walked behind the bar, took two beers from the fridge and returned to his table. He didn't put any money down, didn't write anything on a tab.

Turning to the blokes next to him, Nic said: "What does a fella do here to get a drink?"

All three looked at him.

The one in the middle was short, but built like a tank. Looked like a rugby player. "Who the fuck are you?" he said.

Then one of the others rested a hand on the shoulder of the tank and laughed as if it was the best joke he'd heard. "You wouldn't be the new grease monkey by any chance, would you?"

Nic nodded.

He held a hand out to Nic and said to his mates, as if they hadn't heard: "This is the new grease monkey. Welcome to Gimbly."

The tank also held out his hand, said: "Why the fuck didn't you say so?" and laughed too. He shook his head and shouted over the bar to somewhere beyond: "Mary, you've got a customer."

Mary King appeared a moment later, wiping her hands on a floral apron, but when she saw it was the mechanic, the frown she wore disappeared. She clapped her hands together and shouted. "Listen up, everyone. This is our new mechanic. Nic. As you know, we're giving each other a few months' trial, to see whether we suit, aren't we, Nic? Look after him. Be nice." Then she lowered her voice toward Nic. "What'll you have?"

"A beer'd go down a treat. The Special Draught."

He shuffled the coins in his hand while she pulled a glass of beer.

"Don't worry about that. Everything's covered: accommodation, meals, drinks, the lot. Call it Fringe Benefits, if you like. All your immediate living expenses within reason." She drew the glass along the bar flannel to kill a drip. "If you want another, or nuts or chips, you help yourself."

"Really?"

"We run an informal pub here, for the locals at least. It's the way things work."

"So everyone's on the same sort of contract, are they?"

Mary fixed him with an eye and tapped the side of her nose with one finger. A gentle reminder to mind his own business. "Dinner'll be ready in five," she said instead. "Seven o'clock sharp." Then she dropped a couple of empty bottles into a bin and returned to the kitchen.

Tank said: "The name's Tank. This is Whitey and Watto. So you're the new grease monkey, huh? Wasn't sure who you were. Can't be too careful, eh?"

"Careful of what?" Nic asked.

Tank grinned and shook his head. "You've got me there."

Whitey said: "What footy team do you barrack for?"

Archie arrived from the kitchen, with Bluey a few late steps behind. He grabbed two beers from the fridge, twisted the cap off one and took a long gulp. "Ah, that's better," he announced. Then he came round the bar to join them. "Giving you a hard time, are they? You gotta look after my new off-sider, fellas," and he slapped Nic on the back, winked at the others. "I suppose you'd be used to fancy nightclubs and flamin' discotheques. Our spit-and-sawdust pub a bit of a come-down after the city, is it?"

A mild dose of mockery, but there were rituals everyone went through to fit in.

"Nightclubs? Too right," he said. "Every night of the week and twice on Sundays. But I don't mind slumming it for a while. See how the other half lives, eh?" He winked back.

Whitey said: "You should get a karaoke in, Archie. Put it in the corner there. We could have a Karaoke Night once a week or once a month."

Tank groaned and Watto said: "Or once a never."

Archie nodded. "That's something else I should do, is it? Put a bleedin' karaoke in?"

"Yep," Whitey said. "Definitely. It'd be a winner, you'd see."

"Anything else your lordship fancies?"

"Nup. Just that."

Archie studied him a moment. "I could fart higher if my arse was further off the ground, you know. Would you like me to manage that too?" The four of them cacked themselves laughing.

At seven o'clock, dinner was served. Seven o'clock sharp. Archie and Nic sat at a table together and shared a dish of Stargazey Pie – a row of stuffed fish tucked up snug in a crusty bed, their tails sticking out from the blanket of pastry at one end and their heads poking out the other, one eye of each staring blindly at the ceiling strip-lights of the lounge. There were another two place settings at their table, but no one joined them.

"Don't worry about the others," Archie told him. "They need a while to get used to a new face, and then you'll be right – they'll be right. They were all new faces once, too. They forget that."

"Probably fifth generation Gimbly-ites."

"Nah, you're definitely wrong there. Gimbly was all but a ghost town for an age or two. Even the ghosts would've left if they could. Everybody's a blow-in now. Not just you." He glanced at the assembled diners. "A bit of reticence ain't a bad thing though. Pretend they're shy, if it bothers you."

Nic nodded. "Are they?"

"Are they what?"

"Shy."

"God no!" And he laughed his deep, phlegmy laugh.

There was vinyl flooring underfoot, the buzzing brightness of fluorescent lighting overhead and several cheap prints depicting tropical paradises on the walls. It had the ambience not of a hotel or pub restaurant, but of a factory canteen. Except, while Mary served a variety of three or four dishes, he'd heard no one place an order.

Archie noticed him looking around. "You see a meal you'd rather have? Don't you want Stargazey?" He seemed disappointed.

"No, it's not that. Really. The meal's fine. It's great. I was just wondering how everyone orders their meals, so I know for tomorrow."

Archie smiled. "Pot luck. Just like at home. But if you want something particular, then let Mary know and she'll make sure you get it. This is one of my favourites." With that, he cut an extra slice of pie and dolloped it onto the mountain of food in front of him.

"So there's no daily menu?"

"This ain't a restaurant, you know." He tucked in and, after a couple of chews, said, "It's a perk of the job is what it is."

"Oh. I see. Now I see." But he didn't. Not at first. Then he said: "So, everyone who eats here – who's eating here now – also works here?"

Archie looked up. "That's about the size of it." Then he gestured for Nic to eat his food. "You ain't waiting for me to say grace, I hope?"

"Nup."

"Well, let the dog chase the rabbit, eh. It'll go cold otherwise."

Although talking with Archie was initially like talking to a brick wall, they eventually talked more that evening than they ever did in the following weeks.

"So Gimbly was a ghost town, was it?" Nic said. "I've heard of places like that, where everyone moves away – deserted streets, deserted houses. What happened? What brought it back to life?"

"No big deal," Archie grunted, between shovelling the food in. "Small towns like Gimbly either manage or go under."

"What about the school? When was the last time they had classes there?"

"Small schools ain't viable these days. No loss here. We ain't got no nippers in town. Not a single one." He barely lifted his focus from pastry, potato, fish and peas. "Bet you went to some flash private school, did you? Best years of your life, were they?"

"Left as soon as I could. Was dead-set on an apprenticeship. All I ever wanted to do was work with cars."

"Good lad. That's the way."

"So what's the story with the security company? Seems strange having a business like that in a place like this. Guess they're linked to that laboratory place, are they?"

Archie paused with his knife and fork in mid-air and stared at Nic. He seemed to reappraise him now, and he chuckled. "Shit a brick, fella. You ask a lot of bleeding questions. Has anyone ever told you that? Must come of living in the city. Different pace of life in the country. You'll discover that for yourself soon enough – find out everything you need to know in good time. And what you don't know won't hurt you, eh?" He lowered his knife and fork again and continued eating. "I've always said, what we don't need to know, we won't miss. Ain't that the truth?"

It would've been rude to persist. For one evening at least, it looked like Gimbly would have to remain a story-less town, somewhere in the middle of nowhere in particular.

In return, Archie began tossing questions at Nic. About his family, where he grew up, about his E-Type. Preferred him to rattle on, it seemed. Occasionally Archie would pause in his chewing to pass the dog a scrap and he'd nod or shake his head at Nic to show he was still listening.

Nic answered the questions out of politeness and because he felt he was a guest in a strange house in a foreign land. A large, strange house, with unusual routines and manners.

When Archie's plate was all but clean, Nic's was only half-started and Mary had already served one table with dessert.

"What about you, Archie? What about your family? Got any kids?" By this point though, he doubted he'd get a straight answer.

However, Archie King wiped his mouth with a paper napkin and chuckled. "Oh yes," he said. He aligned his knife and fork across the middle of his plate, picked up the remaining fish head and slipped it to Bluey, then began to speak. He had a story to tell after all.

"I'm just an ordinary sort of bloke, if you really want to know. If you must know. No different to most other blokes of my generation. Grew up on a farm just a spit and a kick away. Didn't have two pennies to rub together when I was a littl'un. My old man and me mam did it hard, like lots of others back then. Might have had a few acres, but that didn't make us rich. They inherited a bit of land and built it up from there; got a flock of sheep together, got a herd of milkers, got a few chooks.

"The bank egged them on to buy more and more in the sunny years – gave them loans during the fine days – but whipped away the umbrella the moment it began to rain, the moment times got hard. Mam and Dad went under, drowned, lost everything. That's how the bastard banks get rich. Scumbags, the lot of 'em."

Nic nodded. It was a popular refrain.

"I'll tell you something for free, if you're not too smart to learn from an old fart."

Nic nodded again and caught up with some eating. "Okay."

"Life's a cucumber."

"A cucumber? Not a box of chocolates? How's that?"

Archie smiled and leaned forward. "You think you're gonna cut it up into neat little slices for dainty cucumber sandwiches – la-di-dah – but, just when you're feeling comfortable and mighty pleased with yourself, it gets shoved up your arse instead." He roared with laughter. "Life rarely works out as a plate of dainty cucumber sandwiches. Rarely ever."

"You've done okay for yourself," Nic said. "You and Mary." He didn't really know for sure – knew stuff-all about them, in fact – but it seemed the thing to say.

Archie considered this as he sucked a piece of food from between his teeth, ran his tongue round his chops searching for more; drained his beer and opened the second bottle. "Guess you could say I'm a self-made man," he agreed. "Was never one for staying stuck inside a school-room, or studying more than the friggin' barest minimum, especially if I could be tinkering with a motor instead, or putting a bet on the horses.

"Yet I haven't done too bad for myself, have I? Got a garage, got a hotel, got stakes in a bit more besides – got half a town. Archie King's kingdom." He put a hand down to Bluey and scratched him under the chin.

"You know, I reckon if I'd stayed on at school and got a bit more learning I could've been a better writer, reader and arith-metician than I am now. I'd have got a few certificates to prove what a clever bugger I was. And then, if I was lucky and minded my manners, instead of doing what I wanted to do and ending up running my own garage and owning a big stake in all of this, I could've spent my life working in an office for some other bleeder, probably counting profits for the bastard banks. I'd have got sucked into working for someone else. And, at the end of the day, all for the sake of a measly gold watch and bugger-all pension. Instead of that I'm a dumb so-and-so who's wealthier than half-a-dozen bank managers put together. Ha! So much for education, eh?"

"Qualifications and certificates aren't everything," Nic agreed.

"Everything? They're nothing. Just bits of paper, good for lighting the fire. Experience is what counts."

"And family?" he prompted, now the guy was talking. "You got children of your own?"

Archie looked at him a moment, and it was a cool, calculating look, and Nic was ready to be told to mind his own fucking business; then he warmed and took a gulp of beer. "We had four kids, me and Mary. Our youngest lad took after his old man and was always in strife as a nipper and a teenager, but then he went away, travelled the country looking to make his fortune, came back home and signed up with the constabulary, and now he lives next door. He's the local copper – you'll meet him soon enough. Can't miss him." Shook his head and laughed at the absurdity of the notion, and Bluey briefly raised his head off his paws before lowering it again.

"I grew up in the country, but worked in the city like yourself for a few years. That's where I met Mary. You can never tell where you're gonna meet the love of your life, can you?" At that, he paused and pushed his plate away from him. "There. That's more than most bleeders here know about me, so I hope you feel bloody privileged."

Nic smiled, nodded. Maybe he should feel privileged. It was the stuff of dinner chatter, but maybe with Archie it was more than most people got. He reckoned they'd get on okay, Archie and him. He'd be alright to work for.

8

The silence that shrouded Gimbly that night was more substantial than the simple absence of city traffic noises: the absence of tyres screeching on bitumen, of engines revving at traffic lights, the ebb and flow of sirens. It was spun fine, but woven closely, like a mist, and drawn over the valley and wound round and round, under and over, binding the trees and undergrowth, dampening the river and muting the sheep. It was the densest of shrouds, this silence, spun from the lightest of threads, and it smothered the life from the day.

Nic lowered the window until it was all but closed and pulled the blind tight shut, pushing away the black stillness of night. He yawned. It had been a long day and he was more than ready for bed.

A deep, dark sleep swallowed him. Swallowed him whole at first, but then began to spit him out towards a haunted half-sleep, with poisoned dreams of journeys and death that were many deaths and many journeys bound into one.

He woke shortly after two o'clock in a cold sweat. He dreamt he'd run over his new boss's dog. He'd swerved to avoid a branch and hit Bluey instead. It dragged itself off the road, up the stairs of the hotel and into his room, where it gushed blood as it whined and licked the mangled remains of its hind-quarters.

However, as it licked and licked, it turned into a grease monkey like himself – a figure in blue overalls – except he knew it was his predecessor. Panic set in then, until it broke the pattern of his half-sleep and he realised it was a dream, not a vision. It was then he heard a long scream and was quickly wide-awake.

A sharp scream. The hotel was silent. But, yes, he'd heard it. He was sure of it. Even though there was no rush of footsteps, no shouts of alarm. All was still, all was quiet. So quiet he could hear the night breathing through the narrow gap of his window. It was a woman screaming, somewhere in the attic above him, or it could have been an animal caught in a trap or snagged in barbed wire. It was terrified, desperate and final.

He listened, tried not to move, and waited.

He then heard someone fiddling with the door to his room. There was someone outside, and he strained to hear whether the handle was turning. Maybe. Perhaps not. But there *was* someone there. Someone listening to him listening.

Slipping silently out of bed, he slid through the darkness of the room and stood next to the door.

There it was again. They were quiet, but they were there. And they were waiting.

He took a breath, released it, and in one swift movement he grabbed the handle and latch and swung open the door.

In one swift movement, the cat turned and sprang down the hallway, with just the briefest of glances back at him.

"Silly bugger," he laughed, and shut the door again. "Silly, silly bugger."

Fumbling with the blind and the window, he raised the sash and stood there until he felt the chill dark rush in and settle on his skin in a shiver of goosebumps. Which is when he heard it again – another scream. Piercingly close. A blood-curdling shriek.

Except he was awake enough now to realise it was some sort of animal – not a woman at all. It sounded like the thing was sitting on the roof, just above his head, but sounds carry strangely in the still of night and this place was huddled within an amphitheatre of hills. All the same, he shut the window and locked it tight.

9

For some reason, he'd assumed the previous mechanic had worked until recently, but it turned out that Archie had been struggling like a trout on a line for months; so his first task was to catch-up with the backlog of work. Nothing too desperate: a broken headlight, servicing two portable generators, repairing a brake line, replacing a couple of tyres – that sort of thing. His boss had obviously been a good mechanic and could teach Nic a thing or two, but had lost the dexterity in his hands, the strength in his arms, the ability to crouch, stretch and reach into the awkward guts of a vehicle – to do the things a grease monkey does.

After months of being little more than a loose end, the simple fact that he was working and covered in oil and muck again began to restore Nic's sense of who he was and who he had it in him to be. He was a mechanic again and had a purpose; it made him lift his shoulders.

At first.

However, Gimbly was a strange, dark town. Not simply because it was remote and secluded, hemmed in by hills and a snaking valley of forest, but because he couldn't shake the feeling that there was something out of place with the town, even if he couldn't put his finger on precisely what that something was. It was difficult to fathom Gimbly despite its compact smallness and there was a darkness of mood about it despite the brightness of each spring day. And with each day that passed it grew, out of all proportion to its size, even more bizarre and bewildering to him.

It overshadowed his satisfaction with working again and left him, instead, with the sense that he was drifting further away from the relevance of his past and the world as he knew it. It stopped feeling like a fresh start to life, but more as if he'd got lost somewhere along the way and shouldn't be in the place he'd ended up.

"It's so quiet," he said to Archie, standing at the open door to one of the service bays. Down the street, along from The Crown and the derelict church, small flurries of dirt and leaves blew across the pot-holed bitumen. In the other direction, the valley road was swallowed from sight by the over-arching canopy of trees, and only the cut of the river and its narrow flood plain served to define a passage out to the world beyond.

"Quiet?" Archie said. It was the end of the afternoon and he'd just hobbled back from the hotel when he stopped to ask the mechanic what he thought of their town. "You're used to all the piss and hot air of city-slicking, that's why: everyone running around going nowhere, except up their own arses at a thousand miles an hour."

"But only one car's come into town all day, and that van – for whatsit-Laboratories – wanting fuel. It's not normally this quiet, is it?"

"Never really thought about it being quiet. What else do you expect in a place this size?"

"Well, a bit more traffic for one thing."

Archie laughed. "I'll see what I can arrange."

"So you're saying this is normal?"

"This is normal," Archie replied.

Twenty minutes later though, the sight of a car – stabs of reflected sunlight flicking between the low line of trees – caused him to pause as he was bolting shut one of the bay doors. Watto pulled up at the garage and climbed out of a spanking new silver Chrysler Crossfire. Top-of-the-line. Nic knew the model – he'd conned a salesman into letting him have a test drive once.

"G'day," Watto said. "Is Archie in the office?"

Nic nodded. "That's not your car, is it?"

Watto waved a clutch of papers in the air as he walked past. "Says it is on these." He laughed.

"You're back already? Hope you didn't break any bleedin' land-speed records," he heard Archie say as he shut the office door.

They were in there five or ten minutes and Nic had time to sweep the garage floor. When Watto came out, he was looking down and seemed to be examining the keys in his hand.

"Fine set of wheels," Nic observed. "Had a test drive in a Crossfire once."

He looked up at the sound of Nic's voice, but carried on walking. "Good for you," he said, and got back into the car, started the ignition and drove round towards the motel.

When Archie emerged a few minutes later, Nic wasn't going to say anything. It was none of his business. Not yet. But Archie said: "So you fancy the Crossfire, do you?"

"It's alright, but I wouldn't trade in my E-Type for love nor money."

"There's sweet fuck-all to spend a wage on in Gimbly. Fit in and stick around, and you'll be able to afford both, no worries."

"It doesn't bother you that he bought it in the city? That he didn't buy it through you?"

"Couldn't give a toss about that," Archie said and pulled out his hanky. "We ain't bankrupt yet, nor close to it. It's no skin off my nose."

Nic shook his head. "He's got one of those lock-ups round the back of The Crown, has he? Haven't seen a single car parked at the motel."

Archie glanced at the mechanic, then blew his nose loudly and took a moment to fold his hanky over before shoving it back in his pocket. "You're probably worried about the paintwork on yours," he said, sniffing. "Might get scratched with all the grit blowing around, eh? Tell you what, if you want to get it off the road, you can park it in the spare bay here, next to the tow truck. Or there's even space in the showroom with the others, if you like. I don't mind which. It's up to you."

"Really? Yeah, that'd be good."

"No worries. Besides, if some foolish bugger did break into the garage, they'd have to get rid of your Jag before they touched the stock, wouldn't they? And the same goes for working on it. Just grab the garage keys from the hook in the kitchen. These ones." He drew a bunch from his jacket pocket, jangled them in the air, woke the dog. "Help yourself."

"Thanks, Archie. I appreciate that."

"Call it a perk of the job, eh. We like to look after our own here."

All the same, it felt more like an easy ploy to change the subject than a concession. In those first weeks, he often sensed that people were holding something back and regarded him from the corner of their eyes. It wasn't just that the chatter grew a tad more subdued when he strolled into the bar at night, nor that everyone seemed guarded when they spoke to him, but that mostly everyone avoided talking to him if they could help it. Or so it seemed. He expected it from the bloody cat, but everyone was like it. Remote people in a remote town.

Back in his room, he'd grab an apple, bite a piece off to give to Polonius, and think about what hadn't been said. Sometimes it left a bitter taste.

10

Saturday morning saw scattered gobs of cloud scudding over the valley, as if the sky had curdled, but the forecast promised a bright, dry weekend. All the same, Nic dispensed with breakfast quickly so he could grab the best of the day for peering underneath his E-Type and lifting its bonnet, tinkering and tuning, replacing the spare tyre. Not quite cooing over the precious beast, but never far from it – unscrewing and inspecting each spark plug, checking the rotor arm, the fuel flow, the carbs, looking at the timing; making sure everything was synchronised and finely tuned. Man and machine.

On the other side of the street, pottering among the roses, was Archie and Mary's son – the local constabulary. He cut a comical figure: a bear of a man in beige overalls and straw hat, clasping a pair of secateurs and moving slowly, ponderously, along the narrow grass pathways, dead-heading and gathering withered flowers. The police car sat in its usual position in the driveway, the garage door was open and, dozing in its shadow, lay a chained German Shepherd.

When Nic finished, he cleaned up, pushed his car onto the forecourt and locked the service bay door. It badly needed a wash and polish, but that'd have to wait. More than anything he wanted to drive. Fast. The need was compulsive. Why own a sports car if you didn't treat it like one? Compulsion in propulsion.

First though, he strolled across the road. The policeman had finished weaving the new shoots of a rambler through the trellis of a rustic arch, and was dispatching a few barely-visible weeds by the front fence. Nic had heard him referred to as the Gnome, but this was the first time he fully appreciated the irony of the nickname. He took in the man's height, his considerable bulk, his straw hat, and introduced himself with a grin. He held out his hand, until it was clear the Gnome wasn't in the habit of shaking hands.

"I know who you are," he replied.

"Thought I should introduce myself, seeing as how we're almost neighbours." It was a weak joke for a town where everyone was a neighbour, but friendship had to be initiated somehow.

"Well, now you have, so you can fuck off again." He pulled out his secateurs and returned to snipping off old flower heads.

Nic blinked, thought he'd misheard, knew he hadn't. Maybe the guy had a dry sense of humour, and he waited for him to laugh. Either way, he'd feel like an idiot if he walked away now. "Nice garden," he said. "I thought the birds were real first time I saw them."

"My mother... " he began, and then stopped. He stood upright, appeared to straighten an ache out of his back and looked down at Nic. "You've left your car out. Where are you going?" The tone was more interrogative than conversational.

"Need to check a few things out," he said. "It was playing up on the way here."

At that moment, a pager buried inside one of the Gnome's pockets began bleating, and the German Shepherd sprang from its sleep into a fury of barking – ripping at the throat of the day.

"You take care on that road," the Gnome said, unbuttoning his overalls as he strode along a narrow ribbon of lawn towards his patrol car. "That road's more dangerous than it looks. Might have a nasty accident." More officious warning than official advice, it wouldn't have taken much to sharpen its edge into a threat.

"Moron," Nic muttered and watched him reverse out of the drive. By the time he opened his E-Type's door and slid into the seat, the policeman had torn down the valley towards whatever crime or accident he'd been alerted to, lugging the chip on his shoulder with him.

But that was the copper's problem. There was no way someone like that should spoil the day. Right then, Nic craved little more than to cushion himself in leather upholstery and to turn on the Jaguar's ignition. There were few things as sweet as igniting the power of a V12 engine, and then holding it there: thrumming, quivering to be unleashed. And then releasing it and holding onto it. Energy, power, speed and the exhilaration of freedom. The world lay stretched before him and its roads became his – kilometre upon kilometre, waiting to be peeled back and possessed.

The clouds were higher and sparser than earlier, with one vast firmament of clean blue sky behind. No smog at all. The trees broke the glare into fragments that bounced off the windscreen as the road edged beneath the fringe of their canopy, but he pulled the visor down all the same. A few hundred metres out of town, his attention was caught by a large stick shimmering across the road, moving with an uncanny momentum of its own. He braked to avoid it when he realised it was no stick but a black snake slithering forward, from the forest down towards the river, heading for water; the glimmer of red scales clearly visible on its belly. A beautiful, dangerous thing.

Ten minutes later, he came across the barricade of flashing red and blue lights blocking half the road that was P.C. Gnome and his patrol car. Bailed up in front of the spitting lights, nose-to-nose, forced half onto the verge, was a white Commodore wagon, and sitting in the back, bouncing with excitement, were three young children. The mother and father looked as though they'd begun arguing with one another as the surly policeman inspected their vehicle and provided a Gimbly welcome for day-trippers.

This can't have been what his pager had alerted him to.

Poor buggers, he thought. Big bastard, he thought. Small-minded, big bastard. And turning a bend, Nic planted his foot to the floor for a glorious kilometre of straight, level road.

By the time he reached the bridge, he'd begun to notice the steering was pulling to one side. He doubted it was anything major, but wouldn't be able to relax until he'd checked it out. There was nothing for it, but to turn back and put on his overalls again. Have another tinker, make some adjustments. He drove cautiously, listening for unusual taps, trying to separate the effects of a poor road surface from what might be a mechanical judder. A few kilometres out of Gimbly, the white Commodore was heading along the road towards him; no longer going in the direction of the town but away from it. With a flash of head-lights, the driver warned him of traffic police ahead, but the patrol car was parked in the Gnome's driveway when Nic arrived back at the garage.

11

Sunday morning. Pausing to read the headlines from the top of the stack of newspapers sitting on the sideboard – 'ORGA-NIZED CRIME FIGURES JAILED', 'HOPE FADES FOR LOST CHILDREN', 'HOMELESS MAN WINS LOTTERY' – he felt a hand on his arm and Mary said, "Take one."

He flinched, spun around. "Jeez! You're a quiet mover. That's the second time."

She smiled. A genuine smile, not just a polite smile. "The newspapers are there to be taken," she told him again. "Help yourself."

"Thanks. Thought they might be spoken for." He picked up the top one and folded it.

Apart from her habit of creeping up on him, he'd begun to take a shine to Mary. Everyone did, it seemed. Beyond her occasional brusqueness, she was a friendly old chook and certainly knew how to keep a place like The Crown ticking over with only a skeleton staff. It might have all been a tad basic but the place was comfortable enough.

"Come and join me in the kitchen a while," she said. "I'm about to have my elevenses."

Outside, the warm stillness of the air and the cloudless sky suggested the most tranquil of Sundays. Ideal for washing and waxing his car.

"I'll make you a coffee," she said, leading the way. "We'll have a chat and a piece of that gingerbread you like. I want to know how your first days have gone."

"I've only just eaten thanks," he said to her back.

"A late breakfast, eh? Had a bit of a sleep-in, did you? It's been a busy week for you. All the same, I'm sure you can find room for a bite more. Look at you, you're all skin and bone. You need fattening up. Besides, I've been too busy to have a proper chat with you yet."

She was a tiny woman – petite – now that he looked at her properly. He found it hard to imagine the Gnome was her son. How could someone like her produce someone like that?

"Fair enough," he said, following her into the kitchen, where she seated him and poured two cups of coffee and cut two slabs of cake. A large room with stainless steel benches, two industrial cookers, a walk-in freezer and, in an alcove, an industrial dish-washer.

"We get through mountains of dishes," she said, following the direction of his gaze. "I was going to ask if you'd take a look at it sometime. Not now. In the week. I reckon there's something loose inside. It's been getting louder and louder."

"I'm not much of a plumber," he said.

"I think it's mechanical. Wouldn't mind you having a look at it anyway. Rather than calling someone all the way here to tighten up a nut or replace a bolt or something. Archie would've taken a look once, but I don't even like to mention it to him now. He used to do most of those jobs."

Nic nodded. So, he'd been brought in not just as a mechanic, but as an odd-job man too. "Okay," he said. It wasn't like he'd be short of time. He looked at his coffee, blew on it and looked out the window.

"And you're finding your way around the workshop okay? Arch doesn't always remember to ask these things."

"Yes, thanks. No worries." He felt he should be saying more. That she might be expecting something from him.

"So everything's fine?" she said.

"It's all good. It's fine... really." He took a sip of coffee and swallowed hard. A couple of words remained lodged in his throat.

"But...?" She smiled, lifted her cup, looked at him, then replaced it in the saucer again without drinking. "What is it, Nic? I'd rather you told me."

"Nothing really. It's probably nothing."

She waited.

"Well, I know I'm a blow-in and I've only been here a few days and all that, but, still, there's things about the town that don't make much sense. Yet every time I ask someone... Look, it sounds stupid, I know, but..."

She nodded, as if this wasn't unexpected in the slightest. As if this was precisely the reason they were sitting at the table now. "What in particular doesn't make sense? Tell me. I want to know."

He turned the coffee cup in its saucer and then turned it back again. "The laboratory, for starters. Almost everyone seems to work there, but no one'll talk about their jobs, as if it's some sort of national secret. Then there's M.M.T. How can a place like that survive in a town this size? And how come Gimbly has its own police house?" He paused, picked a crumb from his plate and put it in his mouth. "Like I said, if I ask anyone they give me the cold-shoulder."

"You think they're hiding something from you?"

He shrugged. "Maybe. Or there's something I don't understand."

She pursed her lips, then held a finger in the air as if to test how the wind blew. "Of course, you're absolutely right. We're in an unusual situation here. A privileged situation. It *is* like no other town. And we have to be careful about what we say, if we're to keep things the way they need to be." She reached down and stroked the cat, and a moment later it leapt up to rest in her lap. "But it's only fair that you know what that means and why everyone's a little cautious about what they say. If you're going to stay and be a part of Gimbly, that is."

"I'm here, aren't I? I signed a contract."

"That you did. Although it might be a little early to decide if you're going to stay."

"Fair enough."

She paused, settled herself, and then began again, as if telling a story that she'd told often enough to know well. "None of us talk much about the lab because we don't want to lose it. You see, while one section of the unit deals with pharmaceutical disposals – secure collection and disposal – its main business is research and that's a very competitive market. The chemists – pharmaceutical engineers – and the technicians don't talk about what they do because they're not allowed to. They'd be fired if they did and it'd be professional suicide. Industrial espionage is rife in their business and companies invest millions in each program, which is why M.M.T. is here. It wouldn't exist without the research unit, but neither would The Crown or the garage. We'd all be without a job, including you. And Gimbly would be reduced to a ghost town like it was for ages before. Instead, we have the lowest unemployment rate in the country."

"Is anyone unemployed?"

"No. Even Mog's on the payroll, aren't you, Mog? Rat catcher extraordinaire." She buried her nose in the cat's fur and then kissed it. "The town's relationship with the company behind the research is, let's say, one of mutual benefit: we help it keep a low profile – be invisible – and we have a cosy lifestyle with unbelievable financial security. Better wages than in the city. And that's really all you need to know, isn't it?"

He considered this. Is that what everything boiled down to? A steady stream of dosh and a cushy job? "I suppose," he said.

"Everyone here knows they'd never get the same sort of money elsewhere. So, we all do what we can to play down the presence of the lab, particularly the research side of things, and our location is the key to this. After all, not many people come this way, do they?"

He shook his head and smiled. He thought of how P.C. Gnome had stopped the white Commodore and the icy reception he'd received that first night in the bar. It made a sense of sorts.

"You know, you work for the pharmaceutical company as much as for Archie and me. We all do, one way or another, directly or indirectly."

She took a breath, then stopped the story, perhaps in the hope she'd said enough. She stroked her hand across the cat's head – once, twice, three times – and it narrowed its eyes to two slits, staring at him.

"What sort of research? What are they involved in?" He imagined the horrors of animal testing and remembered the terrified shriek he'd heard in the night; he guessed what sort of stink would be kicked up if the animal rights activists got wind of it. "Surely you can give me a clue?"

"That I can't." Her coffee and cake remained untouched; the coffee was going cold, the cake uneaten. "There are some things you must know not to ask. Answers to which I might not even know myself, might I? It's best that way, believe me. We've got a good thing happening here and people don't take kindly… well, try not to be too inquisitive. Be circumspect in what you ask and talk about. That's really the only thing to remember and everything'll work out fine and dandy. You've got a good job; an excellent job. We want the garage to be a success and to make its own way, independent of the other business. I'd like you to fit in, stay and become part of the town, but that requires discretion."

"And that's why the guy who worked at the garage before me didn't last the distance? Too nosy, was he? Or a bit of a mouth?"

"Something like that. And it's why I'd rather you look at the dishwasher first, before I bring someone in from outside. If you don't mind?" She pushed Mog onto the floor and stood.

"Of course. No worries."

He was pleased with himself and threw himself into cleaning his car with the feeling he'd discovered an essential truth about the place; chewed over it as he washed away the muddy tracks of a raven and the paw prints of a cat, until the reflection of an unclouded sky appeared.

12

The mechanic might've uncovered why that tight cluster of buildings, nailed into the horseshoe of a valley, remained as quiet as it did, but, by Wednesday of the second week, he wasn't convinced he could stomach its quietness for three months, let alone longer, and stay sane. He was ashamed to admit it, even to himself, but Whitey was right: even a Karaoke Night would increase the class and culture of the place ten-fold. And that was saying something.

There was no café to stroll to, no passers-by to observe from a table on the sidewalk, no cinema... nothing, and no one to meet. He'd finished the two books he'd packed, found precious little of interest among the stack of titles sitting on a shelf in The Crown's lounge; he'd watched more TV than he cared to, and had even jotted down another of his dad's stories (*Little Red*). He was at a loose end and sick of his own company.

When he'd showered off the grime and sweat of that day's work at the garage, he fed Ophelia, opened Polonius' cage door and let his rat run up his arm and onto his shoulder. Nic slid the window open wide and stood staring out. The view took in the roof of the derelict general store, the long paddock with the beginnings of the river cutting through it, and the hills opposite, but he wondered what lay beyond. He took another apple from the bowl and polished it against his shirt sleeve until its glossy redness reflected his distorted image: a parody of Long John Silver.

"Pretty Polly," he said to no one in particular, and was reminded of his sister. Then of his mother and his father. He doubted he'd ever have found himself in a place like this if they'd been alive. That's what came of being adrift in the world, without family and friends as anchors. Without them it was too easy to drift and get lost; to become storm-wracked or becalmed. Was he lost? Had he marooned himself in this place? He wasn't sure.

Siobhan had been his anchor for a while. He missed her – the smell of her, the curves and sex of her, the wit and warmth of her – wished he hadn't cut her loose that last time. Wished, wished, wished. They could have found a way to stay together. He was sure of it.

"Pretty Polly," he said again.

Pieces of eight, pieces of eight.

He took a bite from his apple and straightaway spat it out. Spongy and brown inside, at the base of the stem was a tiny bore-hole where a maggot had burrowed through to the core, rotting the flesh. He threw the apple into the bin and stroked Polonius.

"Get out," he told himself, and knew it was good advice.

He'd get out of his room and go for a walk. Before dinner. Maybe climb to the ridge of that bloody horseshoe. Look over the top. Get some exercise and explore a little.

And Polonius. The old rat could come too. Little sis had sometimes perched him on her shoulder as she strolled through the city park opposite their home, and her friends had squealed and laughed, and once a woman had screamed... once upon a time.

It was shortly after five. Almost two hours until dinner. Plenty of time.

A dry, hot wind had scorched every particle of the working day, leaving his skin feeling as if it had been sand-blasted, but, while the sky was still clear, the wind had swung from north to south-west, which made the air cooler, fresher. Inside, it was still warm – the fabric of a building soaked up this kind of heat and released it slowly – but it was refreshing to be walking outside now. The moment the road passed the overgrown blocks beyond the hotel, it shrivelled to little more than a track. Couch grass had matted across from both verges to reduce it to a narrow, pot-holed lane, defined by tyre tracks instead of bitumen. It clung to a fence-line for about another hundred metres, parallel to the creek bed on its left and running alongside a thicket of trees to its right, before coming to a farm gate.

This thicket appeared impenetrable at first and all he saw at its fringe was a tangle of briars and creepers (ivy, old man's beard, straggles of dog rose), nettles, shiny leaf, deadly nightshade, until, shortly before he reached the gate, the brambles had been cleared and another set of tyre ruts peeled off into the wood. He found himself standing in what must once have been Gimbly's Botanical Gardens.

It was the extravagance of space between twenty or so grand trees that hinted at a formal scheme; this and the suggestion of a rough lawn in places, which must've been slashed just a few weeks back. The air was moist, sweetly dank, even at the end of a day that had brought the desert's heat with it. He took a deeper breath. It was the taste of damp moss, lichen, leaf mould, peaty soil and something else a little bitter.

One tree was a magnificent gum loaded with layers of yellow and crimson flowers; these hung like fragments of a ragged dress, bobbing up and down, up and down, as the uppermost branch tips danced drunkenly to each gust of wind. Close to, a blue spruce wore its robes with upright sobriety, aloof from such frivolity. And in front of both, at what had once possibly been the centre of the park, were the crumbling remains of an ornate pond, blanketed in leaves, pine needles and twigs.

It was a secret garden within a secret town. The valley was a Russian doll of secrets.

He followed the tyre tracks. They led to where the horseshoe of hills reared directly over the back of the township. A stretch of this had been quarried – perhaps for the stone to build The Crown – and formed a sheer glistening wall of looming rock, while the remainder was defined by the tangle of scrub and native trees. Dotted like jewels, a few late, blood red and glossy black berries beckoned poisonously. Overhead, the branches were marred by cankers and witches knots.

Polonius shifted along his shoulder, dug his claws into Nic's shirt, wrapped his tail across the contour of his collarbone for balance.

"You'll be right," Nic soothed, stroking him. "We'll just see where this goes." And the suddenness of his voice made him realise how quiet it was, beyond the bluster of wind and the creaking of trees. Not a single bird. Not a sign of one.

The track carved a route uphill. It zig-zagged a couple of times early on to gain extra height and avoid a precipitous outcrop of rock and scree, but settled into a gentle climb. The worst of it was the flies leaving their shadows to pester at his face, and Polonius risking his perch to snatch a fresh meal.

"Now, now," Nic said, and tucked him inside his shirt.

At first, it provided a view of the township's roofs, but the track looped back then, away from Gimbly and into the shade of gums again, straight towards the top of the hill. It was steeper there, but he stuck with it. By the time it reached the ridge, the track had left the woods for cleared pasture. There was a stronger breeze – a galloping wind – and he could see for kilometres in all directions.

It was possible to make out the cut of the river and, through fire-breaks in the immense, dense forest, the road into Gimbly. The town, though, was hidden at this angle. Beyond the ridge, as far as the eye could see, was a landscape of folds and creases, undulating hills and broad valleys, patterned by bleached, paddocks and dark forests, like an illustration from a children's picture book. A vastness undisturbed by road or rail; merely dirt tracks and two sets of buildings – farmhouses probably – to suggest an inhabiting humanity. Sheep and cattle were specks and, far off and high up, the fleck of an eagle, but there was little else except the vast, unpopulated, inhospitable landscape – only the knowledge of life in the township below.

He was standing at a split in the track. One branch headed off to a paddock gate about twenty metres away, and the other led, he guessed, in a circuitous route back to Gimbly, or somewhere close to the road on the other side. He cradled Polonius in his hands a minute or two, enjoying the bony softness of him, the tremor of his body as his whiskers sniffed at the air, the faint, rapid beat of his heart, before placing him back on his shoulder and taking the second path.

The route descended more gradually, but was less direct than he'd hoped. Checking his watch, he hurried his pace. No one was late for Mary's dinners. So he kept his eyes open for a short-cut. And then he stopped.

It was as if someone had placed him in their sights and was watching him; suddenly he felt conspicuous on the open hillside. Just a sensation, a slight bristling, that might have been nothing at all. He waited a moment for the betrayal of a movement, but didn't see anyone. Only the trees were moving, and the shadows between the trees.

Then he spotted an animal track; a more direct route. It took him across rougher ground, between nettles and goosegrass, and forced him to climb over the rotting corpse of a fallen tree – strangled by ivy, pole-axed by a storm and now harbouring bizarre fungal growths. But once started, there was little choice except to thread between thickets of invasive shiny leaf and around lantana and brambles (Polonius tucked inside his shirt again). Until, with fifteen minutes to spare, he paused to find himself looking across at the rear roof of The Crown and, closer to, at the back of the research unit.

There it was, but from a different, higher angle. The roofs of both warehouse units were dotted with skylights on one pitch and covered in solar panels on the other, and there was a roller door at the back of one, tall enough and wide enough for a semi-trailer; also, a couple of smaller, detached buildings to one side and what looked like a self-contained generator and pump sys-tem. Close to the fence, two enormous water tanks were set into the ground, and a few metres from these an industrial-sized propane gas container.

Clambering down the last stretch of hill, he came up close to the perimeter fence. No tell-tale sounds escaped the building, no vehicles were parked in the compound and there wasn't a soul to be seen. Like M.M.T.'s old school building, wherever there was a window it had been covered in reflective tinting. It was disappointing, yet he couldn't help but admire the way P-R.G. Laboratories contained its secret. A deep, silent secret.

No longer rushed, he was strolling towards the side of the perimeter fence, heading for the back of The Crown, when a giant of a man and a German Shepherd straining on a short leash came striding round the corner.

"Oi, you, come here!"

Nic stopped.

"Now! You! Come here!"

For the second time, Nic came face-to-face, or face-to-shoulder, with Gimbly's policeman. The height and bulk of the man commanded caution, if not fear or respect. The uniform added to that; the gun, the baton – the hardware. He'd have more than filled a doorway, and it would've taken a battering ram to move him if he decided to stay put. Even so, though he looked heavy on his feet, it was obvious he could move pretty damn fast.

The dog would be even faster. It didn't let up straining to be at Nic's jugular, nor with growling a fierce, low growl, which it ground between its side teeth as if grinding bones.

"What the fuck do you think you're doing?" the Gnome demanded. "This is private property." He looked the mechanic up and down, and his round, piggy eyes became tighter, angry circles at the sight of a rat on Nic's shoulder, crawling into the neck of his shirt. "You've no right being in this paddock. You're trespassing."

There was no suggestion of a common humanity to link them; nothing except humourless officialdom. It was in his tone, his bearing, in everything that was missing from the man. More than that, there was a vicious bestiality in the way he positioned himself (poised to strike), the snap of his words (hungry to bite) and the dig of his eyes (keen to disembowel and quick to dispense).

Taking an instinctive step back, Nic said: "Just out for a walk. Round the gardens and up the hill there. Lost the path on the way down. Ended up here. Thought the paddock was just scrub."

The Gnome let the seconds pass in what was a predator's playful pause. The arrogance of dominance. When he finally spoke, it was a deep rumble that was deliberately slow, beat out word-by-word.

"I know you've got a suspended sentence. It'd take bugger-all to get you thrown in the nick, *Nic*. Trespass? Not a problem. I've a mind to charge you here and now." He began to smile.

Nic opened his mouth. "What?"

"Either that," he continued, and smiled some more, "or you'll end up getting shot. Start sneaking about these woods, across this paddock, and you'll be mistaken for a rabbit. Guts splattered everywhere." He pulled the dog to the other side of him and jabbed a finger at Nic's shoulder. "You mind your manners around this town, you hear, and don't end up where you've no right being. I've got more than a few doubts about you. You shouldn't be here."

"This is ridiculous."

"Someone like you wouldn't last long inside. You'd be eaten alive." The Gnome laughed at that – a short, dismissive snort – and Nic felt himself being picked bare. A carcass after a meal.

"You're joking? It's an overgrown paddock, that's all."

"Snoopers don't last long in Gimbly. Remember that."

And he was escorted along the side fence, towards a gate and the road at the back of The Crown. The dog panted at its leash. They were two wolves padding at his heels, keen for him to run, keen to chase and pounce and rip out his throat, peel off his face.

When they reached the back of the hotel, he wouldn't be marched any further. He stopped. Made them stop. The dog started growling again and the day's absorbed heat radiated from the stonework of the hotel.

"I'll find my own way back from here."

The Gnome hesitated, as if he'd rather grab him by the neck and drag him into the bar. "Make sure you do," he said.

If Nic had been hungry before, now he felt sick. Hollow and nauseous. It left him with no appetite for food and less appetite for bar-room small-talk. What hunger remained would be eased by an evening of licking his sores.

13

Brooding on a nest of anger, he responded to an impulse. He dropped the telephone directory on the bed and searched first for P-R.G. Laboratories and then for M.M.T. Security & Couriers Ltd.

Nothing. He found no listing.

He turned on his mobile to ring Directory Enquiries, but it still wasn't picking up a signal in this narrow valley; hadn't been since he arrived. Instead, he used his room phone.

Curiosity had hooked him. He wanted reassurance; to feel comfortable once more. Having just got the mysteries of Gimbly to hold together, he didn't want everything falling apart again.

Twice he repeated the initials to the operator, sounded them out in case she'd misheard him: "M for mother, T for Tango."

There was a slight echo on the phone; there had been several clicks when he picked it up and dialled out. It was a bad line.

"I'm sorry, sir. There's no listing under that name."

The phone carried on clicking after the operator rang off. He listened, wondered if he'd got a crossed line, whether somebody was listening.

Next, he looked up the telephone number of The Crown. At

least that was listed. It'd be too bizarre if it wasn't. Then he phoned Siobhan.

One impulse after another.

The number was still loitering in a messy corner of his memory. He thought he might have tried to forget it, that it might be better if he had, but it remained there, doggedly refusing to slink away. There were too few others to push it out.

However, as soon as it began ringing he knew he'd only get her answer machine. She'd rarely answered directly, seemed to filter all her calls.

Sure enough, the computer-generated voice switched in after several rings and gave him a prompt to record his message. What should he say? He'd planned nothing, had no rehearsed words.

He recited the telephone number of The Crown and, needlessly, the time and date. After this, a spur-of-the-moment message: "I'm in a place called Gimbly. Took the job. Sorry about the other week, Siobhan. Sorry we parted like we did. I've been thinking about you – us – lately, wondering if we could meet up sometime, talk things through properly. Don't call me on my mobile though, 'cause the reception's useless here." He paused, was about to hang up, but added: "This is a weird-as-shit place, Siobhan. But thanks anyway. Thanks for getting me the job." Then he laughed, partly at the confessional tone and also to make light of the comment, and rang off.

Afterwards, even though it had only been the echo of his own voice he'd heard, the return to silence was like being engulfed in fog. For a few minutes, with the telephone to his ear, he'd felt connected to the world and not quite so alone. Now he was alone again. He looked about his room, wondered whether he should phone the operator for a chat, see if she'd tell him her life story.

He should have a snack at least. Anger had only masked his hunger. But of the three apples remaining in the fruit basket, he knew they'd be either bitter or rotten.

Ophelia mouthed sweet nothings at the glass of her tank and

Polonius had disappeared into the depths of a nest of his own making. Tonight, Nic's only solace would be in the meagre pleasures of solo sex, followed by regret, a shower, an early night, and the hope that in the morning the world would've turned into a brighter place again.

14

He was ready to let it go, this business with Archie and Mary's son, because there didn't seem much else he could do, except stay out of the bastard's way. The guy obviously had a major personality problem – he didn't possess one for starters.

Even so, there was a tension during breakfast, as though something had been said and word had got around. It permeated the dining room like the stink of stale food. When he walked in, one of the guys responded to his greeting with a curt nod, but it was an automatic gesture, cut short. Breakfasts were being eaten behind a screen of subdued chatter and the clatter of cutlery. And then he caught a glimpse of the policeman's jacket sleeve through the kitchen's serving hatch and he reminded himself he'd done nothing wrong.

Collecting his cutlery and about to load his plate with bacon, eggs, sausages, tomatoes, he watched a large paw rearrange several cream and pink roses it had propped in a vase, and he wanted to stab the bastard. To lunge through the serving hatch and pin the bastard's hand to the counter with a blunt knife or a fork.

Five minutes later, Mary came across with two cups of coffee. She put one in front of him and sat down opposite with the other. Heaping two teaspoons of sugar into his cup, she stirred it. Her own cup she left unsweetened. He hadn't the heart to remind her he didn't take sugar. Doubtless she liked 'her boys' to have a sweet tooth too.

"Archie's had to cancel his trip today, so you won't be on your own after all."

Nic had forgotten about that. "No worries."

"Our son's gonna run a few errands instead." She slid the salt-cellar towards herself and absent-mindedly traced several large circles. "From what I know of you," she began, "I understand you might be a little sensitive about the police – the law – these days. After your... experience."

He paused in his eating. Did he bristle at the sight of a uniform or a cop car without realising it? Did he see them all as bastards? "I don't think so," he said. "If people treat me fairly, I try and do the same. Doesn't matter who they are. It's that simple. Some cops do their job well and some are arrogant... some are plain arrogant."

She stared at him a moment and persisted. "But the law hasn't done you any favours, has it?"

"Like they say, the law can be an ass." He took a sip of his sweet coffee and glanced at his watch.

Mary smiled at this. "You're right. You know, there've been laws passed against playing football on Sunday, and even against eating mince pies at Christmas. Laws are just measures that governments introduce to control people; they're not unchangeable, absolute. It's more a matter of what's fashionably acceptable or unacceptable, don't you think?"

"But I didn't break any law. I never have. I was framed."

She lifted her hand and, for one moment, he thought she was going to wag a finger at him. Instead, she let it drop again. She was a difficult person to read at times. Maybe she was simply searching for a way forward.

"About my-son-the-policeman and your run-in with him yesterday. His bark's worst than his bite, you know. He plays gruff, but, if you follow a few simple rules, you'll soon find out he's not such a bad fella to have on your side."

Nic focused on the breakfast in front of him. "I don't doubt it," he said finally.

"He might be... well, once you've been here longer you'll realise he's not like the cops you've come across. I know some of those aren't worth the time of day." She smoothed a hand across the table. "Remember what I said the other day? Well, he's looking after this place for all of us. At the end of the day, it's us he's looking out for."

"Hmm."

"You'll soon get used to the way things get done round here."

"Perhaps."

"Just give it a chance."

He shrugged. "Okay," he said. At that moment, he wanted her to go away and to be left alone.

With a grating scrape of chair legs, Mary stood up. She seemed happier than when she'd sat down.

15

Sometimes there was traffic in the night. Sometimes the sound would break into his dreams and he'd slide out of bed to peer through the window into the narrow blackness of the valley and see lights – demon-red eyes blinking between the trees or piercingly bright eyes the size of plates – either leaving the town or entering. Yet, the following morning, there was never any sign of who'd come or gone or why; just dust tracks of ghost tyres. Sometimes it was one vehicle, sometimes two together.

Often, he guessed, it'd be a delivery for the laboratory: pharmaceuticals to be disposed of or materials that were required to do whatever it was the place actually did. Other times, he figured, it'd be one of the M.M.T. vehicles – probably the box van or the panel van – driven by Whitey, Tank or Watto, taking mail to the nearest sorting office or leaving to collect supplies for the town. They brought in everything from fresh milk, newspapers, perishables, general groceries and alcohol, to farm equipment and the incoming post.

A couple of nights after leaving his message on Siobhan's phone, he woke in the night from dreaming about her to hear a car idling close by and then pulling out, down the valley and away from Gimbly. As he lay and listened to it, he convinced himself it was a Porsche he was hearing. The engine had a similar purr. And then it was gone.

Possibly, the memory of the dream made him think this, or the sound of the car crossing his sleep made him dream of Siobhan in the first place. One or the other.

Quite simply, he dreamt that he'd woken to find her kneeling at the side of his bed, in the same manner she'd appeared in his apartment that last time. That was all. The entire dream.

It was 2:47 and he clambered out of bed, went to the bathroom and drank a glass of water.

Maybe the cat was outside his door again. Maybe that's what had disturbed his sleep. He opened the door, but the hallway was empty. Not a soul, not a glimmer of light from downstairs. Nothing but the faint aroma of a perfume he thought he recognised. A scent he associated with Siobhan.

Inhaled deep, slow. But by then it had gone. Too faint to know whether he'd imagined it or not. So he headed back to bed and tried dreaming her next to him once more.

16

On too many days, there was little to do except wash dust from the cars in the yard, tidy the garage, sweep the floor, follow the minute hand as it crept round the clock. With hindsight, he should've strung out the initial backlog of work across a couple more days, instead of hurrying to complete it. Anyway, it was the closest thing to excitement his job offered when a car transporter arrived. Hearing the grumble of its engine and the shudder of its compression brakes reverberate down the valley, he stood next to the bowsers to see what was coming and heard two or three awkward transmission shifts before it came into view. It was loaded with six sedans.

Archie and Bluey hobbled next to him. "A bit of business, eh?"

Nic smiled. "Are we expecting this?"

Archie stabbed a finger at a document he was gripping and then pushed it at him. "I need you to help the driver unload and then you'll have to bring these six out of the yard so he can take them away." On it were listed half a dozen cars he'd washed that morning.

The transporter had ground to a halt a few metres away and the driver was climbing down from the cab.

"Where are they off to?" Nic asked.

"City auction. Let someone else sell 'em. We've got these new ones from a Fleet Car company. No more than forty thousand on each clock."

"You're joking? We're just swapping six for six? Won't you lose out on that?"

"Time to shift the stock around. We won't lose out. Got good deals at both ends. Don't you worry about that, sunshine."

Nic shrugged. "You're the boss."

"Too bloody right."

It didn't make sense. Nic couldn't see how money could be made from this. Maybe old Archie was cooking the books in some kind of elaborate tax fiddle, or had the whole place so negatively geared it didn't matter if he declared a loss – the profit came from elsewhere. Maybe P-R.G. Laboratories agreed to underwrite any losses. Why else would he prefer a quick turn-around to actually turning a profit? Mind, there was a heap Nic didn't know about running a business and, before long, when the old fella was out the way for the day, he'd go through the books more closely to see if he could learn a thing or two.

17

On Friday of that week, and less than an hour into the working day, Archie stumbled from his office to the yard where Nic was hosing bird-shit off a couple of cars. "You can stop wasting your time with that," he snapped. "I've got a job coming round for you."

"I'm almost done. This won't take long to finish." It was corrosive stuff, bird-shit, and needed to be washed off before it left a mark.

"Nah. Now. I want you on this straightaway. Time for you to earn your keep instead of farting around with all these Mickey Mouse jobs."

With that, the Gnome arrived in a lime green Falcon. Yet another car Nic hadn't seen before. He pulled into the service bay, swung himself out of the driver's seat, tossed the keys at Nic to catch, nodded at his father and walked out. What a creep.

Nic said: "What's the matter with it? What's the rush?"

"Go to the driver's side and you'll see." Archie stood next to a workbench, one hand against the drill stand to steady himself. Looked like he could do with a walking stick.

Tracing a line, which reached from the bottom of the rear passenger door to the handle of the driver's door, were three puncture holes. Each perforation was a fraction smaller in diameter than the tip of his little finger. The metal had been pierced neatly, with force and speed.

The mechanic crouched on his knees to examine the damage.

He stroked the outline of one hole with his finger. "Bullet holes?"

Archie nodded. "Spot on. There's no flies on you, are there, Buster?"

"You're kidding?"

Archie shook his head. "Nup. Not today."

He opened the driver's door and saw fragments of broken glass littering the floor pan. The window wasn't wound down, but shattered. Perhaps another bullet or two. He glanced at the upholstery and the dashboard, expecting to see blood, but felt the blood drain from his head instead. He leant against the car, his hands on its roof, until the dizziness passed.

"What's going on, Archie? What's all this about?"

Archie smiled. "You alright? You look like you've seen a ghost, boy."

"I'm fine. Got up too quickly."

"Well, it ain't no major drama, sunshine. There was a domestic at one of the farms. My boy and a traffic cop got called to sort it out, but the boyfriend let off a bit of steam. Did a bit of damage to the car, silly bugger."

Nic stood looking at the car, then across to where Archie stood. It didn't feel right. "Then, whose car is this?"

His boss let the question hang and Bluey started growling. "Enough!" he barked back at his dog, and it shuffled sideways a couple of steps. To the mechanic, Archie snarled: "What did you say?"

"I asked whose car this is."

"What the fuck's got into you? I just told you, didn't I? Not that it's any of your bleedin' business. You're just the organ grinder's monkey here and don't you forget it."

Nic pointed at its interior. "This isn't an unmarked police car. It's just an ordinary car. I can't afford to get mixed up in anything that isn't kosher."

Archie laughed at that. "Of course it ain't a police car,

Einstein. God, you can be a daft bugger at times. Anyone ever tell you that? It's the boyfriend's car, stupid. He shot up his own car because his girlfriend said he was too pissed to drive it." He pushed himself away from the workbench and tried to stand up straight.

"Just like a spoilt kid having a temper-tantrum, who goes and wrecks his own toys. I'd have told him to save a cartridge for himself, but my son got close enough to knock the fuck-wit flat and take his gun off him. One punch and down he went. Out cold. When he came round, he was a right mess; full of remorse when he realised what he'd gone and done. Crying like a baby, he was. I reckon those sort are all the same: big mouths once they've got beer in their belly and a gun in their hands, but weak as piss without. Basically okay though, which is why they decided to fix things up on the q.t., if you know what I mean. No charges and no insurance company. That's how real community policing is done."

Nic tried conjuring an image of the Gnome as a caring community policeman, but could only picture the prick jumping at the chance to pull his service revolver and bury some poor sucker.

Archie paused, stepped towards the mechanic and rested a hand on his shoulder. "Now, is that okay with you, Your Royal Highness? Am I allowed to keep running my bloody business now?"

Nic bit his lip, then said: "As long as you're sure it's kosher. I can't afford to get mixed up in anything that's not by the book."

"Kosher? Look, all I give a stuff about is that we'll get paid for repairing the car – the panels and the window – and you don't even need to friggin' worry about that when all's said and done." The fringe of a snarl had returned, but then he forced a laugh again, as if he realised Nic was teasing him. "Anyway, it's a bit bloody late for playing Mr Precious, ain't it? I thought you'd already cooked your goose and we were the ones giving you a second chance."

"That's not what I meant. Forget it."

Archie moved back towards the bench and put a hand out to steady himself. "Well, get used to it, boy. This is the country. Things like this happen out here. It might well happen again."

Archie sighed. "We had a hunting mishap only shortly before you arrived. A couple of the boys went shooting foxes and rabbits and got careless; came back round on themselves and ended up peppering their four wheel drive with shot. Never seen two more shame-faced hoons in my life."

Nic took a deep breath, nodded. Maybe he was being an idiot and jumping at shadows. Too wild an imagination. "Lucky no one was hurt."

"Yeah. On this occasion our fella has won himself a black eye and a bruised ego, but that's not a bad result and might do the prick some good." He paused again and pulled himself up straight; Bluey stood too. "Now, Ali Baba, just get on and do your job, huh. I'm not paying you for your conversational skills. The van'll drop off paint and parts later."

All the same, Nic wasn't easy about the job. Something still didn't ring true and Archie had been way too defensive, too quick to attack, even for a cantankerous old bastard. He worked slowly on the car, and every once in a while Archie and the dog hobbled over and stood behind him, trying to hurry him.

"Haven't you finished that yet? Wish I could do the fucking job myself, the rate you're going."

Third time around, Nic came back at him. "Help yourself," he said, throwing down a pair of grips and beginning to stand up. "Or leave me alone to get on with it." It was the first time he'd growled back at his boss. There was little to lose.

Archie stomped off to The Crown, spitting on the ground as he went, and the dog trailed behind. Fifteen minutes later he brought back a cold beer for the mechanic.

"You're doing fine, lad," he said. "Shouldn't have shouted at you. Bloody rheumatism. Enough to piss a man off." With that, he left him to get on with the job.

Nic pulled a bullet from between the door panel and its lining sheet. The winding mechanism was wrecked. Across the road, the Gnome was scratching away in his garden, picking roses. The garage door was rolled up and the dog was chained to its shadow. There was a hate growing deep inside him. It had germinated and sent down a long tap root. He didn't know why they were opponents, the two of them, but that's the way it was. He held the bullet up to his eye and put the Gnome in his sights.

"Arrogant bastard," he muttered, and dropped the bullet into the pocket of his overalls. He wished he knew what it'd take to shake the bastard up and knock him down to size.

As he worked, he wondered if the yobbo boyfriend was one of the local farm-hands. If he was, he guessed he'd see him in the bar at the end of the day, sporting a black eye and bragging about his latest adventure. But no one like that turned up, either that day or the ones that followed, and the Falcon, which was ready the next morning and picked up by the Gnome at lunchtime, never appeared in town again either – not in the few weeks the grease monkey had left in Gimbly.

The only injured person who showed up that day was Tank. He saw him in the afternoon, coming out of The Crown with his right arm in a sling, getting into the delivery van, which was being driven by Whitey.

"G'day, Tank, Whitey," Nic called from the garage forecourt.

Whitey waved and Tank called back, "See you later."

"Yeah."

He never did though. That was the last time he saw Tank.

18

Nic's chance to mooch through Archie's office and examine the books came in his third week. It was a blustery day – overcast and dusty – and looked as if it should be cool, but there was warmth to the wind coming from the desert.

Shortly after he'd unlocked the garage, he turned to find Mary standing by the bowsers.

"Archie's a bit under the weather today," she told him. "I've got him an appointment with the doctor later."

"The doctor?" Nic said. "Gimbly has its own GP?"

She smiled at that, but he wouldn't have been surprised. "No, there's a clinic a couple of hours down the road. About a hundred-and-fifty k. away. So don't get sick in a hurry."

He looked down the valley in the direction of civilisation, as if he might see it.

"Anyway, you'll be on your own today. Apparently there's a fuel tanker arriving later." She reached into the pocket of her pinny and took out a slip of paper. "We've written down instructions for you. It's straightforward, he says."

"No worries," Nic said, and watched her walk across the road towards The Crown. She leant down to stroke the cat, sunning itself on the veranda, then picked up a dead mouse or bush rat or something and tossed it into the gutter. She looked back at him as if she knew he was watching. Nic nodded and began reading Archie's instructions.

A fuel tanker? That'd probably be the only business of the day, unless he got lucky and some other moron decided to shoot a car or two. He looked at the clock over the office door and realised this was becoming a habit, like a nervous tick. A person might grow old, watching away the hours. He doubted whether he could stomach more than three months of Gimbly.

However, just before eleven, an off-road motorbike was brought in on the back of a ute from one of the farms. There was nothing wrong with it, but it needed servicing, he was told, and so that's what he did... and he still had time on his hands.

By mid-afternoon, the fuel tanker had delivered its load and he had nothing else to do.

Archie's office was dark and dingy, tidy and bare. It was unlike any garage office he'd set foot in before. There were no out-of-date calendars advertising oil brands or brake pad manufacturers, no pin-up posters or charts of big-breasted, bikini-clad beauties promoting radial tyres and air pressure specifications, no letters or order books lying about on work surfaces.

Thinking he'd take a look at anything he could find – account ledgers, work logs, bank statements, anything – he lowered himself into his boss's chair and found that every drawer in the desk was locked. He stood and tugged at the handles on the two filing cabinets, the doors of the metal cabinet, but these too were locked. Even the computer wanted a password before it'd boot up. On the desk sat a calculator, a few pens and a notepad, and the routine work log and invoice book, but that was the lot.

He drew Archie's chair closer to the desk, pulled the work log and invoice book towards him, and flicked back through old entries, but there was nothing of interest – not even the initials of his predecessor. The names of M.M.T. Security & Couriers and P-R.G. Laboratories Limited cropped up on almost every page, and occasionally a private name appeared, but these always listed The Crown, the motel or a Gimbly farm as an address. It was poor pickings. There was bugger-all to find, no secrets ready to be discovered.

Working his way back through the books, towards the beginning of the financial year, Nic looked up and jumped. The Gnome was standing in the doorway.

"What the fuck do you think you're doing?" the bastard barked.

Nic let the book flick shut. "G'day, officer." He refused to be intimidated. "Got another job for me, have you?"

"You've no call to be snooping about in here." This time it was a growl.

"I'm not snooping about anywhere. I'm making sure the books are up-to-date. What's it to you?"

The Gnome reached the desk in two strides. He turned both books round to see what they were and flipped them open at the latest entry. "Have you been asked to do that?"

"What are you on about? I work here, remember." He'd taken too much crap. A person could be too slow to anger, too tolerant. "Jesus! Your dad's sick today. If a job needs doing I do it. I don't have to ask your bleeding permission." He wanted to stand up but resisted the temptation; knew it'd only heighten his disadvantage. "Get off my case, will you."

The Gnome side-stepped the desk and reached out for Nic, who rolled the chair back and retreated. Needed to do some quick-talking.

"Look, I'll make a deal. But just lay off, will you? Leave me to do my job... I'll leave you to do yours. Okay? But get off my case, eh? If you've got a problem – don't want me here – take it up with your mum and dad. They're the ones who employed me. Okay?" By then he was up against one of the filing cabinets, trying to keep the desk between them.

The Gnome smiled – a smile like a cold threat, served on stale toast – and quietly, almost gently, directed two words at Nic before turning and striding out of the office, out of the garage. "Fuck off," he said.

19

It was about eleven o'clock on a Friday night. He saw bright lights flooding from the laboratory and two vehicles leaving. Didn't know if it was lit up every night and it was only because he was out walking that he saw anything at all. The bar had been at its fullest and he'd sat leaning over a couple of drinks for the evening, pretending to watch a soccer match on TV. He'd had trouble sleeping those last few nights and thought a long walk might help. So, without grumbling a goodnight, he grabbed a jacket from his room and slipped out into the dark.

He pretty much followed the first section of track he'd followed before, except he was slower this time; thinking things through, chewing them over. He could cope with the shot-up Falcon and the secrecy surrounding the pharmaceutical company, and even with the Gnome's hostility to a point – the guy was just an arrogant prick – but the fast turnover of secondhand cars was bizarre. Selling luxury cars over the internet made a sense of sorts, but not the business of having a car yard in a town no one visited. Especially not Archie's strategy of rotating the entire stock through city auctions every few weeks. He'd barely break even doing that. Must be pulling a swift one somewhere, somehow. Either the business was dodgy or the old guy was the worst businessman in the history of used car sales.

Or maybe Nic was being stupid and his imagination was running feral. After all, it had been a shit of a year and it wouldn't be surprising if he'd grown a tad paranoid. And why would anyone employ someone like him if there was anything illegal going on? Unless, of course, they'd got it wrong and, because of his suspended sentence, thought he'd have no qualms about being involved too. Jeez, he didn't have a clue what to do.

About three-quarters of the way up the hill, he pulled the collar of his jacket high around his neck and looked back down at the town. It was then he noticed the lights at the laboratory and crouched down to see better; moved beyond the path and crouched against a tree. Almost straightaway, a burst of bright light streamed from one of the warehouse units.

A roller door had been raised and two vehicles were pulling out. The glow lasted for a minute or two, until the door was lowered again. A sedan followed by a box van – the Gimbly delivery van. He stood to watch them move past the security gate and snake out of town in convoy, and he followed their lights sneaking between gaps in the dark smother of trees as they wound along the valley, further away from Gimbly, until there was nothing left to see.

Whatever business they were about and wherever they were going, he envied the idea of a journey, a departure, and driving someplace else – any place other than where he was. Driving, driving, driving.

Brushing bark and leaf litter off the seat of his pants, he made his way downhill, quickly now, returning the way he'd come, hoping the keys to the garage were still on the kitchen hook. The idea of driving grew stronger. Took hold of him. Thank God he'd fixed the alignment on his car. Tonight, he'd drive for two or three hundred kilometres, no worries. Didn't matter whether the world was asleep or not. He'd make the nightscape swim past. Forget where he was and think about being other places.

The downstairs of The Crown was in darkness as he approached its back door, but a couple of lights shone on the first floor. Making his way towards the kitchen, he yawned, but the hunger to be somewhere other than Gimbly and to feel the contours and twists of the land unravel between bitumen and tyre was too much to resist.

Memory and touch guided him through the kitchen, between the benches and Mary's large table, and he widened his eyes to adjust quicker to the interior darkness. Reaching across the counter, groping for the key hooks, he glimpsed a shadow rise to meet him and stifled a cry, a curse. He took a step backwards and the shadow sprang to the floor, glided towards the cat-flap.

His hands found the bundles of keys and quietly read the braille of each until he identified the one he was looking for and pocketed it.

Stepping outside, he drew the door slowly, quietly shut behind him.

A piercing scream. The same scream as his first night in Gimbly. Except now it was clearly an animal. Not a woman being murdered, or a screaming banshee. Sounded too close, but could've carried from the laboratory.

Dropping the handbrake and slipping the E-Type out of gear, he gave a gentle push to roll it onto the road. Whether he did this to avoid waking anyone or alerting anyone, he wasn't sure, but even the crunch of gravel seemed too loud and the service bay door creaked shut in a way it never had before. Nevertheless, nothing stole from the sweetness of turning on the ignition and hearing – feeling – the engine turn over and the power of life pulse into the beast. Then gliding darkly, as smooth and powerful as a jaguar, out of the town and along its valley road.

Driving beneath the canopy of trees made the night darker, the road narrower. Branches stretched across the road, fingers-to-fingers, reaching down. An intermittent breeze scuttled flurries of leaves across his windscreen, across the road like swarms of mice, and the breeze blew up into eddies of wind that charged ahead of him, throwing pins of dry twigs and daggers of small branches in his path. Still, he listened to the engine and tapped a rhythm on the steering wheel, and smiled.

An owl flew across the road in front of him, swooped down across his windscreen, clipped the glass. All he saw was a white blur in the night, against which he instinctively pressed the brake and might have skidded off the road, to sink into the ditch or smash against a tree. But he kept a straight course, just eased back on the accelerator. He'd learnt from the ravens and wouldn't be caught out twice – not so soon. Tonight he could drive forever.

Look forwards, move forwards, never back.

And then, when he was little more than seven kilometres down the road, he saw the flicker of lights in his rearview mirror, pursuing him, strobing through the pillars of the trees. He paused long enough to see the red and blue beacons gnawing a hole in the night.

The Bogey Man was coming to get him.

"Fuck!"

What could he do but take a deep breath and pull over? He mustn't let the bastard rile him.

The Gnome parked behind and got out. The mechanic wound his window down, left the engine running.

"You're out and about late," Nic said, faking calmness, forcing politeness. "No rest for the wicked."

"Turn your engine off, sir." He shone his torch at the mechanic's face, made him turn from the glare and shield his eyes. "I had a report that someone was snooping around the town again, sneaking about. Guess it must have been you."

Nic said nothing.

"You unlocked the garage to get your car out?" He shone the torch at the passenger seat and into the rear of the car.

"Yes, of course. With a key." He'd volunteer no more.

The Gnome pulled out his baton and Nic knew he was in deep shite. He used the baton to prod the front tyre – the driver's side – as if he could gauge air pressure from that, and then stepped back again.

"And where are you off to at this time of night?"

"For a drive. Nowhere in particular."

The Gnome smiled and walked around the car, made a show of inspecting it; he stopped at the rear and the mechanic felt a slight tap communicate itself to him through the body of the vehicle, saw the policeman bend down, pick something up – presumably a piece of red plastic – and toss it into the undergrowth.

"Did you know you've got a tail-light out here, sir? Rear passenger side. I'm afraid I'll have to ask you to return to town; this car's not roadworthy. Tut, tut. And you a mechanic, too."

Gimbly's toll-keeper troll. Fol-dol-de-roll. Nic began opening the door, determined to get out and look at the light, as if that would change anything. "You can't do that," he said.

But the Gnome, who he'd think of as the Troll from this point on, held the door shut and put up a warning finger. "I'd think twice about that if I were you."

"What the fuck..."

"Unroadworthy car, reckless driving, obscene language, assaulting a police officer." Once more he wagged his finger. He was in a playful mood. "I hope you haven't forgotten our deal."

"What friggin' deal?"

Again that sick smile; smug, self-satisfied. "That you don't tell me how to do my job... Remember?"

Nic clenched the steering wheel, bit into his lip and drew blood. "Well stuff you, I've had enough of this town. Contract or no contract, I'm done."

And with those words the look on the Troll's face changed. In an instant the playfulness vanished. "I'll escort you back for your own safety, sir. You're a road hazard without proper tail-lights. Who knows, a truck might not see you and run you off the road, or simply steam-roller over the top of you. Could be very messy. You turn around here and I'll follow."

20

Cooked breakfasts weren't provided at the weekend. The usual boxes of cereal, jugs of milk and juice, a few loaves of bread and a toaster, were left on the dining room sideboard until about mid-day. But no ham and eggs, pancakes or mixed grills. Gimbly's residents surfaced as and when they would.

Nic sought out Mary the moment he came down from his room. He'd barely slept. Well, until about six, when daylight began greying in from behind the blind and he'd finally drifted off for a couple of hours. She was in the laundry and he knocked on the door.

"Can we have a chat?" he said, pushing his hands into his back pockets. "You, Archie, me."

She stopped what she was doing – measuring scoops of powder into the row of washing machines – and looked at him. "Sounds formal."

"It's important. Ten minutes would do."

"I see. Archie should be back within the hour and I've got a few jobs to sort out," she said. "Have you eaten?"

"No."

"Then have your breakfast and we'll talk at ten."

He rehearsed his words in the interval. Had no remaining doubts about what he had to do, what he needed to say.

The two of them were sitting together in the kitchen when he returned. Archie was on the phone and said, "I'll get back to you," and hung up. Three empty coffee mugs sat on the table in front of them, and Mary cleared these to the sink when he entered.

"Come in, sit down," she said.

Archie said: "Now, what's all this about?"

Nic then knew they'd already heard about last night. He sat down, thought he should be as direct as possible – no point in putting it off – but it wasn't easy. "I'm on a three month contract, right?"

"Right."

"I've done three weeks."

"Yes."

He looked down at his hands, then looked up and shifted his gaze from Archie to Mary and back again. "What would be the chances of cutting it short, finishing early?"

There was a pause. "Why?"

"Well, it's like this…" he began, then stopped, took a deep breath and hurried on. "Things aren't working out here. Not for me. The town might be fine for those who come from the country, but it doesn't matter what I do, I don't fit in. I appreciate the chance you've given me and all, but there's something about the place..." He took another breath and bit his lip. "And, not only that, but your son – the policeman – seems to be going out of his way to make life as difficult as he can. Hell, I can't even go for a drive at night without him knocking out one of my lights with his baton and slapping an unroadworthy on me."

He looked for something to hold onto – a salt cellar, a drink mat – but played with the ring on his finger instead. "It's like he's setting out to provoke me, and I can't afford to tangle with him. There's nothing for me here. I'm not taking on anything I haven't done before and, well, you know..." The words petered out. He'd explained himself as well as he could. Anxiety out-paced him.

Archie smiled, looked at Mary. She nodded. He thought they both looked relieved.

"You want out?" Archie said.

"Yes."

"Unless there's something to hold you here?"

"There isn't."

"A contract is a contract," Mary stated.

He began to slump.

"They're not usually re-negotiable," she continued (and yet there was something in her emphasis that gave him hope, made him sit up again). "But we wouldn't want you to be unhappy. Heaven forbid. An unhappy worker isn't a productive worker, don't you agree?"

"I agree," he said. "Definitely."

She considered. "Tell you what, how about you see how things go in the next fortnight? We'll have a word with... well, we'll have a word. If nothing improves for you by the end of that time, then we'll say you can pack your bags and start looking for other work, no hard feelings, and Archie here will even give you a reference. Two weeks. It'll give us a chance to line someone else up, if we need to. Do you reckon you can manage that?"

"I'll manage that. Thanks. Thanks for understanding."

Afterwards, Nic felt happier than he had since first arriving in Gimbly. He could almost see himself walking through the front door of his apartment again. Back to the city.

*

Three days later, Siobhan arrived.

Interlude

"Tell us a story, Jackanory.
Tell us a story, do."
"Pin back your ears, my little dears,
And I'll tell you a story true."

Once upon a time there was a little girl called Skinny Malinks or
Lizzie Dripping or Little Red Riding Hood or some such. Her
name has changed many times because her story, like all stories,
has changed and grown with each new telling.

One day, the little girl's mother said: "I'm sending you to stay
with Granny for a week. She lives in a cottage in the middle of
the forest and it's time you got to know one another. Make sure
you behave and do what you're told, and be careful not to get
under her feet."

Her mother baked an apple pie, wrapped up half a roast duck
and told her how to get there, and the little girl packed her
favourite doll and walked and walked until she arrived at
Granny's cottage. The cottage was tiny and swamped by the
damp darkness of trees, but Granny was as sweet as the apple
pie and as tender as the duck in the little girl's basket, and she
ruffled her hair and gripped her hand and the little girl knew
what a happy week together they'd have, until she stepped inside
the cottage.

It was no bigger than a single room and stank of rotting cab-

bage and damp animal. There was a stone sink against one wall, with a small window above, and a narrow bed along the opposite wall. There was an open fireplace, with a tall, skinny cupboard to the left and a pile of chopped wood on the right; there was a battered black kettle hanging over the fire and leaning against the hearth was a poker and a wood-splitting axe. In the middle of the room stood a rickety table and two chairs, and right next to the door, stretched out upon an old piece of sacking, was an animal with big teeth and fierce eyes.

The little girl and the beast saw one another at exactly the same moment. But, while the little girl froze on the spot, the beast fixed her in his eyes and, with studied casualness, got up and took two menacing steps towards her, licking his lips and baring his fangs.

Granny said: "Don't just stand in the doorway letting the cold in, child." While to the animal, she laughed and said: "She's not for you, Doggy. Not today. Now lie down and be good." And she leashed him to a ring in the wall with a length of old rope.

When the girl was sure the animal was firmly tied up, she said to her granny: "Would you like to have a tea party with Patch?" And she held up her doll by way of introduction.

"Foolish child," Granny snorted, before spitting on the fire. "There's work to be done." From under the bed she pulled a box of fine clothes – trousers and dresses, shirts and jackets – on top of which sat a small basket with bobbins of different coloured thread and needles and a thimble and scissors. And from the cupboard she uncorked a flagon of stout. She sat on a chair and pulled out a fine gown with a tear in the hem and began threading one of her needles.

"We could play hide-and-seek or hunt-the-thimble, if you like."

Granny screwed up her eyes, stabbed her thimbled finger toward the child and said: "Your mother promised you'd be a quiet brat and wouldn't get under my feet, so make sure you do *as you're told or... or I'll have to lock you in the cupboard. There are jobs to be done and, seeing that you'll be eating my food and enjoying my fire, you'll need to make yourself useful and do your fair share." She looked at the dirty floor and the ash-covered hearth and the greasy window. "You can start by collecting more firewood."*

The little girl remembered her mother's words about doing what she was told and went outside with her doll to gather wood, although, apart from some tree trunks that were too big to move and too hard to split, all the fallen branches close to the cottage had long been collected. The little girl searched and searched until the cold and the dark began thickening between the trees, but she returned with only five little twigs.

"This is all I could find," she said.

Granny snatched the sticks and threw them on the fire. "Well, you certainly haven't earned your keep today, have you? But then, you're probably not cold in that lovely warm coat your mother's sewn for you and she probably stuffed you with food before you left home. My, oh my, I do hope you're not a spoilt little brat. Never mind, I'll let you off this once; you go to bed without any fuss and I'll make do with some of your mother's apple pie for my supper." And with that, she ate half the pie in one bite, cut a sliver into the beast's tin bowl and, after she'd licked her fingers one-by-one, put the remaining pie high on a shelf in the skinny cupboard.

The little girl quietly cried herself to sleep, but woke when Granny squashed her against the wall. It was crowded in the single bed and Granny threw the girl's doll out and kept stealing the bedclothes and kicking and farting in her sleep. So in the morning the girl was hungry and tired.

However, the fire was blazing, the wood pile had grown and the first thing Granny said was: "Shall we have mushrooms for breakfast?" So the little girl was happy again because she knew that day was going to be a better day.

"Yes please," she said.

"Then go into the woods and fill this basket."

The little girl headed out into the forest once more and searched and searched, but could only find one little mushroom. One little mushroom in all the forest.

"This is all there was," she said when she returned a long while later, but Granny didn't say anything at first because she had her mouth crammed full of roast duck.

As Granny licked her fingers, carved three slices of meat into the beast's tin bowl and put the remaining duck high on a shelf in the skinny cupboard, she said: "That's all you found in all this time? What sort of fool do you take me for, child? Just by looking at you, I can tell what a greedy little piggy you've been: you've eaten all the mushrooms as you picked them." And, with that, she snatched the one mushroom out of the basket and gobbled it up herself.

"But I didn't and I'm hungry," the little girl whimpered, "and I'm not a pig."

"Don't lie to Granny, little girl, or... or I'll feed you to my dog, shoes and all. You'd be a tender morsel for sure."

The little girl, who was crying now, stamped her foot and said: "You're not my granny; you're a mean old woman, that's what you are. And that's not a dog, that's a wolf." And, quick-as-a-flash, she took the three slices of duck from the tin bowl on the table and popped one into her mouth and the other two pieces into her pocket.

The mean old woman shrieked and reached forward to grab the little girl, who ducked and ran round the other side of the table. The animal howled at its loss and tugged at its leash.

"You're a bad girl and you deserve a hiding to teach you some manners," and the old woman picked up the poker and pointed it at the girl. "Now put that meat back or it'll be the worse for you."

"You're a wicked old woman," the little girl said and popped

the second slice of duck into her mouth.

The wicked old woman then roared and turned into a fat, lumbering bear and chased the little girl round and round the table in the middle of the room, waving the poker at her. The wolf barked and barked at the commotion and pulled tighter and tighter at its leash, until first one strand of rope frayed and snapped, and then another strand frayed and snapped.

And the little girl was so scared with running and running, she didn't know what to do next. She wouldn't be able to get out the door quickly enough and the window was too high to reach – she was going to get caught any moment and fed to the wolf. She looked at the fire, glanced back at the old witch, noticed the axe and decided to act: first, she let the old woman almost catch her and then, at just the right moment, she dropped to the floor and curled up like a mouse.

This was too quick a surprise for the lumbering granny, who tripped over her, flew through the air and hit the middle of her head on the blade of the axe, so that it split like a pumpkin as she fell into the fire.

After the scream and the thud, came a moment's silence, as both the girl and the wolf held their breath. But then the wolf leapt forward and tugged and howled, and the little girl saw his leash was held only by a single thread. Quickly, she clambered to her feet and, just as the last strand snapped, she jumped into the tall, skinny cupboard, pulling the door shut after her.

At first, all she could hear was the scrabbling of the animal's claws at the cupboard and the panting of his rank breath through the cracks in the wood, and there was nothing she could do but hope he didn't knock the door's small latch undone. She couldn't help but imagine his big teeth and fierce, hungry eyes and large, empty belly, and she shoved her fist harder into her mouth to stop herself from whimpering. However, after a short while, the little girl was surprised when the sniffing and snorting and scratching and clawing at the piece of thin timber between them stopped, and even more surprised by the smell of cooked meat drifting into the cupboard.

The smell of the old lady cooking on the fire made Doggy forget how angry he was and remember how hungry he was. How little he'd eaten for so long. It was the smell of juicy pork and crispy bacon, and he licked his lips, dragged his mistress out of the fire with his teeth and began gobbling her up, shoes and all.

That very morning, a woodsman came walking through the forest. Attracted by such delicious and tantalising smells wafting from the old woman's cottage, he thought she must be cooking up a rare feast and could surely spare him a slice or two of pork or bacon. Except, when he peered through the window, what he saw was a huge beast, which had killed the little, old lady and which was now eating her. So he forced open the window, took aim and shot it with his gun.

The little girl would say very little about what happened at the cottage. A word here, a word there. If anyone asked too much, she'd shove her fist in her mouth, curl up small as a mouse or run off to hide in a cupboard. And so it was that the woodsman told one story of what he believed had happened and the little girl's mother told another story of what she believed had happened, and the people who heard these stories added a detail here and a suggestion there until the stories changed and grew into many different versions of the same story; even though, strangely enough, most of them carried the same message: that grandmothers exist to be loved, that wolves can never be trusted and that the smartness of little girls should never be underestimated.

However, there's only one moral to the story I've told, which is this: truth is often a matter of perspective. It's the slippiest of eels and will wriggle and jiggle every which way depending on who's holding it, and in order to know it better we have to hold it ourselves and look at it from all angles.

Part Three

1

Nic stood at a bench, unpacking a delivery of parts – a replacement carburettor for a Massey Ferg, brake pads, a couple of batteries – and was gearing up to phone the suppliers and ask why they hadn't tracked down his replacement tail-light, when a silver Porsche Carrera screeched into the service bay. It slid on the concrete as the driver braked and almost collected a compressor sitting in the middle of the bay. A cloud of dust and the stink of hot rubber. The engine was revved once – a piece of theatre that placed the driver centre-stage – and then turned off. But no one climbed out.

He leaned down to the window and peered against its tint. With one smooth whirr, the window unwound and there she was, beaming at him. Siobhan.

"I wonder if you might look at my brakes," she said. "They feel a tad spongy." Then she whooped in delight and reached out of the window to grab his overalls, pull him closer, as if she'd drag him into the car and onto her lap.

Within seconds, all past doubts evaporated. Hey presto: vanished. As he knew they had to. They were one another's future. Love demands a leap of faith. If he could've slid through the window he would.

She was out the car and wrecking a sleek, black dress by squeezing a close impression from his oily overalls. Pressing against him, into him. The acridity of hot rubber was replaced by an exotic scent with a hint of vanilla. Forgiveness was immediate and absolute. His hands were locked behind the small of her back, then dropping to caress the curves of her bum, then reaching up to hold her beneath the arms and lift her. She bounced up and down on tip-toe, dancing with delight.

"Talk about an angel and a prayer," he said, taking a moment to drink up the sight of her. "It's a bloody miracle. Magic. What are you doing here?"

"I came to save you." She still had her arms around his neck, needed to lean back to look him in the eyes. "I got your message. You sounded bored so I thought I'd drop by for a few days." She held her arms up and out, let him hold on to her as she swung back, like an acrobat on a trapeze, or Superwoman.

He smiled. He grinned. "You're nothing less than an angel. And I'm more than ready to be saved."

"Not a minute too soon, eh?"

"No way. Perfect timing."

"And you've forgiven me?"

She'd done what she'd thought was right. She'd been terrified of going to the police – and he could see why now, more than ever. In her own way she'd tried to look out for him. Maybe it was time to see it as a comedy of errors. After all, life had to move on.

"Water under the bridge," he said.

He brushed down a seat for her, hoped Archie wouldn't be back anytime soon. Everything could wait a while; they owed him that.

"And look at you," she said. "Your hair. What happened to your hair?"

He'd kept it cropped, preferring it that way; had run the

shaver over it that weekend. "Thought I needed to reinvent myself. A new image. Don't you like it?"

"I don't know. It's a bit radical." She reached a hand out, ran her fingers over his head. "It's alright, I guess. You look a bit meaner like this. A tough guy – or tougher, anyway."

"Good. I reckon that's what I needed. Less of a soft touch."

She glanced over her shoulder, seemed uncertain about telling him something.

"What?" he said.

Instead, she shrugged and smiled wearily; it must have been a long drive. "Looks aren't everything. It's what's behind them that counts."

"I know."

*

When Archie returned with Bluey, he said to the mechanic, "I see you've got company." And to Siobhan, he said, "Hello, young lady. What brings you to our neck of the woods?"

She gripped the sleeve of Nic's overalls and said, "Love. What else matters?" She drooled the word, made it longer: 'lurve'.

The mechanic raised his eyebrows at Archie and Archie winked. Bluey barked, waddled over and licked her hand.

"You best go over and see the boss then; see if she can fix you up with a room. If you're staying, that is."

"I will. I am."

"Let my fella here get on with his work, eh?"

"Sure thing." She kissed Nic – a dainty peck on the cheek this time – and whispered, "I'll catch you later. When you knock off. I'll be waiting."

Then she was gone again. She got in the car, reversed and parked in front of The Crown.

2

Archie let Nic finish a good hour early and Siobhan rushed up to him as he clattered through the front door. She'd been watching the garage from a window on the first floor, she said, and leapt downstairs the moment he left work. They were in the bar, which smelt of spilt beer, stale carpet, air freshener and freshly cut roses, of which there were three tall vases teeming with soft yellows and pink doubles; each set against a flatter, darker contrast of jagged fern fronds. A dramatic display.

"Hmm. I love the scent of roses," she crooned.

"I have to take a shower," he said. "I'm filthy."

She whispered, "I'll wash your back."

And she did.

"Love's a sticky business," he murmured as they lay in bed late that afternoon. He had one arm embracing her thin, delicious shoulders and knew what a king-size fool he'd been to push her away. Could never make the same mistake twice. He loved her, wanted her and, from now on, he'd fight to keep her. It wouldn't matter what life threw at them, they'd tackle it together head-on.

"You mean sex," she teased. "Most men are the same when it comes down to it: one track minds."

"No, I mean love. Seriously. Sex is straight-forward; it's love that's messy." And he was right: since he'd first loved Siobhan, his life had grown stickier and messier. Nonetheless, he'd rather that than not have her. Some people managed fine being on their lonesome, but he had no stomach for it; was inept.

"But you're glad I'm here? You're happy I came? Despite the mess?"

"Despite the mess, yes. Definitely. Wouldn't have it any other way. But what if I hadn't phoned you, Siobhan? What then?"

"Then I'd have paid you a surprise visit anyway. I'd have tracked you down and proved my undying love. And you – you wouldn't have been able to resist my charms any longer."

"So sure?" he asked.

"Absolutely. It's in the script." She stroked a finger around one of his nipples and then pinched it gently between finger and thumb. "You didn't stand a chance."

"You always get your man?"

"Of course." She pulled the pillow from behind her back, punched it into shape and dropped it in place again. "I'm glad you're here," she said.

"In Gimbly?"

"I'm glad we're here together now. At this moment in time. Although Gimbly doesn't seem such a bad place, Nic. I've seen worse. And you've got a good job. You should hold onto it."

"It's a dead-end job, Siobhan, in a dead-end town. There were a couple of days when I thought it might be more than that. Not that I don't appreciate what you did – for pushing my name forward. But it's not for me, sorry. I've had it with the place and especially with the local cop. They're a bunch of unfriendly bastards on the whole, but he's the worst. You'll see for yourself when we go down for dinner. Seven o'clock sharp."

With one finger he stroked a circle on her forehead as he spoke, drew a line over the bridge of her nose, across her mouth, her chin, her neck, between her breasts to her navel; he rested a moment in her pubic fur, before tracing the contour of her thigh, the calf of her leg, an ankle, and ended up stroking her toes, weaving between them. "I wish there was a decent restaurant I could take you to."

"If you didn't have a job, you wouldn't be able to afford to."

"Catch-22," he said.

She ran a finger across his stomach, arched a foot in response to his caresses and purred. "I've missed you," she said. "I thought I would and I did, but everything'll be OK now."

The mood in the bar was different that evening. Everyone was livelier, more animated; the laughter was never muted. It made a liar out of him, but that didn't matter tonight. Maybe Siobhan brought out an affability in him that allowed others to lighten up. Perhaps he'd been sending the wrong signals since he'd arrived. For one night, he'd happily pretend that was the case.

"How're you going?" they said when he walked into the bar. And: "How's the town's maestro mechanic?" or "G'day, matey. What's new?"

Whitey was pulling a beer for himself behind the bar. "Let me get you both a drink while I'm here," he said. "What'll you have?"

For the first time, Nic chose a table in the middle of the room, rather than trying to hide himself by a wall or blend in with the bar by huddling over a beer and staring at the TV.

"Weirder than weird," he said.

"What is?"

"This place. Suddenly I exist again. With you here, I'm no longer Mr Invisible."

"It's my charisma, my pure charm; I make you glow too. It's the gift of the Irish," she giggled.

"Seriously," he said.

She said: "Being invisible isn't so bad; in the right place, at the right time."

3

Swinging arms, kicking gravel into the dark, they ambled in the direction of the old Gardens. She bent down and picked something from the road, turned it so it glistened in the moonlight.

"A washer," she said. "I thought it was a coin." She placed it across her thumbnail and index finger, flicked it up in the air and tried to catch it, but missed. She picked it up again, took another look, drew her arm back and sent it skimming into the grass.

"I heard about it through contacts – business contacts," she told him, returning to the question he'd asked. "They owed me a favour and so, when I heard you'd lost your job, I called in the favour."

"So you don't know anything about the research lab – P-R.G. – you don't know what they're about?"

She shook her head, shrugged. "Sorry."

He stopped when the track split; wasn't sure where he was leading her. But Siobhan squeezed his hand and drew him forward, towards the gate at the side of the paddock. Nic hesitated when she opened it.

"I'm not sure, Siobhan. I don't know whose paddock this is. People get a bit shitty about private property around here. Perhaps we should stick to the road."

"Don't worry, Nic. Life's too short to worry about everything. If anyone threatens to shoot us for trespassing, I'll throw some more of my charisma at them."

"Hmm."

"Besides, I checked with your landlady. She suggested it."

They walked in silence a while, following the track as it crossed the paddock and climbed to traverse the horseshoe that was the valley's end. The cattle ignored them, the sheep clustered and trotted uphill. They followed the ruts of the track, crossing two ramshackle, timber bridges made from railway sleepers, until it wound back and around upon itself to reach the opposite side of the valley, where they sat on a slab of rock on the crest of the hill. The moon was a lick short of being full and he could see well enough to know it wasn't such a different view to the one he'd gained from the opposite ridge, except the town was exposed. It seemed idyllic, with the early spring night air folding around them and the moon smiling down and a few lights glowing in Gimbly.

"Might look cosy at night," he commented, "but they're just lights in the darkness."

"Homely," she said.

"The place gives me the creeps. No two ways about it." He drew his coat tighter, pulled the collar up. Sitting still, the chill was reaching into him.

Then, remarkably close – too close – a strange bark. Twice. Short and angry. Nic looked around and Siobhan did too. He couldn't see anything and began to stand. Then two more barks, but far off, from down the valley. A response. A pack.

"Perhaps we should go," he said.

"Okay," she said. "If you want."

Peering into the near-darkness, he tried to see where it came from and to find a stick or a branch. But there was nothing.

And then the scream. But a woman. Clearly a woman. In agony. Being tortured. Or mad. From nearby.

"Fuck," he said. "Who *is* that? What's going on?"

When he looked at Siobhan, she was doubled up; was hurt. Crying with pain. Then she sat up, drew a breath and laughed some more. "Your face!" she panted. "You soft bugger." Gasped for breath. "That's just an owl. An owl!" And she creased up again.

A few minutes later, as they headed back down the hill, she pointed across the paddock, but he'd already seen it. Ghost-like, an owl broke from the cover of an isolated tree to scoop across the grassland in a flawless, measured flight. It plucked a rat or a field mouse from life and, without breaking rhythm, coasted back into the cover of woodland.

4

So much for Siobhan booking a room of her own. Her suitcase lay open on the middle of Nic's carpet and by the following morning her clothes were strewn everywhere except in his wardrobe: knickers and bras across the desk; trousers, skirts and jumpers, shirts and jeans, draped over his armchair and desk chair and on the floor where they'd fallen from the bed; a large nest of socks and pantyhose lay next to the kettle. The bathroom was a similar story. She'd disordered his world again and he couldn't stop grinning.

"For someone with such a tidy mind," he said, picking his way around the room, getting ready for work, "you're a messy bugger."

She was lying in bed, warm and curled with sleep, and he would've climbed back in with her to catch up on the missed months, if there hadn't been work to go to.

"I know where all my clothes are," she said. "It's only you who sees a mess."

As she unfurled across the mattress, she let the sheet slip so her shoulders and most of one breast was exposed, and she pushed her foot out and stroked his back as he sat on the edge of the bed to tie his bootlaces. She was wearing a ring on one of her toes and a silver ankle chain.

"So what'll you do with yourself today, Lady Muck? I'll give you two hours before you're bored off your face with this god-forsaken town. Two hours tops. Reckon you'll be sitting in your car and raring to leave by lunchtime."

"Oh, I'll fritter away the hours relaxing. It's been in short supply lately and this seems the perfect place to unwind. I'm not so shallow that I can't create my own entertainment, you know. I've got a book to finish and a few accounts to sort out. Who knows, I might have another walk or go for a drive. No doubt I'll even meet some of the locals. A place like this is what you make of it."

"Perhaps." He wasn't convinced that anyone could make Gimbly into anything other than what it was – or wasn't. "Watch out for that copper, though. There's a rotten one in every barrel, and he's it. *It* with a capital S.H. A real bastard. I'm surprised he didn't pull you over for a roadworthy on the way in."

"I'll look out for him and I'll be my most charming. He's probably just a lamb in wolf's clothing." She yawned and stretched, cat-like, allowing the sheet to drop further.

As she drew her arms back, above and behind her head, he followed the accentuated curves of hip, waist, abdomen, shoulders, neck and breasts – lithe and delicious, her nipples erect – as she knew he would.

"Siobhan, play it safe, eh? He's a nasty piece of work. Don't give him an excuse to tangle with you. Promise."

She saluted and covered herself. "He was probably just having a bad day, Nic. Being a copper can't be easy at the best of times. He'd probably be okay if you got to know him. Besides, people are just people, wherever they are and whatever they do. He's got to have one redeeming quality at least. Just look at that garden of his."

"You noticed that too? Well, if that isn't the work of an obsessive lunatic, I don't know what is. The guy's a sandwich short of a picnic."

"That's just you being angry," she said. "And fair enough too. He shouldn't have done what he did. But a rose garden is a rose garden, and I think it looks great." She took his hand in hers. "Is that what this is really about? You and... the policeman? Is that the only reason you're thinking about giving up such a great job – a once-in-a-lifetime opportunity? Because of two little spats? I bet he's like that with everyone when they first arrive. Sees it as *his* town. Why don't you give it time and let him get to know you?"

He stood up, but she patted the bed at her side. "I can't. I must go to work, Siobhan. Otherwise they'll sack me before I've served out my notice."

"You don't have to go yet."

He stood by the door. "I was going to grab some breakfast. I'm ravenous. I'll bring something up for you, if you like?"

She dragged the sheet up to her neck. "Don't I even get a goodbye kiss?"

"You're wicked," he said. "And I'm a sucker for you."

"Hmm, don't be too hard on yourself. It's because of your chromosomes."

"What?"

"It's because you're male."

"Aha. Got me there."

He sat down on the bed and put one hand on her leg and stroked the fingers of his other hand through her hair and against the small of her neck. She curled round so her head was in his lap and he leant down to kiss her, but she put her arms round his neck and drew her face up to his. He kissed her and let her tongue push and slide across his own; felt her teeth clink against his as she gripped and bit his bottom lip. She nipped once, twice, let him bite back, but not too hard, then pressed her tongue so that it slid over his again, and began tugging at the buttons on his shirt.

"Delicious," he sighed, helping her with the buckle of his belt.

5

Fewer chains dragged against the hours for knowing that Siobhan was nearby. She gave purpose to his day, was someone to look forward to; the simple knowledge of her presence made him more substantial and resilient – better able to cope with this place. He was fully alive again.

Archie was in pain. Nic could tell by the way he measured each awkward sequence of movements, by the tightness of the creases at the corner of his eyes and the strain that froze his mouth half-open whenever the pain found him – as if he was concentrating on something but couldn't remember what. Bluey was stiller when his master was like this, spending the hours stretched out with his head on his paws, looking up, watching.

"You look like you should be at home, in bed, not at work," Nic told him.

"Don't you bleeding start."

"Is there anything I can do?"

"Yeah. Mind your own bloody business and get on with your work."

Archie didn't last the morning though; a morning of cussing and swearing, an angry few phone calls with the office door shut, while Nic did an oil change and replaced a couple of tyres. Then Nic was shown how to fill out documentation for the sale and transportation of the five showroom cars – a hint of greater involvement, if he didn't quit.

"Are they being picked up today?" he asked.

Archie tried pushing himself out of his chair but knocked his stick over. When Nic stepped forward to offer a hand, he waved him off and lowered himself into the seat again. He took a breath. "In the next couple of days," he said. "Business is booming. We've got five going out and six being delivered."

"What's coming in?" he said. "Similar models?"

Archie began reaching into his desk drawer, but the movement faltered, collapsed. Nic waited and listened to his boss draw two slow breaths before he could carry on. He blinked, refocussed on Nic. "Have you got work to do, or what?"

Forty minutes later, Archie and Bluey shuffled over to where he was working.

"I'm going home. You're in charge. Let me know if there's any problems."

"Okay. Fair enough. Look after yourself. I hope you feel better."

"And don't fuck up."

That afternoon, he knocked off early again. There was nothing else to do. Archie's car transporter company phoned to say they'd be arriving the next day, and there was only so many times he could sweep, wash down and tidy the tidiest, cleanest workshop in the country. He stood in the doorway and watched the sky darken, felt the day grow ominously still.

For ten minutes before the first fat drops fell, the air was sweet with the scent of oncoming rain. From the shelter of the work bays, he watched the theatre of the downpour from beginning to end. He couldn't remember the last time he'd done this, nor listened to the deafening tattoo it beat on a tin roof – as a child on holiday, perhaps – nor been amused by the cascades of water pouring over roof gutters and leaf-blocked spouts into torrents streaming and flooding the road. Not from beginning to end. Not like this. There were some things you paid less heed to in the city.

It lasted fifteen minutes at most but was the first rain he'd seen since his arrival and the air remained sweet long after it had stopped. The surrounding hills seemed to lift a little, as if they'd been stirred and taken a breath, and the crickets sang about it and the sheep didn't stop bleating about it for the rest of the day.

He walked straight into the kitchen at The Crown to hang up the garage keys and ask Mary how Archie was. But found Siobhan there instead. Wearing an apron, washing dishes.

"What are you doing, Cinderella? Can't you pay your bill?"

She spun on her feet, laughed, pushed the hair out of her eyes with one arm and leant back against the sink. Every movement was light, smooth, fluid. A dance. It charged the impulse in him to scoop her up and drink her in, to drown in her. Who was it that said beauty should be edible? They weren't wrong. Sometimes the longing was close to pain and he thought he might drown anyway. Might happily drown.

"Washing dishes," she said. "What does it look like? How was your afternoon, lover-boy?"

The smell of gingerbread baking reminded him of the day he'd turned up in Gimbly. Spicy, sweet, warm, soothing – inviting and comforting. The cooling trays were laden with six cakes.

Standing in front of her, he drew a finger along her forearm to remove a line of detergent suds and flicked them into the sink. "Why are you doing that?"

"A good cook always washes her own dishes. Didn't you know that?"

"You baked these? I didn't know you liked cooking."

"There's lots you don't know, thank goodness, and don't you forget it. Life would be too boring otherwise. There'd be sweet nothing left to discover or wonder at."

The cat was under the table, eyeing him imperiously. This was its domain and he a visitor.

"There are dishwashers, you know. You don't have to do that."

"Phooey," she said. "It's not the same. I've had a good day. Got to know a few people." She scraped more suds off her wrists and dabbed them onto his chin. "What a nice goatee you have." Then: "Mary's up with Archie at the moment. He's not at all well today."

He wiped the suds off and dried his hands across his overalls. What was it she did that he didn't do, to get to know people so quickly, so easily? To get them to open up to her? Was it some extra quality that made her special, or something ordinary he was missing? He'd never been aware of it before, nor felt he was lacking something; not until he arrived here.

"I gathered," he said. "He's often like that, but worse at the moment. Miserable and moody with it; like a bear with a sore behind."

"She told me how much they value having you in Gimbly. She's worried they might have to sell up if they can't find a replacement. If you decide to go, that is."

He almost laughed at the bullshit Mary had fed her, but held back. Absolute bullshit. Instead, he said: "I'm sure she is."

"Good mechanics are hard to find out here."

"They'd recruit from the cities if they had to. Hardly anyone here's a local," he told her. "But even if they did have a problem, that still wouldn't be *my* problem." Then he sneezed; knew it was the cat. "Look, I should get showered and changed. Thought we might grab a drink or go for a wander, if you like."

She turned back to the sink of dishes. "I'll join you in a while. I promised Mary I'd help out until all the meals are on."

"Oh, okay," he said, but was irritated now. Maybe Mary was a lot more conniving than she seemed and Siobhan more gullible – a bit of a romantic, perhaps. Even so, as he stood in the shower and let the heat stream over his neck, across his shoulders, down his back, he knew it was pathetic to feel the slightest pang of jealousy and that he should appreciate Siobhan's generous, gregarious nature all the more keenly instead.

6

It rained through the night. As torrential as the afternoon but relentless. Rivers of water overshot the roof and the guttering, cascading onto the veranda. Slightly after three o'clock, Nic turned the light on. He'd been woken by a constant drip, tip-tapping on the ceiling above their bed, breaking into his dreams, but there was no wet patch visible. The only stain was the stain on the carpet, hidden by the rug. Afterwards, his brain put the two impressions together – the dripping and the bloody stain – and created a scramble of unpleasant dreams.

With daylight, the world was grey and gritty. It was drizzling, but there were deeper, dark puddles along the roadside, and a wash of red soil and stones across the bitumen, where the water had streamed and spat through the verge. There was more debris of leaves and bark strewn across the street and, from where he stood, the river appeared to have risen – higher, muddier, faster.

Mary caught him as he made his way downstairs. "You'll be on your own again today," she said. "Archie's in no shape to get out of bed."

"Right you are."

"But he said to phone if anything untoward crops up."

"I will."

The car transporter arrived late-morning, bringing two black Ford Mustang GT500s, another Persian Blue Lotus Elise, along with a Peugeot 607 and two S-type Jaguars in silver. Nic helped unload both tiers of cars and then, reversing the process, with loading the cars from the shed. He pored over the paperwork, scrutinised it again, and wasn't going to put his signature on a single docket until he knew the details were spot-on.

"That's a bitch of a road," the driver said. "Had to stop twice to clear frigging branches. Enormous fucking branches. Am I the only poor sod to use it?" It was the first time he'd done the Gimbly run.

"Doesn't get much use," Nic said. "Last night's storm would have brought plenty down. It was bad enough yesterday."

"Would've turned back if I could. Don't get paid to risk breaking my bloody neck. Bastard of a place to get to. Hope they serve a decent meal at the pub there?"

"I'll have a word with Mary, the landlady. She'll see you right."

"Not exactly the centre of the universe, is it? Thought I must have the wrong road or the wrong load. Farm town, is it?" He was talking for the sake of it, probably desperate to chew the fat with another human after hours on the road with only a CB or a mobile phone to yak at.

"Yeah, farm town," he said. "Not much but farm and forest round here."

"And no such thing as a poor farmer, eh? Not if they're buying this stuff. These cars are worth a mint. Should give up driving and buy a piece of land, I reckon. I'm in the wrong bleeding job."

Nic nodded, smiled, let him rabbit on. He found himself unwilling to enlighten the driver, and wondered at this.

The new cars were rain-spattered, but he soon brought them back to their fine polished finish once he'd lined them up in the shed.

He was sitting in one of the Mustangs with the driver's door open when Siobhan appeared. He'd been peering at the instrument panel and examining the cockpit interior, taking in deep draughts of the newness of it. When he glanced up, she was standing there, watching him and grinning, arms crossed. "Boys and their toys, eh?"

"Perk of the job." Gripping the leather-wrapped steering wheel in both hands, he pushed himself back into the upholstery and pressed his foot against the accelerator.

"Looks like you're in your element," she said, but the rain began pounding on the tin roof and she had to shout to be heard.

"You're not wrong there," he shouted back.

She moved next to the open door and leant down to see the Mustang's interior, and shook her head at him sitting there, playing. "Aren't you hungry though? You haven't had lunch and it's almost three o'clock."

He looked at his watch. "Starving," he said. "Didn't realise."

7

Several minutes after the evening meals were served, Mary returned to the dining room, took a spoon and rapped it on the sideboard. She held the spoon in the air and the conversation vanished into silence.

"Listen up. Whitey's come off the road about five kilometres down the valley. The van's in a ditch, wrapped around a fence post, and some of the load has spilt." Her voice had a note of urgency but there was no panic, only decisiveness. "We need two or three extra pairs of hands to help out. Perhaps you three." Still clutching the spoon, she pointed to a group at a table. "Watto and Hamish should be outside with the replacement van and a car in a minute; they'll get you down there. You'll need waterproofs."

Without a murmur and with just a couple of extra hurried bites, the three abandoned their meals and moved off to get jackets. Maybe this was the way you paid your dues in a country town; it wasn't just a matter of helping out in a crisis but dropping everything to do it and minding to ask no questions. It was a different pace and approach to life than in the city; a different way of connecting.

Mary came over to Siobhan and Nic and said, "You too, Nic. Archie says to take the tow truck. Get the van out of the ditch and back to the garage tonight if you can. He doesn't want it sitting there. But finish your dinner. Let the others tidy things up first." Placing the spoon on their table, she pushed both hands over her bun of white hair and tucked a stray strand back in place.

"How's Whitey?" Siobhan asked. "Is he okay?"

"Just a couple of scratches by the sounds of it, that's all. But we'll get him checked over. Make sure there's no broken bones." She picked the spoon back up and pointed it at Nic: "This is exactly why we need a good mechanic in town. Not much might happen for weeks at a time, but when it does we'd be stuck without one."

Siobhan looked at Nic and he shrugged, pushed his knife and fork together and began to stand.

"No need for your food to go cold, Nic. The others can sort out whatever mess it made of its load. Give 'em ten minutes or you'll just be standing around getting wet."

"No worries," he said and sat back down, but felt he should hurry all the same. Seemed the thing to do.

As he made his way back through the hotel to pick up the keys, having pulled on a pair of overalls and a jacket, he poked his head into the dining room to wave goodbye to Siobhan, but couldn't catch her eye. She was talking with Mary, who'd taken his seat.

8

Against layers of darkness and teeming rain slanting across the headlights of the tow truck, Nic pulled up as the cluster of men in fluorescent weatherproofs were transferring the last of the ditched van's contents into the replacement van. With the vehicles filling the road and the van at a crazy angle in the ditch, it resembled the scene of a major accident, but it wasn't. It was too dramatic by half. He clambered out of the truck to the reverberating whine of a chainsaw. Up ahead, a tree was down, blocking the road, and the Troll was stationed over it, wielding the saw, dissecting it branch-by-branch, log-by-log.

Nic watched a moment, thinking it might not be such a bad thing if the bastard slipped and lopped off a leg or something, and in that moment the rain eased. He lowered his hood and walked over to where one of the blokes was doing his best to rearrange and secure a van full of damaged freight.

Almost every box had taken a battering and a couple had been totalled; reduced to flattened shreds of cardboard. Quite a few had been roughly repaired with parcel tape, while a couple of black bin liners must've been filled with loose stock.

It was the sort of merchandise he'd often seen in the van whenever it delivered goods to the garage, on the way round to The Crown and the laboratory: cartons of potato chips (salt and vinegar, cheese and onion, chicken, plain), boxes of biscuits (custard creams, ginger nuts), large boxes of toilet paper, bottles of detergent. Yet it seemed strange these items should be leaving Gimbly. He'd always assumed the town was the one and only destination.

Stacked next to the biscuits were three damaged boxes of lollies (Love Hearts, Sweet Violets, Sharp Shooters) with simple banner labels: *Sweet Things Confectionery Company, Wholesale Manufacturers & Suppliers*. He hadn't tasted a Sweet Violet since he was a kid and had never really liked them, but he remembered now that they'd been his sister's favourite as a child. She'd lick them and wipe them on her lips, pretending they were lipstick, before eating them.

Climbing down the bank to take a look at the van, Watto was in the freight compartment, working against the awkward tilt with a dustpan and brush and a clear plastic bag. Had his back to Nic. Looked like he'd been sweeping up a spill of Love Hearts or some such. He tied the bag and snatched off a dust mask; shoved it in his jacket pocket. The whine of the chainsaw was at its loudest. He was removing a pair of latex gloves when Nic thumped the side of the van.

Watto jumped, grasped at something to hold onto, dropped the dustpan and bag.

"Sorry," Nic said and couldn't help but laugh.

"Shit! Fuck! Thought it was rolling." He took a step forward, then stopped and picked up the plastic bag. "Don't you ever fucking do that again."

"Sorry, Watto. Didn't mean to. Just wanted to say I can hose it down at the garage, if you like. You don't need to sweep it."

9

The van's radiator and lights had copped the worst of the damage and there were a couple of crumpled panels, but it wouldn't take much to get on the road again, as long as the parts suppliers got their act together. What he really wanted to examine wasn't under the bonnet, but in the freight section, where Watto had been. Friday evening or not, once he'd unhooked the van from the tow truck, he raised the engine's bonnet to make it look like that's what he was inspecting, in case anybody walked in, and then he climbed into the back. All it'd take was one Love Heart, one lolly, to prove or disprove what was running through his head – that imagination of his. He'd even eat the thing himself if he needed to.

It was too weird, a tough-nut security guard like Watto wearing a protective mask and surgical gloves to sweep up a few lollies. Too much fuss all round. And why would the van be carrying boxes of lollies anyway?

There were no gaps in the pressed tin that lined the sides and floor of the freight area, where spilt goods might fall, but several metal struts were bolted to the main frame, so that shelving might be attached. It was behind these that a Love Heart or two might have slid out of sight. But there was nothing. He even poked a screwdriver behind each one, hoping to prise something out, but it was just cold, bare tin that had been swept clean.

10

A wild wind rattled the window throughout the night and it was still rattling when he properly woke the following morning. The day had a weak, diffused light to it that struggled to stretch across the veranda and find its way into his room. He'd slept only fitfully and lay awake between two and three-thirty, going over the events of the evening, rearranging the jigsaw of ideas he'd formed about Gimbly. At one point, shortly before he fell into sleep again, he was ready to get up, grab a torch and walk back to where the van had come off the road. Except, even then, he knew how ridiculous that was and that a better plan would be to return in the light of day – as long as it didn't rain too much.

"What's the matter?" Siobhan asked, as he crammed their dirty dishes onto the breakfast tray he'd brought from downstairs and cursed too quickly, too loudly, when a knife smeared in marmalade slipped from a plate onto the bed.

"Nothing," he said, but then slid the tray onto the desk and peered out of the window for the second or third time. An armada of clouds was sailing too slowly over the valley. There wasn't space for the faintest patch of blue in the sky, just fleet after fleet of full-sailed clouds. In the distance, but drawing closer, they seemed darker, larger.

"What's the matter, Nic?"

"I'm feeling cooped up, that's all," he said. "Hope it doesn't rain."

"Well, let's go somewhere then," she said. "Once we've showered, we can go for a drive or a walk or something. It doesn't matter if it rains or not."

"Along the valley road," he suggested.

"I don't mind where we go, Nic. Really. Wherever you want."

He took his impatience with him. He knew he did. It trotted along between them, getting between them. It snapped at their conversation and left an uneasy silence. He wished the wind would hurry and push the clouds away and dry the grass out. No rain. Mustn't rain.

Siobhan mentioned the previous evening's accident – small talk, to draw him from wherever he was – but he'd say little more than he'd said before: a big fuss about nothing.

She took his hand and stroked it. "You're very quiet," she

said. "Are you sure everything's okay?"

"I'm fine," he said, looking across the valley beyond the short horizon of the opposite hill's crest – a ridge that stretched from one end of the valley to the other, like a crease in the landscape. He increased the pace a little. "Didn't sleep too well last night, that's all. Probably tired."

She continued stroking his hand as they walked. They avoided puddles and pot-holes, half-heartedly dragged a couple of fallen branches out of the way, onto the verge, and occasionally fell into kicking at the detritus of twigs and leaves. The air smelt damp; of rotting wood and sweet mildew.

The site of the accident was further out than he'd realised. At night, it had been hard to get his bearings because he didn't know the road well, it was teeming with rain and, of course, he'd travelled in the tow truck, which made it seem barely any distance at all. But now, every once in a while, he slowed, paused, looked for signs of flattened vegetation, a nest of muddy tyre tracks across the grass, writhing across the bitumen; a logged tree to one side, scatterings of sawdust from the chain saw streaked across the road. Surely, it'd be impossible to miss.

The second time he did this, Siobhan said, "What are you looking for?"

"Nothing. It doesn't matter. I'll tell you if I find it."

"Do you want to turn back? Have you had enough?"

"No, not yet." He stroked her hand the way she'd been stroking his.

"I don't feel like you're really with me at the moment."

"Huh?"

"Nic?"

"Just a little further," he said. And to gloss it over, because if there was anything to discover he wanted it to be his discovery, so he could share it with her: "It's good to be out, the two of us."

She nodded. "Maybe we should have brought a picnic." But something humourless had crept into her tone.

The wind caught them fiercely, face-on, as they rounded a bend; funnelled and accelerated by the kinks in the valley. The trees roared and rocked now and their branches scooped down as Nic and Siobhan walked beneath them. Leaves flew in all directions and every so often there was a groaning or a creak and he thought a bough might split, sending a ton of wood lurching onto them, skewering them to the bitumen. For a short while it became like walking against a massive hand that was being held against them, so they were breathless and it would've been difficult to talk even if there was anything to say.

Only when he'd started to accept that they must've missed the site and walked a good deal past it, did they turn a bend in the road and he saw what he was looking for.

"Is this where the van came off?" Siobhan asked.

"Yep."

"And this is what we've walked out to see?"

"Yeah."

"Why?"

"I want to look for something."

Siobhan raised her eyebrows, crossed her arms, stood at the side of the road and made a show of examining the twigs and leaf litter at her feet. She stabbed the ground every now and then with the toe of her boot, kicked at pieces of bark, ambled across to the piles of sawdust. Nic clambered down the slight embankment and swore at the sight of so much churned-up mud and flattened grass. It was wetter than he'd hoped but he began pacing the area, tracing a pattern, pushing clumps of grass back with his hands, peering among the fronds.

"What is it, Nic? What *are* you doing? Let's go back." She'd moved closer to where he was searching, began grinding one heel into the loose gravel.

"In a minute. I want to check something out – see if there's anything to find." Crouching down, he parted a few long stems, and added: "There was a spillage. You should have seen how much trouble they took to sweep up a few lollies – lollies of all things – but I figured a few might have got dragged out as the first cartons were shifted to the other van. It was weird, how much care they took."

He paused and looked up at where she was standing. "One of the guys – Watto – was wearing a dust mask. And latex gloves. Thought I didn't notice. The others probably had been too. That's why they didn't want me down here right away. Dust masks and surgical gloves, Siobhan." As he released the stems, he saw a dab of dark pink. "Here we are. This is the stuff." Delight and then foreboding.

"Lollies? So what?"

Nic said nothing. Should he pick them up or leave them? Now he'd arrived at this point, he wasn't sure what to do next. Using his bank card, he scooped up three Love Hearts which were cradled among the grass, depositing them carefully in the palm of his hand. Two were soggy and would have crumbled into powder if he'd picked at them with his fingers; the third was damp round the edges but still dry in the middle. "Most people would've swept them into the grass without a second thought. Why go to so much trouble for a few Love Hearts?"

"Let me see," she said, joining him.

He held his hand out for her to see, cupped it against the wind with his other hand. If they really were what he thought they were, then one way or another he was in deep shit. They both were. They'd quickly have to put as much distance between themselves and Gimbly as they could. His gut tightened.

Siobhan stood looking at him staring at the dabs of pink in his hand and didn't say, "If they're not lollies, what do you think they are?" Instead, after a few moments, she shook her head and began walking away. Back towards Gimbly.

He ran his tongue across the top of the dry one. Didn't know what it would tell him, but that's what cops did in the movies. There was certainly no sweetness in it; no sugar. He tried again, but couldn't get any taste at all. So he picked at an edge of a soggy one and dissolved it at the front of his mouth in a little pool of saliva. Nothing, except a slight bitterness that he spat onto the ground.

"These aren't lollies, Siobhan," he shouted after her. "This is ecstasy. Eccies. I reckon they have to be. Shit! I was right. What else could they be? Christ! Wait up, Siobhan. That's a shit-load of drugs. How much would three boxes fetch on the street?"

She stopped and turned. She said nothing for a moment. Opened her mouth to speak, then closed it. The wind blew through the trees and there was a whispering among the skitterings of leaves. Then she said: "Throw them away, Nic. Here, give them to me; I'll throw them away."

"They are eccies, aren't they? What do you reckon? Eccies or something similar."

She took a deep breath. Nodded. "Yes. They are," she said. "But they could be lollies too... if you wanted them to be."

Beyond the flush of initial excitement, the knot in his gut tightened again, another notch. She was telling him much more than he'd asked for. And the world span.

"What?"

"If you want them to be. You heard me. There's no reason they can't still be lollies. You can throw them away if you want to, can't you?"

He felt himself being sucked forward to the brink of something. A vertiginous moment, with little chance of stepping back.

"Oh fuck." Mesmerised by what she'd said, he stood staring at her. "You know. You already know about it, don't you? Jesus." What an innocent he'd been. Always. Even at his most sceptical. "You're part of this... whatever it is, aren't you? Have been all the time. Oh fuck."

Stepping away from the road, he lowered himself onto the broad stump of an old tree. Couldn't walk and think at the same time. Not without buckling at the knees. Siobhan came over and sat next to him. She took his free hand in both of hers.

"Listen," she began. "I'm glad it's in the open now. So bloody glad. There's so much I've wanted to tell you for so long. I was looking to find a way of sounding you out without committing you, and of preparing you. About all of it, and why I wanted you here and why I want you to stay – how much I want you to stay."

Her words were birds flapping. Too close. He thought he might fall. "No. Don't say a word."

"Please. I have to. I can now. Everything."

"No. Not yet. No more words. Just give me a minute without words."

"I love you," she said. "I wish I didn't, but I do. That's the reason you're here."

The tablets were still cupped in his hand. He closed his fist loosely around them and buried it deep in his jacket pocket. He didn't want to drop them; couldn't afford to lose them.

He sat slumped for a minute and nothing was said. She gave him his silence, but it didn't help because he couldn't free himself from the tangle of impressions, information, emotions, to think one new, clear thought of his own. He was stuck on the brink, and teetering.

Then, once more, she said, "I love you, Nic. Always have done. You know that, don't you? It'd be easier if I didn't, but I do."

He turned to look at her and then focused on how her hands were holding his, but she'd never been further away. "I don't know anything anymore."

The wind shouted through the trees, pushing at his back now, and threw bark and leaves across the road. A twig landed on his shoulder, snagged against his jacket, and she let go of his hands to pick it off; then absent-mindedly snapped it in two and tossed it into the scrub. This simple action changed the moment. His dizziness faded, the abyss receded. She was there next to him again.

"Tell me," he said. The words hardly sounded like his words – not his voice – but he held onto the sound of them. "Explain." He took a breath.

She stood up, appeared set to begin walking, then sat down again.

"There's not much to understand. It's quite simple really. The difficult part is changing someone's mindset, so they can at least come at this without a blinding prejudice."

He waited. Couldn't believe it. Tried to measure his words evenly so he didn't lose his balance again. "Try me. You owe me that much. That much at least."

She nodded. "Yes. You should know. There's no choice now anyhow." She paused, then began: "The lab is legitimate. The staff have been carefully picked. It disposes of unwanted and out-of-date pharmaceutical products and it's also a licensed research unit – extraction procedures mainly. That's all legitimate. But it manufactures a range of pharmaceuticals too – "

"Pharmaceuticals? Ecstasy, ice?"

"Yes, I'm getting to that. It manufactures these to a very controlled, safe quality. Unlike anything else that appears on the streets."

"And heroin?"

"Heroin too. But people get so puritanical when heroin is mentioned."

He stared at her. "I can't imagine why."

Once more, she took his unclenched hand in both of hers and began stroking it, the way she might one day comfort a child.

"It's understandable, I agree," she began, "but we're not the bad guys here. Really. Absolutely. I guarantee that." Her voice took on its softest and most seductive lilt. "And if you'll hear me out then you might understand why."

He said nothing, which was all she needed.

"Look, Nic, not many people realise how tragic the drug scene has become. The media have a bit of a splash every now and then if they're hard-up for other news, but when the ripples die down most people prefer to forget about it again. It's easier to pretend that lives aren't being wrecked, that people aren't dying, even though it's nothing less than an epidemic. The problem is that we get used to seeing deaths as statistics and we stop asking why so many people die from overdoses and whether anything can be done about it." She stopped and looked at him.

He looked back and, for those few moments, wished he could be content with that. To hold on to her. But her eyes had become deep pools – bottomless pools – across which he doubted he could swim. Not now. Probably never.

"Tell me then," he said at last.

"I will. I want you to know. I want you to know everything so you can see the sense of Gimbly. Everything or nothing – there's no in-between now. The same as for everyone else." She gave his hand a sympathetic squeeze. "The fault lies with prohibition," she said, "and years of zero-tolerance. And that we've had one Government after another who'd rather pretend it's a Law and Order issue and throw money at policing it than treat it as a Social Health issue. They're short-sighted bastards, they really are."

He slipped his hand from hers and combed his fingers through his hair. Had the beginnings of a headache. "Prohibition? Zero-tolerance? What's that got to do with Gimbly? With putting the things out on the street?"

She took his hand back again. "I haven't finished. Just hear me out, Nic. To the end. Okay?"

"Okay."

"Prohibition achieves a number of things, but reducing drug use isn't one of them. What it does is create a black-market and foster organised crime. Sometimes, it makes a drug like heroin ridiculously cheap and dangerously pure; too easy to get addicted to, too easy to overdose on. You know, when Prohibition was repealed in the States, many of the mobsters went out of business and the amount of general crime declined too. There was no profit in it anymore; no need. Stupid laws make criminals out of ordinary people. That's the way it is."

He couldn't see the connection between what she was telling him and Gimbly. "If you can't beat 'em, join 'em? Is that what you're saying?"

She closed her eyes, shook her head. "No, no, that's not it. Not at all. Listen, Nic, the reason so many people o.d. on smack is because they don't know how pure each deal is. The strength of a hit can change dangerously from one month to the next, from one dealer to another, depending on how its cut – what they blend it with. Everyone plays Russian Roulette each time they shoot up because, unlike more enlightened countries, the Government is afraid to fund safe injecting rooms, where users can at least test the purity of what they're injecting – and get some health advice at the same time. The politicians are frightened voters would think they were condoning drug use. Not that the bastards have any problems building casinos and then funding programs to help gambling addicts. Is that hypocrisy or what?"

She brought his hand to her lips and kissed it. "But that's only part of the story. As for what's being sold as ecstasy… do you know what ketamine is?"

He shook his head.

"Vets use it to anaesthetise horses, among other things. Yet that's what's being passed on the street: a shitty cocktail of drugs that'll include ketamine, paracetamol and speed, as well as weed killer and drain cleaner, for God's sake. Any unscrupulous bastard with a pill press can mix a heap of shit together, stamp a frigging pink elephant on one side and sell them as eccies. They're making a killing, literally, and the Government won't do a damn thing about it. Party-goers get a buzz alright, but not the buzz they're after.

"Here in Gimbly though, and elsewhere, we're doing something about that. There's more than one way to crack a nut. This is the thing, Nic." And, however prosaic the words, her voice slipped into that soft, sing-song intonation she so often reverted to when she was passionate about something or wanted him to make love to her. "We're putting a safety-net in place to reduce the risks, the number of deaths. We're making available safe, quality-controlled products, so that addicts and recreational users don't have to risk their lives every time they pop a pill or shoot up. Word gets around and it never takes long for the street to know what's good, what's safe, what's not. We're creating a movement, Nic – a Social Movement – to change things for the better.

"We could never take on the international suppliers and it'd be suicide to go head-to-head with some of the gangs by undercutting their prices too much, but it's in no one's interest if the customers are dying, and they all know that. They're not stupid. And, you know, we've already created a reliable chain of supply that's actually saving lives. It's quite simple really."

Her enthusiasm made her gleeful. She paused, kicked at the stump of the tree with the heel of her boot and looked him in the eye. "Gimbly isn't a town run by drug barons. Everything here is done for the best of reasons: to save lives and make the world a better place."

He squeezed the bridge of his nose between two fingers. "A matter of arriving at the right place by the wrong path," he observed, as much to himself as her.

"Yes. If you want. But the only path that will lead anywhere."

"And the money everyone's making from this 'Social Movement' is being donated to the Lost Dogs' Home or the People's Dispensary for Sick Animals? How about Christian Aid Abroad? You're not driving around in a Porsche and Archie's not sitting on a stock of Lotus Elises and Ford Mustangs? There's no Cayman Island bank accounts, no money laundering?"

"Everyone who's involved receives a salary to match the risks they take. You too, if you stick around. It's a high-risk venture, although we've obviously got insurance of sorts. And, yes, of course, we have to channel our finances in a way that doesn't alert the Tax Office or the police, but what each person does with their salary is up to them, as it would be anywhere else. I do know that Archie and Mary have donated large sums to charity, if that's what you're asking."

"And why me, Siobhan? What am I doing here?"

She slipped an arm through his and drew closer. "I've already told you that: I love you. I fell hopelessly in love with you when we first met, and nothing's changed. We had a mechanic, but he was unreliable –"

"Didn't he like what was going on?"

"No, quite the opposite. He was fond of the merchandise himself and had too much of a mouth on him. He was a good mechanic, but he'd have blown everything."

"What became of him? Met with a little accident, did he?"

Siobhan looked puzzled, then startled and then she laughed. "God, you've got an over-active imagination, Nic. Concrete boots and a swim in a deep lake, is that what you think? You've watched too many films. The real world's less dramatic."

"So what happened?"

"We paid him off; put him through a detox program. Hopefully, he's straight now."

"And?"

"And we put the fear of eternal damnation into him. He'll never blow the whistle on us. He knows how easy it'd be to put him in prison for a solid slice of his life, and that we have enough contacts inside to make life miserable. We have to protect ourselves."

He shuddered at these words. Her matter-of-factness. "What if he turned state's evidence, or whatever they call it?"

"Was offered immunity?"

"Yep."

"Gimbly didn't just spontaneously happen, you know. It's

backed by the most influential sponsors – you'd be surprised – and it's in their interests to ensure we get the support and protection we need. The right people in politics, in the police force, the media. It wouldn't matter a jot whether he was given a new identity or not."

"And that's why I was set up and framed in the first place, is it? So I'd lose my job and have to take this one? Is the suspended sentence the threat hanging over my head?"

She winced, moved apart to see him better, shook her head. "No. No way, Nic. We didn't fix you up. Really."

"The gun, the boxes of stolen goods, the van?"

"Nothing to do with me wanting you here. Again, quite the opposite. That was exactly the way I told you. This isn't a place for people with too much baggage. It made it harder to get you here, not easier."

"So it was just lucky that I lost my job when a new mechanic was needed?"

"Don't look for too much logic in the way things work out, Nic. Life's more random than that. A couple of crazy things happened at the same time, that's all, but it took all my persuasive skills to get you here. Most people see you as too big a risk."

"So why…?"

"They love me." She laughed, held her hands out in an act of self-display. "Who can resist my charms, eh? Besides, I was determined not to lose you again and so I gave them an ultimatum."

"You did? What?"

"I told them I'd quit."

"You said you'd quit if they didn't give me a job?"

She nodded and grinned – the return of that impish smile. "Not that I would have, but they weren't to know that. I wanted them to give you a try-out, at least."

"Why would anyone frame me, if not for this? Why plant a gun in my car?"

"Who knows? Perhaps he left it there while he went to get the pizza; thought the girl in the pizzeria might feel a bit intimidated if he walked in with a gun stuck down his pants. Perhaps the police planted it. Maybe they thought they could use it to lever a few names from you."

"But I didn't know any."

She rolled her eyes. "They wouldn't have known that, would they? Who knows what happened? But, all the same, you were our gain. Look, I've never reckoned there's much point in harping on about what's passed. The trick is to make the most of what you've got in the Here-and-Now. And sometimes we have to catch what life hurls at us and turn it to our good.

"The writing's on the wall for Archie and Gimbly needs a good all-rounder like you to take over the cars and mechanical stuff. So, voilà! And because I loved you, I saw a chance to be happy; for us both to be happy. You can't imagine the relief it is to have told you everything at last. No more secrets. Make or break, I guess."

She shivered, looked down; appeared less certain of herself. "By persuading them to let me bring you here for this trial period, I've put myself on the line, but I don't mind that at all. That's my decision. I want to be with you, Nic, but openly and honestly, without deceit. I want you to know what I do, what I'm passionate about."

He stood. Had heard more than he could hold on to and needed to move again now. He'd grown cold sitting there, listening to all of this, and pulled his jacket tighter. "A Social Movement?"

"Yes."

"But illegal, Siobhan. Absolutely illegal."

She giggled. "Yes, but name a movement for major social reform that hasn't been outlawed in one country or another at some point in its history. I guess that's a definition of social reform: breaking bad laws to change them for the greater good.

A few toes get trodden on. They need to be. Sometimes it takes a civil war; sometimes, like the suffragettes trying to get a better deal for women, it requires chaining yourself to a fence or throwing stones through windows – civil disobedience. They were imprisoned, went on hunger strikes, were violently abused because they knew the laws were bad and needed to be changed. There's nothing new in any of this."

"Have you got an answer for everything?"

"I hope so, Nic. This is something I believe in. A crusade worth fighting for. That's why I want you with me – it's too lonely otherwise. You don't know how much I want to be with you, nor how unhappy I've been when I've had to stay away."

He walked round in circles and she remained sitting on the stump of the tree watching him. He massaged his shoulders and his neck, looked up at the sky, buried his face in his hands, looked back at her.

"You don't even have to be any more involved than you already are. Nothing you're uncomfortable with. But you do need to know what we're about so you exercise the right sort of caution. And they will need a response from you straightaway. It may be a lot of information to take in, but your gut response is probably the best one – the most reliable one. It's not easy, but you're going to have to decide whether you're with us or not."

The words flapped around in all directions. "Or not? What does that mean?"

"Well, it doesn't necessarily mean you're against us, I suppose."

"But what would it mean?"

"We'd work something out – an agreement. A severance deal."

He waited.

"But... I'd be devastated, Nic. I'd never be able to see you again. I couldn't." She was biting at her lip again, and shrugged. "You'd get a decent reference of course – the best – and a bonus payment, which you could accept, decline or donate to the Lost Dogs' Home, and we'd have to find a new mechanic, but that'd be the end of it. You have my word. There'd have to be some sort of bond to guarantee your silence, but that's the same for everyone; it's our collective insurance policy."

The wind was building up again, shaking the trees, sending leaf litter scurrying around their feet, threatening rain.

"And if I stay," he said, "what then?"

"We'll celebrate."

"And?"

"We'll keep on celebrating. You'll probably take over the running of the garage in a few weeks and you'll get paid a wage that reflects your responsibilities. Perhaps we can both start to relax too, enjoy being with one another, get a larger room, make things a bit more homely. It can only get better. What do you reckon? How does that sound?"

"I reckon you could sell sand to the Sahara, coals to Newcastle."

Siobhan stood, brushed the seat of her jacket, came over to him. She put her hands on his shoulders and drew him towards her so that his forehead was touching hers. "Say yes," she said, and kissed him. A brief, moist kiss that tasted of the morning's fresh, cool air.

He pulled back a little. "It's a dangerous game."

"No, it's not a game, Nic. It's life, it's living. It's what life's about: making a difference. Rather than bludging through each day doing nothing for each breath except watching the clock. Being proactive rather than reactive. Didn't you once tell me that was what your father was really about?"

"Did I?"

Look forwards, move forwards, never back.

He drew her towards him this time, held her head in his hands and smothered her mouth with his own. He moved his hands inside her jacket and inside her jumper, pushed them down into the back pockets of her trousers. He wanted to drink her in deep, to be drunk with her, find an answer in her. There was no one to fall back upon except her.

Pressing her head against his chest, he looked at the forest stretching down the valley, with the river to the right of him. Five or six light blue butterflies danced at the edge of the trees, skimming fronds of bracken – it was the first time he'd noticed them here – and, across the distance, a few ravens flew south. He drank in the scent of her and then leaned back to look her in the eyes.

"Say 'yes'," she urged.

Her eyes were deep and inviting, and he could swim in them forever.

He blinked. "Yes," he said. "Yes. As long as you're here, I'm in."

He'd stay for Siobhan – not for the place. He wouldn't stake his life on a place, nor an ideal, but he would for Siobhan.

"You mean that? Absolutely? No doubts?"

"Yes. Absolutely yes."

She let go of him and stood back, and he smiled, nodded. Nodded again. She stood there and watched him; seemed to be measuring his commitment or the size of the moment.

"God, I love you," she said. "I love you, I love you, I love you."

11

It became a day of celebration. She was right and his old man had been right: what was the point in living if you didn't do something useful with that life or if you spent your time always looking back, holding onto the way things were? It didn't matter whether you spent your life fighting giants, dragons and windmills, or building cathedrals and universities, as long as you didn't sit on your arse doing nothing. He'd stick by her and look out for her as long as she believed in what she was doing and, at the same time, he'd work towards one day running a garage of his own, independent of Gimbly. He'd learn from Archie everything he needed to know about that side of things. And then, when it was time, they'd both quit and move back to the city. One way or another he'd leave, taking her with him.

"Tell me something," he said to her, after they'd made a cele-bratory kind of love that afternoon, and dozed as spring rain washed the streets, flooded the spouting, with the light thin against the drawn curtains, their limbs still entwined.

"What?"

"I don't understand how Gimbly gets its own police station. Or how the Troll – "

"Don't call him that. You mustn't. Please. He's a little protec-tive of me and gets a tad jealous at times, that's all, but he's okay. He'll be okay with you now, but he's a person, not a thing – not a monster."

"Hmm. Well, the station isn't for real is it? He's not a real cop; it's not a real police station?"

Drawing a bed sheet across her shoulders, up to her chin, she said: "There's something you mustn't forget – not ever – and that's how powerful and influential some of Gimbly's sponsors are. And Gimbly's just one link in the chain. Most anything can be arranged if it's needed."

"Even a police station?"

She nodded.

"And the security company is part of the same deal?"

"Partly."

"Partly?" In order to see her better and know, on this bizarre day, that he existed and she existed and that she really was next to him in the same bed, he turned on his side and half sat up, propping his head against one hand, his elbow buried in the pillow. Why hadn't he met her years ago, when his parents and sister were still alive, and without the complications of Gimbly? She was the one he'd have liked to take home and introduce to everyone. They'd have been proud of him.

"Does that mean it's just another way to launder money? Along with Archie's cars?"

"I didn't say that. Don't put words in my mouth. You have to be careful what you say and do from now on. We all do."

"What else is there? Property in the city? The odd apartment block or two?" There were things he needed to understand, but was afraid to know. Should he ask or remain innocent? Perhaps love should remain blind. A finger in each eye.

She turned and put two fingers to his lips and pursed them together. "Hush," she said.

He opened his mouth and nipped her fingers with his teeth, then kissed them. "One last question."

"What?"

"That last time at my flat – "

"When you kicked me out?"

He grinned and nodded. "You said Siobhan McConnell wasn't the name on your birth certificate; not your proper name. That only the tax man knew what it was, or something like that…"

She narrowed her eyes. "Siobhan is my real name. But it's my middle name, not my first name; I haven't used that *in* years, except on passports and that sort of thing."

"Yes, that's what you said. And that you used McConnell because it was your step-dad's name." He paused, leaned closer to her. "Well, now's the time to spill the beans, lover-girl; all of them. A few more beans won't hurt, not after everything you've told me today. Is it something hideous like Hildegard Higgingbottom or Rumpelstiltskin or... or what? I'll still love you, you know, whatever it is. It's only a name."

Outside his door, the cat began mewing. A soft miaow at first, but then insistent.

"Let her in," Siobhan said.

"No way." He reached for a shoe and threw it at the door. "Tell me, Siobhan. I want to know everything about you."

She hesitated. "It's..."

And he thought she was going to tell him, until she smiled, screwed up her nose in delight at the new mischief she could conjure.

"I'll give you three guesses, like in the old stories. If you get it in three then I'll be your slave for life. All yours." She put her hands together and bowed her head; became a pantomime genie for Aladdin.

"And if I don't guess it correctly?"

"Then you can be my slave instead."

He nodded, stroked his chin, made a show of weighing up the offer. "Sounds good either way." He held her hands and eased her arms back so they were on the pillow behind her head, put his face up to hers, nose touching nose. "Out of the millions of names in the world, though, you'll give me a couple of clues?"

Her eyes narrowed again. "Not a chance. I play to win. Do I look like an easy bargain?"

"So it's not Smith or Jones?"

"Are they your first two guesses?"

"No."

"Then I can't tell you."

He'd wait. He didn't mind playing her game. It was who she was, this delight in mystery, mischief, cat-and-mouse. Before long he'd see a letter with her name on it, or he'd find her passport or her driving licence, and then he'd claim her as his prize.

"One thing I will tell you," she said. "Just to be fair."

"What's that?"

"You won't find it on any of my passports or driving licences?"

"Passports? Licences? How many have you got?"

"A few."

"But none in your real name?"

"Not in the name I was born with. Not that you'd lay your hands on."

"Now, that's not fair."

She shook her head and smiled. "I always play to win."

He'd wait. He could be stubborn too. Pushing her arms back a little further, he leant and kissed her throat. "You're a hard woman."

She pulled one leg up so that her knee gently nudged his balls. "I'm putty in your hands," she said.

12

Mary cooked up a feast that evening. There were cheers when Siobhan and Nic walked through for dinner, a candle illuminating their table, a rose in a vase and silver service; the colours of the place seemed sharper, brighter, and the music a notch louder, clearer. There were congratulations and slaps on the back, as though it was his birthday, and Mary gave him a bony peck on the cheek. "I'm so glad you've joined our little enterprise," she said. "You'll do fine. Just fine. We're like a family here."

Archie hobbled over and shook his hand. "Good on yer," he said, loud and cheery. "I'm glad you're staying." Then quieter, so no-one else could hear: "Don't let your girl down now." He hugged Siobhan, kissed her, whispered something in *her* ear.

Even the Troll, who stepped from the kitchen with a schooner of orange juice dwarfed in his mitts, gave a cursory nod of acknowledgement.

And Siobhan – the star from which all this good will radiated

– sat opposite him and beamed. "I'm so happy," she said.

More than a birthday, Nic felt he was at a wedding.

13

Nothing could ever be the same after that, for better or worse. The conversations no longer changed tack or were hushed when he walked into the bar and most everyone looked him square in the eyes; even the replacement tail-light for his E-Type appeared the following day. And although Archie didn't give him the keys to his desk drawers or filing cabinets, which Nic was no longer sure he wanted, the old fella talked more freely about the cars they were ordering.

"At some point, we might register one of those Mustangs in your name," he said. "If you like. Let you have a bit of a play."

Nic tried not to hesitate. "Fine by me. Whatever works."

"Good lad."

For three weeks, the mechanic went off to work each week-day morning and Siobhan did whatever she did. Time danced to a different, faster beat, and she was there at the end of each day – as if her presence alone affirmed that he'd made the right decision. She 'discovered' a couple of boxes of her belongings in a store cupboard and brought them to his room; she talked about renovating one of the old houses so they could move in together. "We could play house," she said.

Of course, there were days when she left Gimbly and had to stay away a couple of nights, but was now reluctant to be gone longer. She spent much of her working day in an office at the laboratory, around which she offered to give him a guided tour although he declined, but for the most part it was as if they were honeymooning: first love all over again.

Maybe, if they'd played this game long enough for it to have become a habit, then he might've lost every niggling doubt; the two of them could've lived happily ever after. The fairytale marriage of a princess and a grease monkey being the most comfortable of spells to fall into. They'd have stayed in Gimbly for as long as she believed in it and for as long as no unhappy ending appeared on the horizon. He might've convinced himself that all he was doing was looking out for the girl he loved, while working towards establishing his business – their future – and might've one day achieved that. Many things might have happened, and everything might have been rosy between Siobhan and the mechanic for ever and a day. Happy ever after.

However, that's not the way this story goes.

14

The season of wild, three-day gales and bouts of heavy rain gave way to dry, warm days, clear skies, but sharper, chill nights. Sometimes, the suggestion of a late frost blanketed the paddocks at night, but these soon thawed once the morning sun found its way into the valley. On these nights, Siobhan and the mechanic snuggled closer, entwined tighter in their nest of a bed, as they slept and dreamed sweet, juicy dreams.

Then, three weeks into their new life together, Siobhan had to go overseas, for a fortnight at least. She couldn't put it off any longer.

"Where to? What do you have to do?" he asked.

As before, she put a finger to his lips and said: "Don't ask. There are details that you don't need to know. It's the same for everyone. It protects you, it protects me – protects the whole shebang."

"Cloak and dagger stuff?" The lightness of the comment masked an abruptly new and sharp awareness of the dangers she might expose herself to. "Gangland bosses, henchman...' He stopped. It sounded both corny and realistically sinister at the same time, but so far removed from the sleepy, rural isolation of Gimbly. At the thought of that other world, he stopped, checked himself, swallowed. How was it she managed to straddle the two worlds so nonchalantly?

She rolled her eyes. "Hardly. Not at my end of things. Although sometimes people can get a little toey."

"Okay," he said, but sensed she was understating the risks for his benefit or because they'd become a way of life for her... as leaping off skyscrapers and cliffs might for a base jumper.

"When I return, though," she said, "I think we should plan a holiday. How about it? It's fine now, but in summer this place gets hot as hell. Too hot; fries the brain. I prefer to be somewhere I can kick back and veg out, like a tropical beach. Perhaps we could spend a few weeks being lazy, making love under palm trees, snorkelling through clear waters, drinking cocktails in coconuts – that sort of thing. We've deserved it, haven't we?"

He saw clear turquoise waters, blue skies, golden beaches; paradise in the Pacific. "Spend some of our ill-gotten gains at a Travel Agency?"

"Just a little."

"Maybe one day we could simply buy an island. Cut out the middle man."

"Are you laughing at me?"

"Or myself. Maybe we could go to Ireland and I could meet your parents."

"Ireland? At this time of year? You'd either freeze your bol-locks off or end up with moss growing down one side of you."

"I thought you might like to see your folks."

"Another time, eh?"

Even then, things might have continued well. Even up to the point at which the alarm clock rang at five-thirty on the Sunday morning of her departure, when she slid out of bed, towards the bathroom; insisting once again that she didn't want him to get up early too, that she was a big girl and could see herself off to the airport – had done it numerous times before and would, no doubt, do it numerous times in the future.

"Make the most of your Sunday morning lie-in," she crooned. "Turn over, go back to sleep, dream wet dreams about me instead."

Except he couldn't sleep. Not now, not with her about to leave. He turned over and burrowed his head under the duvet. He followed Siobhan's movements as she flushed the toilet, showered, got dressed, collected her bags and crept out of the room.

"*Bon voyage*," he called after her. "Travel safely."

But she didn't hear. The latch on the door clicked behind her and she was gone.

He was awake and needed a piss, and the cold tiles of the bathroom floor and the lingering whisper of Siobhan's scent – something expensive and French – woke him further. He'd surprise her and wave her off; she'd appreciate that.

Nic dragged on jeans and a jumper, and pulled the bedroom door quietly shut behind him so as not to disturb anyone else's sleep. She'd be sitting in the kitchen, steeling herself against the long drive to the airport with a strong coffee and, if she was being good, a piece or two of toast.

The hotel was quieter than death. It was as if the building had taken a deep breath at the beginning of the night and hadn't yet exhaled. It was the quiet of stillness, the quiet of waiting – a long, cold pause between one day's existence and another: a breath held.

At the bottom of the staircase, he moved along the corridor, barefooted and shivering. He passed through one door into that part of the building that housed the kitchen and storerooms. The kitchen door was ajar and light spilt out, along with the soft murmur of voices. Three or four subdued voices.

"I best go," he heard her say. "I don't want to have to rush."

"Watch your speed, remember. Don't take risks." It was the Troll.

"Good luck," said Mary.

Nic felt he'd been remiss. He should be there with her – it was his place to be; not theirs. He took two steps towards the door, and stopped. What he saw was an exclusive domestic scene that he didn't belong to: Archie in his dressing gown, sitting at the kitchen table, being kissed on the forehead; Siobhan turning and embracing Mary – as a daughter might her mother.

"You're their daughter," he muttered to himself. "Siobhan King." He had two thirds of her name. And then he didn't. Of course that wasn't it – it didn't fit what she'd told him.

The back of the Troll moved into view and blocked the scene. He might not have been able to see everything, but silence can communicate its own message. He saw her hands reach up to the Troll's shoulders and he saw the Troll stoop to accommodate her. He bowed his head as if about to kiss her, but instead took a deep breath, as if drinking her in, head to toe, inhaling the essence of her. She became the most prized of his roses, with the richest, intoxicating perfume, and for his goodbye the Troll drank the deepest draught from her. His shoulders lifted and broadened with the depth of it.

Was this the act of a brother towards his sister? Or of the closest of friends? Or a lover?

It was beyond anything he'd expected.

At this point he froze. Couldn't move forward, couldn't move back. Was locked to that spot in time. Until the scrape of a kitchen chair made him stumble backwards a step, breaking the spell.

Forcing himself to retreat in silence to his room, he sat on his bed and was numb. Within seconds, he heard the silver Porsche Carrera accelerate into the distance and knew that the tilt of the world had changed again.

15

This alone wouldn't have unbalanced him for long. After all, a kiss is just a kiss and a freaky sniff is just a sniff that belongs to a freak, and he and Siobhan had shared much stronger, more intimate pledges. She'd danced with him inside her, he'd galloped and soared with her riding of him; they'd melted into one another time and time again. Of course, it could've been that he'd witnessed nothing more than a long and tender hug, given the awkward angle from which he'd seen this, and he knew how jealousy provided a distorted lens, how it changed a person's view of the world, made credible things that might otherwise not exist.

The nature of the relationship, though – well, that was another matter. What if they actually were one big, happy family? That whole thing about her parents being in Ireland. It'd be the continuation of the lie that hurt; the omission of significant truths.

He had to talk with her. Shouldn't assume anything until they'd spoken.

Instead, he gave himself up to reading the bulk of the previous day's newspaper; almost every article in every supplement – all seven, hour after hour, dispensing with the morning and cutting into the afternoon – anything to pass the time until she phoned. A forest of paper. Siobhan had taken her magic with her and the days ahead would be empty, lonely, cold and long. He read so he could ignore the flock of unwanted thoughts racing through his mind. Like birds, they might disappear into the distance until they were nothing but specks for short minutes. But then they wheeled around, their wings flashing a change of direction, and loomed in on his awareness again.

Who was she to the Troll?

What was the Troll to her?

Browsing the papers was a way to spend a weekend morning and, in all likelihood, he'd have discovered the article anyway –

Troll embrace or not, happy-snappy family or not. It was a feature article about policing drug smuggling generally, but there was a passage that commented on the production of ecstasy:

'Although the success of Operation Frontline has significantly reduced the quantities of ecstasy being smuggled into the country, home-produced imitations of the boutique drug have risen, often with lethal results. Such deaths often occur, special investigators acknowledge, because backyard drug laboratories are unable to produce MDMA, the key ingredient in ecstasy. Instead, these makeshift factories resort to using a number of alternative ingredients from weed killer to horse sedatives, from Panadol to motion sickness tablets. Consequently, young people who are seduced by the belief that ecstasy is a safe 'party pill' are paying the highest price for a cocktail drug that is often little more than a dangerous combination of garden centre and supermarket products.

"These people have no idea what chemicals they're putting into their body. They might as well be swallowing razor blades or ground glass," Marissa Tate, convenor of the National Forensic Science Forum, said. "Any criminal with a pill press can cook up some of the concoctions we've seen recently." Of equal concern, however, is the recent saturation of the 'party drug' market with herbal ecstasy. Herbal ecstasy is manufactured from ma huang (a source of ephedrine and pseudoephedrine), and last month was responsible for the deaths of teenagers Angelina Browiescz (18) and Michael Evans (16)...'

The article was confirmation, mostly, of everything Siobhan had told him. But there was no mention of untainted products. Surely it would've picked up on that fact, if what was being produced in Gimbly had made any impact at all? There was nothing to suggest a levelling of prices or a reduction in crime; just a simple graph to illustrate an increase in deaths over the last five years.

He went to the wardrobe, took out his jacket, fished around in the pockets and pulled out the one Love Heart and two tablets worth of crumbs he'd collected from the grass those few weeks ago. Flicking away the bits of cotton lint, he placed the tiny stash on a sheet of paper and gazed out the window at a clear blue sky, wondering what should happen next. He needed to do something, but didn't know what. He needed to know more, but didn't know how.

After a few minutes, he took out another sheet of paper, hesitated, then wrote his name and the address of the garage at the top. He addressed the letter to David McKenzie, the guy who'd helped represent him during the trial, and penned his first draft.

Dear David,

I'm writing to ask that you have the enclosed tablet analysed on my behalf. Whether you're able to do this directly by sending it to a commercial chemical analyst or whether you need to do this through a third-party, such as a Private Investigator, I'll leave you to decide. It's just that I'm not in a position to do this for myself and would like to remain anonymous. Is this possible?

Although this probably seems a weird request, I remember you telling me once that your firm is sometimes asked to take on various types of go-between role.

If this isn't possible, then please return the package to me at the above address. If it is possible, then please forward the analysis report and your account to the same. I'd appreciate it, though, if you didn't use an official envelope for your reply.

Assuming the mail from Gimbly would be sorted and bundled before being taken to the Post Office, and to avoid arousing suspicion, he addressed the envelope to David McKenzie, Spare Parts Division, Hepsburg and Conway, and then the firm's address. He felt relieved to have done something.

If the report showed Gimbly's Love Hearts to be a cheap

and dangerous cocktail, or herbal ecstasy, he'd know the place wasn't everything Siobhan believed it was and he'd convince her to live a different life with him somewhere else. He'd do everything to get her out. But if the report proved the Love Heart was genuine ecstasy – the real McCoy, MDMA – then this would confirm everything. Maybe that's what he'd needed all along – confirmation.

16

The next morning, he got called out to one of Gimbly's farms to work on a large generator and, on his return, a damaged ute was waiting in the service bay. It was good to get out of the town for a short while, even if the farm was all part of the same show, and it was good to be busy.

When he crossed the street to the hotel at lunchtime, Mary handed him a plate of sandwiches and said, "She should have landed by now."

"Will she phone?" he asked.

"No. The fewer calls the better."

"No news is good news, eh?"

"Exactly."

In just a few words, they'd reduced the extraordinary to something almost banal.

She poured him a beer; was keen to spoil him, it appeared, because she knew he'd be missing the golden girl.

He worked late that day. Threw himself into finishing the ute. Spent an hour rearranging a corner of the workshop. When he walked over to the hotel thirty minutes before dinner, Mary was heading down the hallway.

"Hmm, you've been baking again. I love that smell," he said.

However, she scurried towards the store rooms. Pretended she didn't hear.

The cat was sitting outside his room when he got to the top of the stairs.

"Shoo," he said, but it didn't move and he nudged it to one side with his foot. "Shoo!"

Someone had been in his room. It wasn't immediately obvious, but he could tell. Perhaps they'd had maintenance to do or perhaps it was Siobhan – maybe her trip had been cancelled. Except there was no luggage strewn about, none of the usual domestic detritus that trailed her.

The bathroom door had been shut properly, but the door to the bar fridge hadn't; his pile of loose change was arranged too tidily next to the bedside lamp and he half-remembered there being some other object next to those coins that morning; and there was a new smell to the room, which didn't belong to him or Siobhan – somebody else's earthy odour. Then, to confirm all this, torn open and placed on the desk for him to see, was an empty package and a letter that began:

Dear David,
I'm writing to ask that you have the enclosed tablet analysed on my behalf. Whether you're able to do this directly by sending it to a commercial chemical...

He froze, felt the world tilt. Again.

"Oh shit," he said and, for the second time in two days, sank onto the edge of the bed. For a couple of minutes he sat staring at nothing, unable to work out what to do next.

On his desk was the photograph of his raven-haired mother, sister and father huddled on a bench on the city ferry, with the river behind them. He'd always seen his sister as laughing in this shot, her hair blowing in the wind, but she could equally have been crying – there was so little between the two expressions at times.

He looked again.

"Get out of there, Nic!" his sister screamed. He nodded. Stood there looking at her.

His eyes were itching and he sneezed once, twice, three times. Whoever had been here had let the bloody cat in too. He turned and paced from one wall to the other, and then back again.

"Fuck. What now?"

"Get out, Nic!" she screamed.

We don't always recognise the things we need to notice in the instant we see them. Sometimes the brain's too busy and skips past, only to play catch-up in the quiet of the night or, if we're lucky, several seconds later. And then we do a double-take.

Several seconds after sitting in front of Polonius' cage, Nic did a double-take. The cage was open; Polonius wasn't in it.

He looked behind the photograph, the cage and the books on his desk; he scrabbled around the carpet on his knees, looking under the bed, behind the chest of drawers, inside the wardrobe, calling, "Polonius. Come here, Polonius." Rattling the box of pet food as he called, and sneezing.

"Bastards!" he spat, and knew he had to check Ophelia.

One glance told him she wasn't in her tank – not swimming behind her rock. The second glance told him that the unfamiliar object floating below the surface of the water, trailing a tail of weed, was Polonius.

"Bastards!" he shouted, and kicked the chair out of his way and across the room.

Nic cradled him out of the water and lay him on his nest of shredded paper at the back of the cage. Death doesn't look like sleep. Death has a deeper stillness to it. Polonius was sodden and dead.

This animal had been one of his last links to his sister. He blew his nose and discovered he was crying. The first time in years.

He was weeping for Polonius, for the crazy predicament he'd got himself into, for Ophelia, but mostly he wept for the loss of his sister, who'd possessed the most vibrant enthusiasm for life of anyone he'd ever known. What he'd never reconciled himself to was the knowledge that in the frantic seconds before the helicopter exploded – the moment it clipped the cliff – she would've realised she was about to die and been terrified. There would have been no peace to her dying, only fear. She'd been too young and vivacious to die.

He should've done more to keep the world the way it was before Gimbly, before the court case, before Siobhan. He should've done more. Too much had gone wrong. Life had shat upon him again. But this time he'd stood centre-stage and allowed it.

He went scrabbling around to find Ophelia. And although he went into the bathroom and looked in the toilet pan, he was convinced the bloody cat smirking at his door had a little golden secret to share. He'd drag the thing into his room by the scruff of its neck, clawing and spitting; he'd grab the can opener to rip into its belly, and plunge his fingers in to wade through its stomach on the bathroom floor... Until he remembered how the fridge door hadn't been properly closed.

Ophelia was a frozen, diced carrot. Tossed in the ice box to die.

He couldn't move. Had forgotten how. But then he couldn't move because there was a noise breaking across his awareness of where he was and what he should be doing. A low-pitched grinding at first, which became a groan, then ballooned into a drawn-out wail. Only slowly did he associate it with himself and realise that he was the groaning and wailing. When he did, it burst into a cry of anger, loss, grief and frustration, until the cry became a shout so loud that the door to his room flew open because of it.

In the doorway, filling it, stood the Troll. The cat had disappeared.

"Shut your racket." He had a grin on his face, a wolfish sneer.

The mechanic recognised the odour he brought with him. "You bastard! You did this." In one quick glance he looked for something to pick up – a weapon – but there was no golf stick, no axe, no whisky bottle. He clenched his fists instead – they'd have to do – and strode towards the Troll, who simply took one step forwards and sent him sprawling backwards, across the coffee table, into the bed-end.

"You did this to yourself. What sort of fucking game do you think you're playing? What do you take us for?"

"You bastard!" He was on his feet again, looking for something to throw. The coffee table for starters. But he'd been left no room to move. He'd smash the Troll's head to a pulp. Needed to. Blood lust and revenge.

"What sort of fucking game are you playing at?" the Troll demanded again.

"Game? Me?" Could barely speak; easier to shout. "You want *me* to explain? To you? Fuck off! Go on, fuck off!"

The Troll drew out his baton and, in one sweeping blow, smashed two of the legs off the up-ended coffee table. They were attached one moment and spinning across the room the next. The message was clear, but the Troll spelt it out all the same, prodding the baton towards Nic. "Start talking. Now."

He tried to focus; tried to think about some point beyond the room, beyond anger and grief, but it was hopeless. Hopelessness, anger and grief were all he had left. His throat was dry, his voice was hoarse. "Information. That's all. The article in Saturday's paper. Whether this place was on the level."

"On the level? What are you fucking on about? On the level with what?" he snorted. "Who do you think you're screwing with? You're out of your tiny mind."

Maybe I am, Nic thought, and sagged a little. Still, he wouldn't be bettered by this bastard.

"What are you fucking on about?" the Troll roared again.

"Had to be sure – myself – what Gimbly's doing. If it's for

real – trying to help – or full of shit!" Practically shouted this last word. He took a longer breath, found his focus again. "You bastard, they were my sister's."

"What? If Gimbly's for real? You're fucking nuts."

"Ask Siobhan. She knows."

"Siobhan? Don't know why she was dead-set on a wog bastard like you." He scratched his leg with the baton and then pointed it again at Nic. "It'd be you floating face-down if not for her. You're vermin. They should have locked you up, kept you away from her; made you disappear. I could tell you were no good. Just like your old man."

Nic blinked. The words stunned him; one after the other. It took a moment to work out why.

"You never knew my father," he said, but even as he did there was a shade of doubt. And that's all it takes.

The Troll smirked. "Who do you think built that complex back there? He was a wash-out too. Just like you."

It was goading, that was all. He was lying. "My dad's company had projects everywhere. That doesn't mean anything." It was a lie. But there was something else he'd said, which now dawned on him. "It was you. You set me up. You got me framed. That van, that gun."

The Troll couldn't help but let half a grin slip between his teeth. And then the grin vanished. "Except you snivelled your way here of all fucking things."

"Shit. You're a bloody fruit-loop. Aren't you?" Nic took a step forward and, even though he was trembling all over, he looked for a way past, but the Troll holstered his baton, put his hand to his gun and grinned again. His little piggy eyes couldn't get any colder. "Siobhan didn't know about that and she doesn't know about this either, does she?"

"She will do," the Troll snarled. "She'll know why too. She'll know I was right all along – how I've been looking out for her. Then I'll be taking you for a swimming lesson after all. Once she knows, she'll wash her hands of you. You're history."

Nic's stomach knotted. A new cold wrapped its bony fingers around him, teased its claws into his bones. The guy was a psychopath.

"She's not your sister?" It was important to know.

"Who? What are you fucking on about?"

"Siobhan's not your sister, is she?"

"You're fucking cracked. She's Irish. Do I sound bleeding Irish? You're a sandwich short of a picnic, you are. What the fuck could she see in you?"

Again, he looked for a way past the Troll; to the door or backwards out of the window. He needed something to hurt the bastard with, to slow him down.

"I've got your car keys," the Troll told him. "Any more fuss from you and I'll roll it out of the garage and set fire to it. Might even fix you in the driver's seat first." He glanced around the room. "Give me your room keys. Without any fuss."

Nic looked at the desk, next to Polonius' cage, and the Troll stepped over and pocketed them.

"Now, stand there and hold the end of the bed."

Nic did as he was told and the bastard handcuffed him through the rails of the bed-end to the bed post. Then, stepping over the smashed coffee table, he picked up the chair Nic had kicked over and positioned it against the wall. "Such is life, eh?" he laughed and, deadlocking the door to the room, added: "Don't you be going anywhere now." He slammed the door shut after him.

17

Nic pivoted round from where he was cuffed so he could perch on the edge of the mattress and close his eyes. If only he could have kept his eyes closed and shut out everything that had happened. If only he could have slept and woken up somewhere else.

He didn't need keys to start his car. He was a bloody mechanic. But he had to get rid of the handcuffs and away from Gimbly. As quick as he could.

He needed to think clearly; to be calm. Had to shake off the panic. Shake it off. Shrug it away.

He pulled at the handcuffs, but they were tight against his wrists. He pulled at the metal bed post, but it held firm. It was tubular – hollow – but wide and firm.

He slid his hands up and gripped one of the cross rails. It was thin and began to bend the moment he put pressure on it. So he worked it back and forward, back and forward, for two or three minutes, until it sheered off at the post. He slid his hands up to where the post met the top rail and began working on that one too, using his knee to push down, then gripping it with both hands and pulling upwards.

Nothing. No movement. So he slid along to the middle of the rail, where it was unsupported, and repeated the process: push down, pull up, push forward, pull back. Backwards and forwards until it buckled. It was still fixed to both posts, but there was a clear gap on one side, exposing a long, thin, connecting bolt.

Backwards and forwards, up and down.

The bolt didn't give way, but the metal around it tore and he pushed even harder with his knee until, with too loud a clank, it separated and one corner of the bed caved in and dropped to the floor. The frame landed on the front of his foot, softening the thud, and he waited a second for the sound of voices or feet on the stairs.

Nothing.

He was free. Well, he was still handcuffed, but at least he was mobile. And he was going to move fast now. He had to. He was going to keep in control of his life; not give it over to that goon.

Whatever the cost, Nic was going to decide what would happen next and how. He would make it happen.

Quickly. Quickly.

He picked up the phone, but the line was dead. Of course it was. Had to check though.

He was parched. Needed a drink.

Quietly, he crept into the bathroom. Ran the tap slowly into his cupped, cuffed hands and drank. Deeply.

Glanced around. What resources did he have? What did he need? What could he do? He looked around again. Quickly. Quietly.

He could start his car – any car – if only he could get to the garage.

He needed to get out of his room. It was a trap. Before he could get away from Gimbly he had to escape his room.

He could break into the garage, through the back – no problem there, that'd be a cinch – and cut through the handcuffs if he had time; but he had to get out and away from The Crown.

The door to his room was locked, but there was a window to the veranda; even if the decking looked rotten, even if it was a long way to the ground. It'd be too high to jump and risk breaking his leg, too exposed to risk clambering down... it was too risky to risk nothing.

Softly, softly. He had to keep the floorboards from creaking, giving him away.

It was drifting through twilight. Before long, it'd be dark. Darkness would help.

He dragged his overnight bag from the wardrobe and tossed in a change of clothes, a beanie, a few snack bars, a bottle of water and the two framed photographs of his parents and his sister; he shoved his wallet in the back pocket of his overalls. Couldn't find his mobile phone, nor remember when he'd last seen it. Then, awkwardly – ham-fisted with the cuffs – began knotting together every long piece of material there was.

From some point in the past – slightly muffled, but unequivocal all the same – he heard his dad say: "You can achieve whatever you put your mind to. Even the sky's not the limit anymore. Never say never, and never say die. Quitters never win."

Well, he wasn't about to roll over and bare his neck now.

It was shortly after seven when he slid open the sash window. Gimbly would be at dinner, all snouts in the trough.

He leant through the window to peer out and the metal of the handcuffs clattered against the frame. Too loud. He lowered his bag and the bundle of knotted material out first, and then slithered over the window ledge and into a crouch on the decking, testing its soundness as he went. Stayed close to the wall, kept his back low. Light shone from two of the eight windows, but that didn't mean anybody was in those rooms, nor that the unlit rooms were necessarily empty. Snagged the knee of his overalls on a raised nail and heard them rip.

"More haste, less speed," his mum reminded him, and he measured each movement with extra care.

It was too quiet. The only sound came from a TV in one of the rooms. Quiet enough to hear a bag scrape on the boards or a foot scuff against the wall. He didn't know whether he heard the clink of cutlery on plates and the low murmur of chatter, or whether his imagination fed it to him, but if he could hear them, then they'd hear him if he fell through a stretch of rotten decking.

When he reached the end of the veranda, he stood and scanned the area. The road was clear. The place was as peopleless as it was going to get. He tested the handrail with his weight and it shifted – dry rot – so he tied a knot around the joint where it met a corner post, and lowered the rope of sheets, duvet cover and shower curtain over the edge.

It was dangling mid-air between levels and Nic was leaning over, looking down, when the hotel's main door rattled and someone stepped out. Whipping the material up into his arms in one rushed movement, he pushed himself against the wall and slid to a crouch. His heart was pounding fit to break, his breathing came too loud. The knot on the handrail stood out like a fluorescent white turban against the gloom.

From where he was perched, Nic couldn't see a thing, but followed the sound of footsteps as they kept to the hotel side of the road; he could tell by their weight and pace which bastard they belonged to. Then, two or three minutes later, there was the slam of a car door, an engine started, and he watched its lights vanish down the valley road.

"Go to hell," he mouthed into the night.

At least he knew where the Troll was, even if it meant he couldn't use the road. Until that point, he'd been worrying about taking this route because it was too obvious, too easy to barricade, too easy to police. He'd have liked them to think it was an option though, just to keep them busy.

Once again he lowered the sheets over the balcony, but they made only two-thirds the distance. The knots had taken up too much of the length, which meant he'd still have a fair drop to the ground.

The best he could do with his overnight bag was sit it on his back with the shoulder strap across his throat, and hope it didn't throttle him. He hauled himself onto the handrail, felt it shift, heard it creak, and switched his grasp to the post instead. Could only use his hands, not his arms, because of the cuffs. Clambering over the rail, he took a grip of the sheets. This wasn't easy but there was bugger-all choice. Painfully slowly, he climbed down grip-by-grip, half-a-hand at a time. But before he came to the end of the last sheet, he grabbed the corner post and found he could slither the last couple of metres down this. He landed softly on top of the geraniums in one of Mary's terracotta pots, stepping quickly down, back to the wall of the building.

The cat, which had been sitting by the front door, got to its feet and slid into the night. If it had slinked towards him, he might have put the boot in to watch it yowl across the street.

Then he realised that the sheets were hanging above his head, beyond his reach. No way of ripping them down. How could he have been so stupid? He had to be smarter than that.

18

Scurrying across the road, he headed for the denser darkness that spilled around the abandoned general store. Between the old store and the garage was a strip of debris-strewn land – broader than an alley, narrower than the road; he stood there a few seconds looking out. He'd got out of The Crown, but how to lose the handcuffs? Couldn't think straight. Emotions and ideas tangled one another up.

He had a vague idea about using the bolt cutters in the garage, though wasn't sure how he'd get the leverage and pressure he needed.

Leave now, Nic told himself. Walk into the woods and disappear. Grab the advantage and scarper into the night, away from this hole. Leave it all behind.

Except for the bloody handcuffs.

And the fact that he could never return to the life he'd had before.

Hell, he couldn't even go back to his apartment. Not anytime soon. He wouldn't even be able to sell his apartment and start over somewhere else. They'd find him. One way or another he had to expose Gimbly, bring it into the open, before he could ever reclaim his life. And revenge too. He wanted revenge. To make the bastard-Troll suffer at least. For everything he'd lost and everything he'd been put through.

It was then, as he focused beyond The Crown and the adjacent block of land, across at the police station and the Troll's pretty rose garden, that the first tendrils of a real plan put down roots in his imagination. And, almost simultaneously, he knew how to break out of the handcuffs too.

He made his way through the long grass between the old shop and the garage. There were nettles, rusting panels, broken glass, old iron, a rusting hulk of a tractor and, in the blackening night, he stung himself, grazed his shin and cursed. He lifted his feet higher, felt his way forward, until he was next to the fibro wall that was the outside of the store room and the stinking, mosquito-ridden toilet at the back of the garage.

The timbers were rotten – a fact he'd drawn Archie's attention to the previous week – and it was only a matter of giving a quick kick or two to the bottom of the wall. Once, twice, and then he paused to listen, to make sure the noise hadn't caught anyone's attention. Gripping the loosened edge with his fingers, he waggled the corner of the fibro back and forward, back and forward, until the rusty nails holding the base plate and the stud together gave way. Then, with one more pull, a whole half of the short wall was heaving outwards.

Because he knew his way around the workshop, he could work methodically and fast, without turning lights on. At the drill stand, he selected and fitted a drill bit, engaged a low speed and turned the power on. He lowered the bit towards the plate and slid his hands across, aligning one keyhole to the drill as a guide and then pushed up until the bit connected. The force of the drill made the cuff cut into his wrist; would have spun if he hadn't gripped the plate and applied more pressure.

He could hear it, feel it grinding, cutting; watched a small twist of metal curl and peel. He applied more pressure – until, with an abrupt release of tension, he knew he'd destroyed the lock.

With one hand loose, it took less than a minute to drill out the other lock, and he was free. Free to run, free to fight back, free to reclaim his life. And he'd formulated a plan – well, more of a reaction than a plan.

He dragged out an old tow chain and a mess of haulier's rope, and estimated how much length they'd give him, but it was difficult to gauge without unravelling the lot. He lugged these to the inside of the double doors, next to where he'd parked the tow truck a couple of hours earlier.

Only two hours. How much had changed in that time. How much was about to change in the next half-hour. He worked with a logic but without reflection. He didn't want to consider exactly what he was doing or what would come next. His anger was a fury that was burning white. Beyond heat, it provided an energy and focus he'd never known before; charging him, yet separate to him. He knew to let the white fury control him. It was quicker this way and neater. It was necessary not to falter and consider, not to pause and reflect, but to act. There were other thoughts he had to address, but in good time.

He took a pair of jump leads, stripped the crocodile clips off one end of each, snipped the socket from a thirty-metre extension cable, snipped back the Earth lead, and twisted the Live and the Neutral onto the exposed jump lead wires. He connected two twenty-metre extension leads and plugged one end into the mains at the rear of the workshop, then ran the two lines of cable across the floor of the garage, through the broken wall of the toilet and as far back and to one side of the building as it'd reach.

It took him close to the ditch and the fence-line that ran parallel to the river, and he dropped his bag there. From this position he could see the police station, the road into Gimbly and, best of all, it gave him a reasonable view of the profile of the garage while offering some cover. He could squat in the ditch and run out when it was clear. No one need see him. The plug of one extension cable and the socket of the other lay next to each other. There was current in one, but not in the other. Connect the two together and the circuit would terminate at the crocodile clips in a two-hundred-and-forty-volt arc of sparks. He hoped.

Back in the garage, he finished his preparations. These were the hardest of all, but he couldn't see another way. He opened the bonnet to his E-Type and wired the starter circuit so that, when he was ready, all he had to do was cross the terminals and the engine would roar into life. He disconnected the cylinder of oxygen from the oxy-acetylene welding area and rolled it until it was next to the petrol tank of his car. Prising off the petrol cap, he fastened the crocodile clips onto the rim of the open tank. Paused at this, but had to carry on. Had to.

He had to get out of this trap, whatever it took. Whatever the cost. This was about survival now – above all else. But revenge too – the sour satisfaction of revenge. And to drag Gimbly into the open.

The energy of the idea drove him forward, step by step. Desperate circumstances dictated desperate remedies. He rested a hand on the roof of his car and patted it.

He'd have liked to push the other cars forward, to crowd them together, but couldn't risk the time. Any minute, the Troll might return, or someone would discover the knotted sheets.

"It'll do," he said aloud to himself. "It'll have to do."

Then, murmuring a prayer to the night – to the darkness of night – he slowly opened the garage doors. Opened them carefully so they wouldn't make a racket. Heaving up his bundle of rope and chain, he lugged it across the road towards the police station.

He should enjoy this, he told himself. For Polonius and Ophelia. To stand by the memory of his sister.

When he was halfway down the drive, the German Shepherd started up with its barking, working itself into a frenzy. It was in the garage, hurling itself against the metal roller door; became the pounding of a giant drum.

He stopped at that, wanted to retreat. Was ready to sprint to the back of the garage, grab his bag and disappear into the wilderness of forest.

"Hurry," he urged himself. "Come on. Do it."

"Hurry, hurry, hurry," the chorus of his family urged. All three.

What he'd planned was to loop the rope around a trellis, through the decorative arch, before lacing it around the stems of as many rose bushes, ramblers and standards as he could, but there wasn't time.

"What the hell," he said, and tied the rope to two posts of the police house veranda instead, through the bench the Troll sometimes sat on.

The mechanic paid out the rope and chain as he strode down the length of the garden and over the wall towards the tow truck. Too loud for comfort, the German Shepherd's barking and thunderous crashing was crazed and hell-bent. The bloody thing would alert the whole town.

When he got no further than the middle of the road with the chain, he realised he should have done things the other way round – should have connected it to the tow truck cable first and seen how much was left – but it was too late and he'd run out.

Along the valley road the lights of a car came winding towards Gimbly. The Troll would be back in minutes; sooner than he'd expected. He stopped, dropped the chain, dashed into the garage, jumped into the tow truck and started the motor with a roar. All caution gone. He reversed across the narrow forecourt into the road, jumped down from the cabin, grabbed the tow cable and dragged it at break-neck speed to where he'd left the chain-end from the garden.

Kept the motor running. Had shifted up a couple of gears himself.

Couldn't avoid noise now. Needed confusion.

Nic linked the cable and chain together and cast a quick glance in the direction of The Crown. Was surprised the rumbling of the motor hadn't drawn everyone out. Not yet. So he raced back to the truck, slipped the clutch on the winch and set it to start drawing in its load. He'd created a little slack in reversing, but it'd be seconds before that slack was taken up and the demolition began.

There was too little time to stand back and savour the destruction. At the bowsers, he depressed and locked the triggers on both nozzles, stretched them across the pavement into the garage, allowing the petrol to wash across the oil-stained cement. He wanted fumes, rather than liquid. Fumes were more explosive and might just punch a hole in the place. Rushing over to his car, he crossed the contacts on the solenoid – it scratched into life immediately – and lowered the bonnet. Then he turned the lights on full beam.

Quickly, quickly.

He opened the valve to the oxygen cylinder, heard the joyful hissing of its escape, and, for good measure, dashed across the workshop and undid the valve on the acetylene too; which is when he remembered seeing the bottles of liquid propane stacked beneath a workbench... He couldn't stop; wouldn't stop.

Petrol fumes, liquid petrol, oxygen, acetylene, LPG, plus the oil and the mass of other inflammable substances in the garage – surely something would catch when he needed it too.

He'd hoped to start all the cars in the garage, creating a roar of noise to confuse and unnerve, but there wasn't time. Outside, an enormous crash and a rending of roof iron eclipsed the chugging of the tow truck – and he knew the veranda of the police house, along with the Troll's garden bench, was ripping a route of havoc through fifty-odd species of hybrid tea rose, double bloom rambler and multi-graft weeping standard.

"Weep, you bastard. Weep," he whispered in a new song.

Nic wished he could stand, watch and cheer, but the sounds of demolition would have to do. It was music itself. He imagined the mess it'd create and, irrationally perhaps, also imagined the body of the previous mechanic being unearthed along with half-a-dozen other corpses. Ex-lovers of Siobhan – anyone who'd not fitted in. Blood and bone.

Running to the back of the garage and out through the hole in the toilet wall, he was about to head for the ditch when the patrol car entered the town. He stopped, threw himself backwards, heard shouts, the clamour of voices, and then the engine of the tow truck being switched off.

He edged further out, into the night, away from the garage, until he came to the ditch, and then he scrabbled, crab-like, until he reached the spot where he'd left the connecting ends of the extension cables. The car yard and one wall of the garage gave him cover, but he could just see the fringe of the gathering crowd beyond. With the engine running and the bowsers pumping, the whole building might ignite before he created a spark next to the vapours of his fuel tank and the growing cloud of oxygen and petrol. If it didn't, then plugging those two cables together would be his detonator and he'd choose when it would happen.

He'd decide. He'd be in control. He'd no longer be anyone else's puppet.

In the beam of his E-Type's headlights, the Troll was waving his arms about, stomping in circles like a mad dog, bellowing at everyone who was there. Mary was at the front, one hand clutching a tea towel, the other hand pointing at something in the garage, her shock of white hair setting her apart. The mechanic couldn't see the garden, just the debris of the veranda across the road, and a portion of the hole in the front fence. He guessed he'd made an impression.

The Troll drew his gun and strode towards the garage, and Nic saw Mary run after him and hold his arm to make him pause. She was saying something, trying to tell him something. He stopped mid-stride, nodded, shook her hand off and shouted into the garage.

"Turn off the ignition and get out of that bloody car. It'll be the worst for you if I have to fucking drag you out."

This is it, Nic told himself, sliding forward to grip the plug and socket. The moment had arrived. But the Troll remained where he was. Taking a step back, he then levelled his gun and aimed into the garage.

There was a flash and a shot. The mechanic expected an explosion to tear the place apart. Nothing happened. He guessed he was shooting at one of the front tyres, or at the windscreen, but against the bright lights he wouldn't see a lot.

There was a second shot and the engine died.

Nic cursed. "Lucky bastard." He watched as the Troll stepped towards the garage, his gun arm outstretched, the other hand steadying his aim.

Again, Mary shouted, tried to drag him back, but he was too wild and arrogant to heed her.

Nic thought of everything he'd lost and counted off the seconds: "Fe-fi-fo-fum." He pushed the plug into the socket. "Now go to hell and don't come back again."

The first explosion rocked the building, made the ground where he was crouching tremble: a screaming bang and a judder that made the walls vibrate, and sent the loosened fibro section thumping to the ground. Then there was the shrieking of metal, the breaking of glass, the oxygen cylinder rocketing through a wall and across the car yard.

Death of a bogey-man.

He'd only expected one explosion. As he was about to begin his run, he saw the two old petrol bowsers catapulting across the road towards the police station, collecting three bodies in the path of their separate trajectories. It made him pause.

The second explosion took out the front half of the service station and a large portion of the road. The ground shook and moved him this time, so that he clung to tufts of grass – it seemed the earth was opening to swallow him.

"Earthquake," he muttered. Then saw the tow truck lift and cartwheel backwards, in a movement that was almost graceful. This time it was the boom of an aircraft crashing, rather than a bang, and a fireball twice as high as The Crown erupted into the night sky, illuminating the town of Gimbly – including his hiding spot, if anybody was left to notice – and was accompanied by a plume of black smoke and, again, the percussion of splintering glass.

A brief shower of concrete blocks, pieces of metal and shards of fibro hailed past him; then it slowly rained ash, burning cloth, into his hair, onto his clothes.

The plume of black smoke grew and rose until it was almost the shape of a genie – an Afrite – taller than the closest hill, overshadowing the town and the darkness of night.

The rear of the garage was on fire now and within seconds a series of other explosions began: one vehicle after another.

"Easy come, easy go," he whispered, and gripped his holdall. It was time to make his legs start moving; to scarper before the back of the garage exploded out towards him. He needed to run as fast as his legs would carry him; to run towards the woods and far, far away.

19

That should have been the end of Nic the grease monkey's story. A suitably dramatic denouement. Having made good his escape, he'd have walked until he found the main road, flagged down the first car he saw, hitched a lift to the nearest town, where he'd have burst into the local police station and blown the whistle. It would've been a long, rambling explanation, but once the cops visited Gimbly the evidence would confirm his story: the remains of a drug-manufacturing town and a few million dollars worth of pills. He'd have dealt the place a knock-out blow and be hailed a hero. He'd be safe.

Or, if not that particular ending, then a more convenient one. If the explosions were heard, if a fireball against the night sky was spotted, then telephone calls would be made, alarms sounded, and the Emergency Services would rush to Gimbly, saving him a long walk through a hostile forest and over rough ground.

Neither of these things happened though.

With barely a backward glance at the bodies left in his wake, Nic sprinted and leapt into the forest. He thrashed forward blindly at first, crashing and stumbling, deeper and darker. Until he saw the danger in this. He'd get lost too easily. With each obstacle – each thicket of thorny briars, each burrow, each fallen tree – he'd get spun around if he wasn't careful and lose all sense of direction. He'd never find his way to the main road.

He had to stay parallel to the river and the valley road. Even though he didn't dare move out of the forest, the occasional sight of river or road would keep him heading in the right direction.

For hour after hour, he stumbled forward, trying to remain on the same level of the wooded hillside, tracing the same contour. Accompanied by the fleet skittering of creatures escaping his passage, the swooping of bats, the groaning of tree limbs, the cut-throat shriek of an animal or owl. Every once in a while he caught the sounds of the river (water coursing over rocks, fish jumping, animals grunting) and a glimpse of breaks in the trees that might mark a road.

Adrenaline kept him awake and moving. Every time he began to tire, he thought he heard a noise in the undergrowth, footsteps snip-snapping twigs behind him, or voices on the road below, and the adrenaline surged again and he increased his speed. He imagined the German Shepherd being released to track him down – pounding along his trail, hunting him – and he moved faster.

Whenever he stopped to catch his breath, or to concentrate on what sounded like a new, separate creaking of tree limbs or a heavier scattering of leaves somewhere behind him, he hoped he'd be able to catch the distant clamour of sirens, as a stream of fire tenders, ambulances, police cars, approached from the distance; advancing closer, closer, to charge down the valley toward Gimbly, where he'd run to the road to meet them, waving a tired victory salute.

But it never happened. And when it continued to never happen, even though hours must have passed, he guessed that the devastation might not automatically be brought into the open for other people to examine after all. Gimbly was too remote to be noticed. He'd have to engineer its discovery too.

The night grew cold. It grew into a bone-numbing coldness that shivered through him and set his teeth chittering whenever he paused or slowed for a breather. And then, once it began, he'd be wracked by convulsions of shivers and shakes, the aftermath of shock, and he grew afraid he might rattle to death. It wore him down, cheated him of energy, until he remembered to calm his breathing – to relax and calm his breathing – and was finally able to take a few cautious, deeper breaths again and start moving forward once more.

Look forwards, move forwards, never back.

Early on, when he halted at the edge of a firebreak, he felt something brush against his face and looked up to find it was snowing; an absurdity: it didn't snow there. Touching a flake, he found it was ash, not snow; ash from the fire. The genie of smoke had swallowed up the garage and was now showering the earth again. Perhaps they were the ashes of the Troll or Mary King falling on his lips; he wiped the back of one hand across his mouth and spat. And half-an-hour later, it began raining. Not a light drizzle, but a torrential downpour that lasted ten minutes and, even though he was beneath the trees, it saturated him, blinded him and made him slip innumerable times. The forest was an angry place. It was an enchanted world and even the elements fought against him.

Each time he fell, he told himself to slow down, take care, unless he wanted to end up with a broken ankle and be easy pickings. But another part of him said to hurry: *Hurry, hurry, hurry. Don't stop. Use the night. Escape.* Low branches boxed the side of his head, snagged him, jabbed at him, drew blood; twigs poked at his eyes, their fingers stretching to blind him; rocks and rotten stumps kicked back, stealing the footing from under him.

At two in the morning, after more than six wild hours in the woods, Nic was brought to a precarious stop when the ground dropped away into a gulley. So dazed and punch-drunk that even the sound of trickling water close by hadn't alerted him, but he felt the edge crumble, managed to hold his balance and teetered back a step.

It was too dark to see clearly, although the terrain he'd been pushing through made him believe that if he jumped he'd be landing on even ground on the other side. It wasn't particularly wide, he thought. Just a small leap to cross it and he'd be on his way.

It was the last mistake he'd make that night. There must've been an old property division running through that area of forest, marked by the gully and reinforced by a fence-line. When he jumped he hit barbed wire, which was firm enough to snag at him rather than twine about him. His arm caught the brunt of it, shielding his face and his neck, but the movement threw him backwards, down onto the rocks of the gully bed and into the water, where he crumpled, torn and further bloodied. It was shallow – little more than a steady trickle – and he only lay in it for a second or two, but his feet and one side of him was sodden.

Nic staggered to the top of the fence-line. Had to stop blundering on. Would be stupid not to stop and rest a couple of hours. Huddled in his jacket, stretched his beanie down.

Exhausted; except adrenaline kept him on edge. It had hardwired his imagination and there was no turning it off. When he finally began drifting along the brink of sleep, it left him somewhere between a state of dreams and hallucinations.

The noises of one creature ten or twenty metres away and the whispered curses and groans of trees shifting their weight became the Troll tracking him down, sneaking forward, playing peep-oh in the dark, behind the trees.

"Peep-oh," he'd snarl, his teeth transformed into drooling fangs. "I know where you are."

If there was a pack of wolves in the forest at night, then they'd be stalking him too.

Later, his imagination pieced together a picture of Mary taking the full brunt of a petrol bowser as the blast propelled it through the air and, then, as he drifted towards sleep again, he saw her riding it like a broomstick, skimming the tree canopy. If he kept his eyes closed too long, she'd swoop down and snatch him up.

"I'll gobble you up," she'd cackle, bony fingers clawing towards him and her shock of ice-white hair like a wild moon in the sky. "I like to feed my boys up."

He found himself replying to the sound of the stream in the gully: "Run, run, fast as you can; you can't catch me, I'm the gingerbread man."

As the first grey light of morning leached into the sky, he was relieved he could stop pretending he was sleeping and could start moving again. Wet and rigid with cold exhaustion, his misery multiplied when swarms of mosquitoes arrived and began eating him alive.

He tried brushing them off at first and then swiping at them, but there wasn't enough fight left in him. So, as the mosquitoes ate him, he ate breakfast: one last snack bar and a gulp of icy water. He filled his bottle at the stream; hoped there was no dead sheep further up or his guts would soon know about it. The sleeve of his jacket was ripped and his hand was bloodied, his face scratched, but that was the only damage he found. It could have been worse.

Half-an-hour after he started walking through the grey light of early morning, he heard the first helicopter. Its flight-path followed the valley line, heading to Gimbly. About bloody time. After it passed, he stepped out from behind the trunk of a tree to sneak a look, hoping it'd be a police chopper or – even better – a TV crew, but no such luck. Twenty minutes after that, he heard another, a different one, also heading down the valley, and again there were no markings. Private choppers.

An hour later, he came across the main road, close to the poorly marked Gimbly junction. It had taken more than eight solid hours of scrabbling and clambering between trees and around thickets to cover about thirty kilometres; he was exhausted, empty, dispirited. It was impossible to walk further. He slumped on a rock at the side of the road, in a spot where the low morning sun had already created a bright niche, and soaked up its meagre warmth and light. He was sick of the damp and dark. He longed to hear traffic.

Grinding in from the near distance, came the shift in a truck's gears – no, two trucks, at least – climbing a steep gradient. Fan-bloody-tastic. If he hadn't arrived at such a tight, blind corner, he'd have stood in the middle of the road and waved the first one down; but why risk the irony of being flattened by his means of escape? They were a short distance off, but relief flooded through him, warming him, knowing he'd soon be ensconced in a warm cab, being driven to safety, where he might unburden his horrors.

The knowledge was as comforting as the sun on his back. He stood and stuck his thumb out.

The first pulled around the bend, began indicating and decelerating almost at once. It was a rental.

"Yes!" he shouted. "Thank you, thank you, thank you." He didn't care which direction it was heading or how far it was going. He clambered down from the rock.

The truck behind it came into view and it also indicated and began decelerating. It was then he realised that neither vehicle was stopping for him but were both turning for Gimbly.

"Shit." He took three steps back and now prayed they'd continue driving, that neither driver would know to be looking for him.

"Keep moving, you bastards," he said.

They did.

He listened to the grinding of gears as they negotiated the uneven road and closed his eyes and breathed properly again. Perhaps everyone thought he was dead too.

Minutes later, and arriving from the opposite direction, a minibus came into view. Nic stepped back now, so he couldn't be seen, and was glad of this when it indicated and turned off. Peering from behind a tree, he had a second or two in which to notice it was full of passengers and that the driver was familiar. He'd recognise that lank-haired bastard, Chris, anywhere – the one who'd planted a gun in his car. He shuddered and gripped the tree until the van was out of sight and the sound of the engine had faded into the distance.

There was little left in him that could be surprised.

"Someone's upset the apple cart," he told himself, pushing back from the tree, grasping at the cliché. "Thrown the cat among the pigeons." He tried to find a gram of satisfaction in the thought, but was too tired. Besides, he still needed to fully expose the whole she-bang and couldn't begin to relax until he had. Wouldn't be safe until it was done. And there were other things he had to think through too, now he'd got that far, like whether his dad's company really had built the laboratories and... And Siobhan.

The only thing to be glad of was that he'd outwitted the bastard Troll fol-dol-de-roll. He'd wrecked his life every way he could, and he hoped there was a moment when the bastard realised he'd been bettered and that he was about to die. What was revenge without that?

20

He trudged along the verge until there was a spot with a clear view of what was coming, and only stuck his thumb out to commercial trucks; ducked out of sight for anything else.

Within forty minutes, he was fighting off sleep in the stuffy warmth of a cab.

"Looks like you been in a fight," the truckie said.

"Yeah. Something like that." Too little energy to talk and his mind elsewhere.

With the old man.

With Siobhan.

Maybe she didn't know half of what had been going on. Or what a murderous, conniving shit the Troll was – had been. A jealous, possessive freak. All the things he'd done. Had framed him and... She'd understand why he'd hit back. Maybe harder than he'd intended, but... They could fight this together. Too tired to think straight.

His eyelids began to droop and he snapped them open; rubbed at his face with his bruised and grazed knuckles. Mustn't sleep. Mustn't think about sleep. Not yet. Not there. Had to keep his eyes open.

"Been sleeping rough, eh?"

He nodded. Grunted. "Sort of."

The truckie mumbled something, then turned up his radio: a country and western song ended and a new singer began crowing the usual stuff about love. Nic slept.

He got dropped off in the same town he'd stayed when first travelling to Gimbly. It was a small town, fifty or a hundred times larger than Gimbly, but there was no police station. He cleaned himself up the best he could in the public toilets, then withdrew a wad of cash from his bank account, bought the day's local and national newspapers, and sat in a milk bar and ate a steaming hot meat pie; washed down with strong coffee. There was nothing printed about Gimbly. It hadn't made the overnight news, though this wasn't surprising.

By nightfall, he was back in the city – two suburbs from his apartment – and booking into a motel room. Too exhausted to do anything else.

"Had a long journey?" the receptionist asked as she scanned his credit card.

He knew he looked like shit; she was being polite.

"You could say that," he said.

The credit card scanner emitted a series of exclamatory, high-pitched chirps and spewed forth a printed message. The receptionist read it and smiled in apology.

"The bank computer's off-line at the moment. I'll swipe your card manually and get it processed in the morning."

"Okay."

At that moment, there was nothing in life he wanted more than to lie his head on a soft pillow and sleep the clock round. Tomorrow, he promised himself, he'd reclaim his life. He'd begin to discover what was real from what was not, what he could believe and what he couldn't.

21

It was as if he'd been drugged, that first hour or so of sleep. But then a motel door slammed and shook him awake. He sat up, listened until he was sure it was nothing to do with him and tried to relax again. Realised he'd been sweating.

There was comfort in hearing the fluorescent strip across the bathroom sink buzz into life, in wiping his face down with a cold flannel, in staring at his image in the mirror and watch it stare back, in drinking a glass of water and letting a drip trickle down his chin and onto his foot. These things told him he was still the person he'd always been and might remain so.

Later Nic dreamt that Siobhan was riding the Troll, piggy-back, and was galloping across country to hunt him down. Tally-ho, she was the bogey-man now.

"Ready or not," he thought he heard her call, "here I come."

Then she was riding him; he was flat on his back in some forest with her, deliciously naked, the world was slipping away from him, on the brink of a wet dream.

"Ready or not," he heard himself call, "here I come."

He woke in another cold sweat, got up, drank a second glass of water, checked the door to his room was still chained and the windows were fastened.

What if he'd got it all wrong? Had overreacted? And what of his dad's involvement with Gimbly? Except that was nonsense; he knew it was. But what if he'd never been in any real danger at all? What if he'd killed decent people who'd meant him no real harm – idealists, dreamers – all because of a psychotic policeman's threats? Shit, he'd raised half a town to the ground!

He scrabbled back out of bed, ran to the bathroom and was sick. Stood up and was sick again.

He was tempted to phone Siobhan to explain, or leave a message if she didn't answer – she never answered – but he recalled Polonius floating in the fish tank, Ophelia in the freeze box. Hadn't Siobhan told him that Gimbly was only a small link in a chain? The middle of the night was no time to make good decisions.

22

Shortly after seven, he stood in the shower, under a cascade of hot water, easing his aches and soothing his sores, until the ends of his fingers began to pucker. It was a good place to think.

He had to untangle himself from the mess of Gimbly. But if he walked into a police station and tried explaining the last few months they'd probably lock him in a padded cell. Or they'd check his record, find he had a suspended sentence, and charge him with wasting police time.

And if they believed him, what then? What protection could they seriously offer? It was obvious he hadn't dealt a knock-out blow at all. If the people behind Gimbly were as powerful as Siobhan said they were, then he wouldn't be safe, even under protection. Power and wealth strut hand-in-hand, and information could always be bought for the right price, or extorted. The sort of people she was talking about would have easy access to every database that mattered, and it'd take next-to-nothing to track his whereabouts and destroy him. He'd seen enough films to guess how easy it might be. No safehouse would be safe enough.

There had to be a way of insuring against this. Of blowing the whistle so loud, so publicly, that the media snapped into its best Pit Bull Terrier impression – bit into the issue, locked its jaws down and didn't let go until it was well and truly dead. First, though, he had to involve someone who'd make the issue their own; someone regularly in the public eye who'd have the clout to see it through and sort it out. No messing with Mr In-between.

Someone like the Prime Minister, or the Chief Commissioner of Police? Fat chance.

Or maybe a prominent member of Government; someone like the Right Honourable William Pennant MHR… Of course.

He was fine when Nic asked for a character reference, couldn't have been more approachable. Besides, dear Slick loved playing at being the mover and shaker, so let him do some moving and shaking. He'd know how to handle this – unless he was involved himself.

Whatever, Nic would play safe. As safe as he could. Blow the whistle and hide.

He picked up his room phone and then put it down again. Gave himself a Brownie point for using his smarts. He'd wander down the street and find a pay phone instead. This mightn't prevent the call from being traced, but it'd stop anyone from tracking him back to the motel. He couldn't afford to trust anyone until everything was sorted.

By eight-thirty, and after several phone calls, he had the telephone number he needed. Five minutes later, he'd persuaded a secretary to put his call through.

"Good morning," the Minister said. "How have things been going, Nic? My secretary suggested there was some sort of panic on." It was the same brisk, authoritative and confident tone. Too confident, too self-assured.

Nic half-wished that someone he didn't like wasn't so frigging pleasant to him, nor that he should feel so sickeningly beholden to the guy already. "Look, I'm sorry to bother you, especially as you helped me out earlier with that – "

"No bother. None at all. I'm busy at the moment, but – "

"This'll sound bizarre," he said, "but I'm in... I've stumbled on something... a major crime ring... I think someone important – in Government – should know. It's... big." In the phone booth, he turned and looked both ways down the street.

There was a pause. The mechanic imagined him signing papers at the same time as speaking with him, half-listening.

"Sounds like a police matter. Have you been to the police?" It was a matter-of-fact response, as if his mornings frequently began this way.

"It's bigger than that. Much bigger."

"Really?" He sounded amused now. There was another pause. He was ready for the pompous bastard to ask if he'd been drinking. Instead, he said, "Hold on a moment, will you. I'll be with you in a second." The conversation in the background was muted and the mechanic held for a minute or two before Pennant continued: "Now, perhaps you should tell me what's got you all steamed up?"

Where to begin? He took a deep breath. He started with what Siobhan told him about Gimbly and jumped to the events of the last forty hours, fed in everything else that seemed half-relevant. His tale lasted for several minutes, and he had to keep feeding the phone with coins. At the end, there was silence and he wondered if the Right Honourable William Pennant hadn't hung up halfway through.

"Are you still there?"

"A drug factory, eh?"

"The mother of all drug factories. But more than that..." Hadn't he been listening?

"Yes, it sounds – well, incredible. Unbelievable, to tell you the truth. More like a plot for a movie."

"I'm not making this up. It may sound far-fetched, but – "

"Do you have any evidence? Any real evidence?"

"I've got a whole town; will that do? It's not a big town, but it's a town all the same." Then he recalled the trucks and the minibus of men and the two helicopters, and added: "Even so, I think a team have gone in to tidy up. But they can't make it vanish completely. Can they?"

There was another pause. Too long a pause. The bastard *was* doing something else at the same time – drinking coffee or having a second conversation. "I don't suppose they can," he said. "Hmm. Look, to be honest, I'm not sure where I should go with this. You've given me a bit to think about here. I'll need to put some feelers out. I take it you wouldn't be overly happy about trotting along to the nearest police station and explaining what's been going on to the local sergeant?

"Tell you what, give me your telephone number and stay put for the next couple of hours, and I'll get back to you. Where are you staying? Witness protection is something that might need looking into, if what you claim can be verified. What do you say to that?"

It was Nic's turn to hesitate. He couldn't afford to take risks and had been on the phone too long as it was. He had to think straight. "It'd be easier if I phone you back. Say in an hour's time."

"That's fine. Very good. Make it three hours though. Say twelve o'clock."

The mechanic caught himself nodding with the phone. "Okay. Thank you. Look, I appreciate your help. Really I do. I hadn't a clue where to go with this."

"I haven't done anything yet, but I'll try and have it looked into. No promises, but we'll see what we can do, eh?"

"Thanks."

When he put the phone down, he felt like he'd let go of a large burden. If only it was that easy and he could pass the whole mess that had tangled about him onto someone else to unravel.

He allowed himself a lazy moment to imagine the Minister making a call or two, setting into train a whole chain of events that would see anxious secretaries scurrying like frightened rabbits through various labyrinths of power; whispers and rumours beginning to leak. He imagined faceless businessmen, politicians – whoever – hurriedly packing toothbrushes, passports, details of offshore bank accounts, ordering taxis in various cities to drive them quickly, quickly, quickly to various airports. He imagined all this and wished and wished and wished, but doubted it'd ever happen this way. At best there'd be exclamations, dismay and a slow unravelling of truths, if he was exceptionally lucky. Claims and counter-claims; deceit and obfuscation. What he knew for rock-solid certain was that the only person in immediate danger was himself.

There were three hours to kill, though he'd have to line-up a different pay phone to use, probably in a different suburb. Just in case.

First though he'd find a newsagent and grab today's papers; then head back to the motel and order breakfast. Eggs, bacon, tomatoes, mushrooms, the lot – it felt like days since he'd eaten properly and he'd at least have himself a feast.

He stepped away from the phone, but then stopped and moved back. The action was almost involuntary. Shoving a couple more coins into the slot, he tapped out the number for Siobhan's mobile. One of two ravens, which had been sitting on a timber fence, flew down and turned over a ripped and greasy, brown paper-bag for food crumbs, keeping one eye on him. He didn't expect the number to ring out, but after a few seconds the recorded greeting cut in. He listened to it, realised there was no message he could possibly leave, and then put the phone down.

The raven on the pavement picked up a piece of crumpled aluminium foil in its beak and flew off, while the old white eye on the fence jutted its head forward and began cawing at the mechanic, at the morning, at the world.

"Jack-jack-jack!" it cawed.

"Naw-naw!" came the reply from atop a distant power pole.

"The same to you," Nic said, and walked on.

Fifteen minutes later, he was propping one newspaper under his arm and flicking through another as he headed back to the motel, his stomach complaining all the way. Again, there was nothing on Gimbly – nothing to say a town had exploded and people were dead. He swapped papers and flicked quickly backwards through the other; past the business section, past the world news, the cultural segment, the local news. He scanned each item, looking for a headline that might mention *Drug Lab Bust* or *Local Mafia Exposed*, or even *Explosion Destroys Garage*, but there was nothing. Nothing at all.

Until, that is, he reached page two. Under a one inch *Crimebusters* column, he found a picture of himself – the police mugshot, taken when he was arrested, when he had longer hair. Beneath it was a caption: *Have You Seen This Man?*

It was a punch to the guts and winded him. Stole the power to keep moving. The brief article described him as armed, dangerous and wanted in connection with a robbery. He felt a constriction in his throat, a tightening crease through his stomach.

Leaning against a wall to steady himself, he drew the newspaper up to hide his face, until he figured how suspicious this might look. If the newsagent hadn't recognised him, he was probably safe from most everyone else too, for the moment. And William Pennant couldn't have read the papers either.

At the same time, he'd been targeted sooner than he'd reckoned. The shivering started again and his stomach tightened once more, then loosened and began churning to a different tune. He should get out of public view, scurry back to his motel room.

Run, run, fast as you can. It had the makings of a new mantra.

Turning the corner into the street of his motel, he took one glance, stopped and stepped back round the corner. Shit! He moved half-a-step forward, bent down, pretended his bootlace needed retying so he could see what was happening without looking as if he was looking. Then, without any warning, he began to retch. He stumbled a few steps back and threw up in the gutter. There was bugger-all in his stomach to lose and soon he was dry-retching, bringing up nothing but bile. Someone spoke to him and he waved them away.

"I'm fine," he said. "A virus." He felt bloody awful; short of breath and shaking. His heart was pounding and every time he thought of the police cars round the corner he began retching again.

It lasted only a minute or two, but in that time anyone might have recognised him and alerted the police. Standing back, he leant against the wall and wiped his face down with his handkerchief; took several deep breaths, crossed the road and walked to a nearby bus stop. Joining the queue, he opened the paper and peered above it, at the motel.

Parked at an angle across the driveway was one police car; across the road in front was another. There were no sirens, but the lights were flashing red and blue and the cars were empty.

Absurdly, he wondered how he'd get his bag and few belongings from the motel room without being caught – was glad he had his wallet on him – then realised that stuff was gone.

More. He was being stripped bare. Reduced to nothing.

Had to get away from there. Had to catch the first bus that came along.

"Pennant," he mouthed to himself. He could taste the vomit in his mouth. But how could the man have known which motel he was at? He couldn't. They might've traced the credit card. Or perhaps the receptionist had seen his mugshot. On that grey morning, he learnt how pathetic and naive his attempts to protect himself were. What an innocent he was. How stupid. Too much was stacked against him. But that wasn't all. That wasn't the worst of it.

Just before a bus arrived a few minutes later, another car pulled up in front of the motel and parked alongside one of the police cars. There was a magnetic beacon attached to one side of the roof, strobing a blue light into the morning. It was an unmarked car, and a man and a woman climbed out from the front; then the rear door opened and a smaller, more petite figure got out. She had the build of a ballerina and an aura of self-assurance, confidence, although this seemed diminished that day. She had the agile step of a dancer too – sylph-like – but this was no dancer. Her paleness was accentuated by the darkness of her hair ('the colour of a peat bog,' as she'd described it once), which she wore bobbed.

What's more, he knew that her eyes were deep, round pools, which he would swim in and drown if he wasn't careful. Even now he was half-tempted to call out and rush over so he could embrace her and hear the sing-song lilt of her voice; even though he knew it would destroy him, as she had all but destroyed him to this point.

As he had all but destroyed her too, perhaps.

He took a deep breath, to stop the newspaper from shaking,

and identified the scent of jasmine drifting from someone's garden.

She looked tired. Could he sense grief in her bearing – a weariness at what life had thrown her way, a weariness at what death had snatched back?

Perhaps. Perhaps not.

They belonged together, which is rarely an easy bond to sever, whatever else gets in the way. She had loved him and drawn him into her world so as not to lose him, and he had loved her and wanted to share a world with her, but it had almost annihilated him. The impulse was to call her name, comfort her grief, bask in mutual recognition (as lovers often do); the impulse was to embrace her one last time. But it would be the end of him.

As he watched her, and measured each long breath to hold from retching again, she spoke to the two police officers in front – appeared to be giving instructions – and then the three walked into the motel together. They were hunting him down, looking for clues, and had too-nearly caught him.

This was the last time the mechanic saw Siobhan. And almost the end of Nic.

23

Along with half-a-dozen other passengers, he shuffled onto the next bus that stopped. Standing room only at first, but then he took a seat at the back by the window, where he let his head lean against the glass and shudder to the vibrations of the engine. Reduced to a daze, he barely registered the streets that passed, stop after stop, or the suburbs he was transported through, unsure where he was heading or where the safest place would be. When, after thirty minutes or so, the bus arrived at yet another crowded shopping precinct he got off, but only because he could think of no reason to stay on any longer. He saw a queue of people at an ATM and knew he needed more money to survive.

Card Error, the machine blipped back at him. *Contact Bank Staff For Assistance*. His bank cards had been cancelled.

So easy was the trap set. Overnight, he'd become a man whose wallet cash and pocket change were his only assets; that and the clothes he wore. So thoroughly can a person be reduced to their core.

Less a human, more a hunted animal. And too easily tracked in the city. He could grow a beard, grow his hair, dye it, and these things would disguise his appearance, make him less recognisable, but that was the least of it. To live in the open required digital signatures, credit cards, proof of identity – electronic footprints, the most obvious of tracks – so he had to learn a new way of existing if he was going to survive. He'd have to get out of the open, disappear into the shadows, step away from the life he'd known before and from the person he'd been; leave it all far, far behind. He had to vanish and never be heard of again.

No choice. It was the only way.

Not an easy step to take, but a ridiculously simple thing to know.

He caught sight of his reflection in a shop window: standing, staring. A stunned mullet.

"A rabbit mesmerised in the headlights?" his mum suggested.

Run, rabbit, run.

"Mobility and adaptability are an advantage," he might've remembered the old man saying. An early business motto perhaps? "You can be anyone and anything you want to be," he added. "But, whatever you do and whoever you become, always make sure you give the bastards a run for their money."

Run, run, fast as you can. You can't catch me, I'm the ginger-bread man.

"Never say 'never' and never say 'die'."

"It ain't over 'til it's over," the mechanic muttered and turned from the window, which is when he noticed the poster. It was an old one, pasted to a lamppost, its corners curling, colours fading, and more recent concert posters lapping its edges.

'CARNIVAL,' it announced. '*Dodgem cars, Tunnel of Terror, magic mirrors, Big Dipper, Ferris Wheel, shooting galleries, prizes, traditional Carousel, and lots more. ALL THE FUN OF THE FAIR.*'

He remembered the carnival he'd visited with Siobhan, once upon a time in a different life. What a night they'd had. Magic. He remembered how the convoy of trucks, trailers and vans appeared and transformed one corner of the park into a province of booths, tents, caravans and brightly-coloured, mechanical rides. A pleasure ground that existed under its own galaxy of lights, separate to the rest of the world.

He remembered the shrill sirens, the overlapping strains of disco, the endless spruiking, the thwack and ping of air-rifles firing at lines of tin-plate ducks; he could almost smell the hot dogs, donuts, candyfloss, hot grease and bruised grass. He remembered the swaggie reciting ballads, telling stories, and the coconut shy and the Show Bag stalls, the games of chance, the fleeing balloons, the bustling queues, the constant motion – up, down, round and round – the gaggle of drunks, the jugglers and the buskers; and he remembered the show hands working in their singlets on one of the trucks.

The poster may have been advertising the same carnival or any other, but that didn't matter. What mattered was that from his recollection grew the germ of an idea. It wasn't a perfect solution, but it had immediate possibilities.

Every piece of machinery, however big or small, needed a mechanic to maintain it – a grease monkey. Every part in every mechanism suffered wear and tear, might need to be repaired or replaced, and every motor had to be oiled, greased, recalibrated – stripped down and reassembled. Never mind the Porsches and Ford sedans, what about the prime movers – the Kenworth trucks and the Freightliners? He wasn't too proud to turn his hand to dodgem cars and carousels if he had to. Anything. All those gears and levers, all that grease and oil; there'd have to be a job for him in a place like that, especially if he could turn his hand to something else too.

As long as he kept on the move, in a world of shadows, out of the mainstream. And who safer to move among than a close-knit clan of travellers? The invisible people, the outcasts and outlaws, ever wary of strangers asking questions.

For that moment, it was a direction to head because he had to leave the city and his old life; and because he didn't know what else to do.

Run, run, as fast as you can.

He peeled back the overlapping posters and discovered that particular Fun Fair had passed through the city's suburbs many, many months back. All the same, it listed the dates of its current tour and was scheduled to be in a place called Dungarvan – a small town, far, far away.

Standing by the lamppost, he rubbed the fingertips of one hand across the bridge of his nose and massaged the pain that had replaced his forehead. If he didn't eat soon and sink a strong coffee, he wouldn't be going anywhere; he had to close his eyes and relax a few minutes too, before whatever it was that came after that.

Half-an-hour later, with hot food and an espresso inside him, he found brief sanctuary inside a suburban library, flicking through the pages of a road map. The chair was comfortable and the room was warm, and he'd found Dungarvan jutting from a jagged and unfamiliar coastline – a toothy promontory three-quarters along a broad but craggy smile. It was tempting to stay seated there for an hour or two, but against the sound of his best hacking cough, he ripped out five pages of maps, folded them in half, slid them inside his jacket and walked casually out.

"Thanks," he said to the librarian, and she smiled in return.

24

That afternoon, a hitchhiker stood to one side of a service station on the outskirts of the city, the roar of the freeway just a few metres away. He watched each truck steam in and each driver fuel up, and walked over a couple of times for the briefest of chats. His only luggage was a sleeping bag – stained on one side but otherwise sound – and a second-hand tin whistle in the key of D. He hadn't been looking to buy a whistle, but when he spotted it on the Charity Shop counter for a few cents, among a collection of tarnished mouth organs, he asked the friendly old dear serving him if she'd include it for free or reduce the price on the sleeping bag.

"If you don't ask, you won't get," his mother might've prompted him.

"Please," he said and offered his biggest smile. He told her he'd lost his job, his apartment, was sleeping rough, and might earn himself a meal with the penny whistle if he started busking. It wasn't much of a story, this first story, but he played a snatch of *Cockles and Mussels* and she gave him one of her toffees and slid his money back to him.

The sky clouded over while he stood outside the service station and the afternoon began collapsing towards a premature dark, which might have increased his misgivings, but the rain abated until he was climbing into a cab and then it pelted down.

"Lucky," the truckie said, his voice raised against the volume of the radio. "Just in time." He flicked on the windscreen wipers. "How far did you say you're going?"

"All the way. If that's okay." The hitchhiker leant forward until he got a view in the wing mirror of the traffic behind. It'd be a long journey and he didn't want anyone waiting for him when he arrived.

The truckie checked the mirrors himself and accelerated onto the freeway. "Travelling light?"

"Too right," the hitchhiker said. "There's no other way."

Run, run, fast as you can. You can't catch me, I'm the ginger-bread man.

The truckie nodded, smiled, plucked a lolly from a bag and shoved it into his mouth. "The name's Bob. What's yours?"

The traveller considered and smiled to himself, as if on this bleak day it was still possible to arrive, by the most bizarre route, at an amusing thought. "Call me Jacka," he said. "Jacka Nory."

Bob increased the speed of the wipers, turned down the radio – the first bars of *No Woman, No Cry* – and offered him a lolly. "I get all sorts hitching lifts on this run. Don't know why. Some like you wouldn't believe." And he laughed at that.

"Yeah?"

"Yeah, all sorts." Bob checked his mirrors again, indicated and pulled into the middle lane. "So what's your story, Jacka Nory?" He laughed at that too.

25

The end is never the end, just as the beginning is never the beginning; life is a journey of stories, one upon another. Although not every story has a Happy-ever-after or an answer to every question – all those unresolved mysteries in life – what I'll tell you for free is this: just as Nic the mechanic vanished, so too did our friend the hitchhiker. It's the way of hitchhikers; few people see them, fewer remember them. At the end of his ride with Bob, he climbed down from the cab at a service station in a place far, far away and became someone else. And then someone else and someone else. All the way to nowhere. He proved it's possible in this world to vanish and be re-born among the shadows... if you have a mind to.

It's surprisingly easy to live hand-to-mouth, with only the

cash in your pocket, the clothes on your back and the world at your feet... if there's nowhere else you need to be and no one else you need to be there for. Easier still if you've got a few skills in hand and can win folk over with a story or two. An odd job here, casual labour there, until you find yourself in a place and among people – misfits and outcasts, perhaps; restless spirits and out-laws, most likely – who'll allow you to be whoever you need to be to survive.

The weeks become months and the months become years and the past becomes a foreign land you hope never to return to. Hands smeared with grease and oil each morning and afternoon; mechanisms to repair, motors to service. Evenings anchored in the fug of familiar aromas – hot dogs, popcorn, baked potatoes, the syrupy warmth of doughnuts and candyfloss – and the regular raucous of overlapping claxons, sirens, spruikers, pop music, shrieks and laughter.

26

The story-teller is a man in his thirties or forties – it's hard to gauge the age of weathered leather. His voice is deep and lined with gravel. It's the sound of riverbed pebbles chattering and grinding against the hushing of fast water. Hypnotic.

"And, before that day had breathed many more breaths," he croons, winding up his tale, "before the sun had climbed much higher in the sky, the boy had upped and gone too." Widening his eyes, he points a callused finger at an invisible distance – it's out there somewhere, beyond the galaxy of lights, beyond the darkness of night, this promise of tomorrow's journey. "Placing one foot in front of another and with the raven barracking for him – 'For-for-forward! More! More!' – he was already heading towards the horizon and the next chapter in his story."

The story-teller pauses and takes the moment to survey his audience one more time. His eyes may be the blue-grey of an overcast sky, but framed by wild fronds of hair sprouting from beneath a broad-brimmed hat, and planted in a face that's brown as a nut or the bark of a tree, they have a piercing brightness to them, even in shadow. From his pocket, a penny whistle protrudes, which he'll sometimes play to conjure up a crowd. And a shaggy-haired dog lies panting at his side, its tongue lolling out and the name Polonius inscribed faintly on its collar. On the grass in front sits a fire-blackened billycan hungry for coins.

"But listen, my friends," he adds, taking half-a-step forwards and shifting towards a more familiar tone, a less even rhythm, "if you remember nothing else of my story, then at least remember this: You may think this is just a fairytale I've told and nothing more, but we none of us outgrow our need for fairytales – princesses and paupers, witches and bogey men – not ever. It's why they inhabit our dreams and plague our sleep.

"Sometimes we pretend we've outgrown them, even though we're still drawn to each day's news headlines and their tales of good turned bad, bad turned good, of macabre disasters and golden treasures, of love and loss, corruption and revenge. We're drawn by each dose of horror and suspense as we have been since childhood, and are left open-mouthed – gobsmacked – to hear that children can still be eaten by wolves and that wicked step-sisters will dispossess all innocence and virtue. (They are, they do, they can.)

"And we're drawn not because we're bad or mad or overly ghoulish, but because they help us survive and be prepared for each tomorrow. They're reminders to keep one eye on where we've come from and one eye on where we think we're heading, so that ill-fortune has less chance of creeping up with a long knife in its paw, or skipping towards us like the most agile of dancers, or alluring us with the sweetest of songs to crash upon rocks, which might or might not be of our own making. They

remind us to keep our peepers propped open, our lugholes pinned back and be wary. More than anything, though, they should remind us we're alive – and to celebrate that."

He stops, nods, takes a breath. Sweeps both arms out in a gesture that embraces the gathered company and leads them to focus on the blackened and dented billycan sitting on the ground. The last words he recites for almost each and every audience are these:

"My tale it is told, my story is done,
But now hear my request before you move on.
The words in my mouth are crumbs I can't eat,
So my bow is your sign to kindly dig deep;
Gold coins in my tin will help me dine well –
A sound recompense for the stories I tell.
May your journeys be rich and shared with good friends,
And your life an adventure right through to The End."

The story-teller places one rough hand next to the other, oil-stained and callused palms uppermost, and then brings them together in front of his face. It's as if he's closing a book, as if acknowledging and releasing his audience, as if saying a prayer, as if silencing his lips. He smiles, briefly shuts his eyes and takes a bow.

Acknowledgements

I am grateful to Tony Bishop for being prepared to engage with *The Grease Monkey's Tale* when it was little more than a rough lump of a story and for his many helpful comments. Also to Siân Burman who has accompanied me at every stage of discovering and revealing its various layers, and for believing in it. Thanks to Lowri and Gwil who, in one way or another, have chipped in throughout.

I have been particularly fortunate in having Tom Chalmers as my editor. His close scrutiny, insight and advice are responsible not only for smoothing many rough edges but also for helping me recognise where to polish and when to leave well alone. Thanks, Tom.

I owe a debt of gratitude to the work of Professor D L Ashliman, formerly of the Department of Germanic Languages and Literatures at the University of Pittsburgh, USA (www.pitt.edu/~dash/ashliman.html). His website was a useful resource in broadening my understanding of folk texts.

The story of the American tourist and the Irish farmer has been developed from a joke told to me, but has many parallels in folk tales, while the story of the girl and the wise raven was inspired by the Confucian quote: 'A journey of a thousand miles begins with a single step'. Jackanory, as a story-telling character, has been associated in my imagination with books and stories for as long as I remember, possibly because it was the title of a BBC television story-telling programme during my childhood. I have adapted the traditional nursery rhyme *Jackanory*, where it appears in each Interlude, to better fit *The Grease Monkey's Tale*. The extracts recited by the story-teller in Part One are taken from Edgar Allan Poe's *The Raven*, while *Cockles and Mussels* is a traditional folk song.